The Day I Died...

The Day I Died...

SAM GODFREY

This book is a work of fiction. Names, characters, businesses, places, events, and incidents are either the products of the author's imagination or used in a fictitious manner. Any resemblance to actual people, living or dead, events or locales is purely coincidental.

Written by Sam Godfrey
Artwork by Sam Godfrey
Edited by Hana Griffiths

ISBN: 9798649333870

www.instagram.com/samgodfreyofficial

**Copyright © Sam Godfrey 2020
All Rights Reserved.**

Dedicated to...

My angels – A dropped stitch in life's tapestry, forever in my heart.
My children – The sunlight on my darkest days, my biggest blessings, the reason I will never give up. So beautiful, so handsome, so funny, (but obviously none of you will ever be as funny as me!) I'm so proud to be your mom, and if I never accomplish anything else in life, I'll be okay with that, knowing I made you! Love you.
My partner – Apart from my dad, the only man I've ever truly loved. Whatever life throws at us we always seem to get through somehow, so here's to believing that love conquers all, to bright days and making more beautiful memories. I love you.
My dog Simba – Yes, my dog! Man's best friend and unquestionably *my* best friend. Simba came into my life at a time when there was a colossal gap to fill, also having been born on my dad's birthday was a definitive clue that the angels sent him. The unconditional love and laughs we share are undoubtedly one of my greatest joys in life.
Family and friends – Thank you for your love and encouragement. Always in my thoughts Dad.
To *everyone* who has lifted me up or pushed me down, you have all contributed in motivating and inspiring me to accomplish this, so thank you!
Myself – Through the chaos of life and countless unforeseen events, somehow this got completed. So proud that I did this, through all that.
For the readers and followers - Thank you *so* much for all your continued support and inspiration. If this book has made *one* person's day, then it was definitely worth writing.

Ultimately love is everything...

Chapter 1

Lana stirs her coffee counterclockwise, taps her spoon twice on the side of her cup and places it delicately onto the saucer. She lifts her cup, takes a sip, then looks up. **"February 14th, 2016, that was a very important day for me... that was The Day I Died!"**

The Meeting...

Lana glances up at the clock and double checks her watch. Her workday has been *unusually* long, everyone's left already, and the silence is deafening. Although she *loves* her job dearly, she's beyond exhausted and this is one time she can't wait to get home. Lana imagines herself sitting in her favourite armchair, feet up, basking in the warmth of her cosy log fire, sipping hot velvety cocoa.

Rubbing her shoulder, she arches her back to stretch her sore muscles, then decides to call it a day and take the rest of her work home with her. As she grabs her bag from the floor and reaches for her coat from the stand, she's distracted by a roar of thunder and the sound of rain beating hard on the window, so moves the blind and tilts her head slightly to take a look outside.

Lana sighs, it was only drizzling a short time ago, but it's steadily turned into a ferocious, torrential thunderstorm. This is one of the worst storms she has *ever* witnessed, with lightning striking every few seconds. She stares despondently. The rain's so heavy now that although she desperately wants to get back home, she's feeling seriously uneasy about having to drive in the current downpour. Recognising the severity of the weather and that it's not likely to improve anytime soon, she decides to go and get a coffee and try to wait it out for as long as she can instead.

There's a charming, quaint little coffee house situated on the corner of the street called *'Sam's'* which Lana visits as often as she can and has actually been frequenting for years. This is Lana's *special* place. She's particularly close friends with the owner, a lovely elderly gentleman, who's chatty, warm and kind. Sam has owned the café for years and it has been in his family for generations. Lana just *loves* the ambience and the unique atmosphere of the place. It has an array of modern décor but also an old-fashioned feel due to the original artwork hanging from the walls. She also *loves* the music, as the jukebox always plays her favourite songs. They sell a variety of different coffee imported from all around the world *and* have home-made cakes, which she just adores.

Lana rummages through her bag for her umbrella but it suddenly dawns on her that she's left it in her car, and as she's parked it a few blocks from her workplace, it patently becomes clear that if there's any point in her even going to the café she's going to have to make a run for it. She gathers all of her belongings together and makes her way downstairs to the entrance. Once she reaches ground level, she can't believe how fierce the weather has actually become now. People are scattering at speed and the streets are emptying fast. She's overwhelmed with an eerie feeling almost like an apocalypse is upon her, as though impending doom is imminent. She stands there sombrely for a moment, staring out into the dense black clouds, daunted at the prospect of having to run into the rain and if she's being honest with herself, more than a little afraid of the lightning. Taking a deep breath, she psyches herself up and swiftly darts out the door.

As she starts to run, lightning strikes and the rain falls even heavier. She sprints as fast as she can trying not to step in any of the puddles, although she can't help miss them all. Even though it's only a few doors down, as Lana reaches the café she's already completely soaked through and dripping wet.

She isn't looking where she's going and in her hurry to get out the rain, she pushes the door open forcefully and trips over the step. As she staggers, one of her heels snaps and she stumbles into a man pulling serviettes out of a rack, stepping hard on his foot. The serviettes go flying... *everywhere*! She looks down and to her horror, there's now what appears to be *hundreds* of them scattered all over the wet floor. Lana's eyes widen.

"Oh, I am *so* sorry!" she gasps flustered and embarrassed, bending down quickly to pick them all up, one by one. There's a pause as she momentarily glances up at the man. Their eyes lock.

"I'm not!" he replies with a smouldering, charismatic smile.

Lana bites her lip shyly as she feels herself starting to blush, she doesn't know where to look. As she sweeps her wet hair back from her face, the man grins and gathers up the remainder of the serviettes. He throws them into the waste bin, winks at her then walks back to his table, leaving her standing there beguiled and light-headed. She quickly composes herself and hobbles off to sit down at her regular seat at the bar.

"Hey, Sam!" Lana greets the owner as she takes off her mac and gently shakes off the excess rain.

"Hi, Lana! How you doin'?"

"I've been better!" she replies wryly as she scrapes her wet hair away from her forehead once more.

Sam chuckles, "Usual?" She nods in confirmation with a broken smile, feeling somewhat sorry for herself.

She dabs her arms and face with some napkins she's gathered together from the counter top, and whilst doing so feels compelled to turn around and check out the guy who has just had such a notably powerful effect on her, but then she contemplates that maybe she's already embarrassed herself enough for one day, so decides against it.

As Sam reappears with her drink, Lana flips off her shoe to inspect the damaged heel. Sam chuckles to himself. "I'm sure I can find you a spare pair of shoes to get you home if you don't mind what they look like!" he kindly offers.

"That'd be great!" she acknowledges gratefully as she continues to dry herself off.

"Dean? Are you listening to me?" Dean's having a coffee with his larger than life, best pal Brad. Brad's talking and Dean's nodding in agreement, sipping his latte but nothing's registering, as he can't stop thinking about the girl who just entered his life so unexpectedly.

As Dean keeps periodically glancing over at her, Brad stops speaking mid-sentence, and turns his head to look over at Lana. He recognises how distracted Dean is by this girl, so coerces him into talking to her. "For goodness sake D, just go over there man!" Dean's mesmerized but he's not sure whether he should or not. He doesn't want to seem too forward and presumes a girl that beautiful must already be spoken for anyway.

"She's very erm... easy on the eye! But she's probably already with someone!"

Brad looks bemused. "What? Why are you being so negative? This ain't like you! Just go over there and talk to her!"

Dean squints and scrunches his face, "Maybe... I dunno," he stutters, unusually unsure of himself.

As he procrastinates for a little while longer, the realisation kicks in of just how much he actually likes this girl. Deciding that he would be a fool to miss his chance, he summons up the courage, takes a breath and slowly walks over. He clears his throat... "Hi!"

Off-guard, Lana turns around, nearly toppling off her seat and choking on what's left of her coffee. She puts her cup down and manages to splutter mildly... "Hello!"

Dean pulls up a stool and sits down next to her, faking his confidence remarkably. He side glances at her hand and sees no ring, giving him a little extra boost of self-assurance. "Erm... I was just sitting over there," he indicates by pointing in Brad's direction as she turns to look. Brad puts his hand up and mouths *hi*, to which she responds with a sheepish half wave. Dean continues, "and I was thinking that we didn't exactly get off on the right foot. Well, I mean you *stood* on my right foot!" Lana lowers her eyes bashfully. "So, I was wondering if I could get you another coffee or... some cake or..." Dean pauses and looks up at her hair, "a hair dryer?" he grins, waiting in anticipation for her response.

Although he's a complete stranger, there's an instant and spellbinding connection that she can't ignore. Lana's captivated by him already and thinks he's exceedingly charismatic and charming, but she doesn't want to seem too forward either, so she tries to subdue her thoughts and act cool. "Lana Anderson," she says while reaching out her hand to formally introduce herself.

"Lana. What a pretty name! I'm Dean by the way." He shakes her hand as their eyes unite once more.

"I'd love a cappuccino, please!" she states boldly whilst obliviously still grasping his hand.

Dean smiles and nods in agreement. "Two cappuccinos please, Sam!"

Chapter 2

To Be Loved...

As the storm waivers and the rain progressively starts to settle, Lana and Dean become engrossed in conversation *and* each other. As he talks, she is *completely* transfixed on him. Drawn to him like a moth to a flame, a magnet luring her in, a feeling she has no control over, and although they've only just met, the familiarity is such that it's almost as though she's chatting to a dear old friend she's known all her life.

Dean's voice turns into white noise as she gazes deep into his vibrant green and hazel eyes. His defined dimples surround his perfectly full lips and she can't help but smile back like a lovesick teenager, staring in wonderment at just how handsome he is. He asks her a question and as if a hypnotist just clicked his fingers, she awakens from her trance.

"Sorry, what did you say?" she stutters, shaking her head and blinking profusely.

He grins at her adoringly. "Your perfume, I was just wondering which one you're wearing?"

"Oh! It's Armani, Si."

"Si? That's Italian for yes?" he queries.

"Mm-hmm," she nods.

"Well, it's lovely!"

Lana wants to say *you're* lovely but stops herself and instead simply smiles timidly and murmurs "thanks" whilst hiding behind a big gulp of her coffee.

"So, what do you do for work?" he enquires attentively.

"I'm a wedding planner, I work in the Madison building."

"Oh yeah I know it, it's just up on the corner, right?"

"Yeah!" she confirms with a bobbing nod of her head.

"So, can't people plan their own weddings?" he asks teasingly as she smiles back demurely.

"Yeah, I guess. It's just that some people can't be bothered, they just want it all done for them, then some don't have the time and some people well, they want us to make them the fairy tale."

"Ah ha! So that's where *you* come in!"

She nods, "Right!"

"So, what kind of things do you *plan* Lana?" he asks flirtatiously.

"Whatever people ask for!" she smiles enticingly.

The chemistry between Lana and Dean becomes increasingly electric with every passing second.

"We've been asked to do some *crazy* elaborate weddings. Some people spend thousands trying to achieve this 'perfect day' but my favourites are always the beautifully simplistic ones, it just depends what people want."

Now Dean's getting her to open up to him, he endeavours to keep the conversation going. "So, what's the *craziest* thing anyone's ever asked you to do?"

Lana hesitates and ponders for a moment. "Well, there was this *one* woman last year, it was *so* strange. She asked me to design her *whole* wedding in *brown*, 'cause that was her favourite colour and when I say the whole wedding, I mean *everything*! She even had a brown ring!" Dean has a surprised, wide-eyed expression on his face as he quietly chuckles under his breath. "Then she requested *only* brown food, but there was only so much I could do with that! She was going nuts and I said well I could burn it all if you want and *make* it brown!" Lana tilts her head and rolls her eyes as Dean laughs. "And then a few months ago there was this other couple, they wanted everything *elephant* themed!" she smirks, "but apart from them two it's usually pretty normal, and magical!"

"Well, it all sounds pretty amazing!" he comments, smiling warmly.

"Yeah it is, it just means sometimes I have to work long hours and that's why I usually end up in here!" Dean *is* listening to her but at the same time thinking how fun, bubbly, and beautiful she is.

Just then Sam reappears holding an old unsightly, battered pair of moccasins. They're tan in colour with tassels and pretty worn. "Now I know these aren't much to look at, I know they're not the best, but they should be alright to get you home for tonight." Lana's deeply embarrassed that Dean's sitting right next to her staring at these beat-up shoes, but she has no other option and doesn't want to appear ungrateful, so she takes them; she thanks Sam and puts them on. She places her broken heels in her bag, but to her amazement Dean doesn't utter a word about it and instead carries on their conversation obliviously.

"So, you come in here a lot then?" he asks keenly.

Lana clears her throat, "Yeah, probably three or four times a week, or as much as I can really. I have a bit of an insane love for coffee and I don't know what it is about this place, but I just feel so relaxed and at home every time I come in here." He nods in agreement as she takes another sip of her drink. The fact that Dean's not in the slightest bit interested in these ugly shoes she's wearing, is heightening her interest in him even more.

"So, what about you? What do you do?" she asks inquisitively.

"I work with Brad down at Bulmer's, you know that big advertising agency two blocks up?"

She squints. "Is that the building next to that new steakhouse that just opened?"

"Right! Well we work out advertising campaigns together, and when I say *we*, by that I mean *me*!" Lana's amused as he continues. "I do probably *ninety* percent of the work, but I don't even mind, I just like having him around, it makes the day go faster and I've gotta say that he did actually have *one* good idea once, and that made us quite lot of money so I think he's alright for a while. Probably another year I reckon 'til he's gonna have to think of something else!" They smile contentedly at each other, "but erm... yeah, I like it in here too. This is only the second time I've ever been here, but the rain was that crazy we just ducked in here quick!" He stares lovingly at her, "but I think I'll definitely be coming back here more often from now on!"

She smiles coyly as she breaks his intense gaze, then bites the corner of her lip as she does when she becomes overly shy or embarrassed. She glances outside at the rain and it's still pouring unrepentantly. She looks downward towards her cup and notices that she's already finished, but she doesn't want to leave just yet. She summons up some courage and turns to Dean. "So, I think it's my turn to buy *you* a drink!"

He shakes his head, "No! I cannot let the lady pay and besides, this would be my third in a row, so I might not be sleeping for a few weeks!" he jokes.

"Please... I insist!" she pursues.

There's a pause as he looks hard into her eyes... "Okay, how about *you* buy the coffee and *I'll* buy the cakes!"

"Deal!" she beams.

"Alright, so there's this thing they do here, that I had the last time I came in, which I think you might like, it's called *the three plate*.

Lana interrupts and states astutely, "With the three mini cakes on one plate?"

Dean squints "Right! You've already heard of it?"

"Yeah, I might have had that a few times already!" she replies grinning to herself.

"Hmm, really! Why doesn't that surprise me?"

"Excuse me?" she jokes.

They both chuckle as Dean orders the cakes. "Sam? Can I have two three-plates please?"

"On the way!" he shouts back.

"Thanks!"

Lana excuses herself to go to the rest room, as Dean takes the leftover change he placed in his saucer from earlier and walks over to the jukebox. Although it's an old 1950's style jukebox, it's been maintained and upgraded and contains a mixture of old and new songs. He looks up and down the list and scans it with his finger.

Brad notices Lana's absence and quickly runs over. "Any progress to report?" he whispers cheekily.

Dean grins, "No, not yet, but I'm working on it! Now will you *please* go away before she comes back?"

"Okay I'm going but hurry up 'cause I need a lift and I need my dinner!" Dean sniggers and shakes his head as Brad returns to his table.

After a few minutes of deliberation, Dean decides to choose an old track, Jackie Wilson's, To Be Loved. He selects the song and as it starts to play, he strolls back to his stool and sits down. Lana's returning too and wonders if Dean put the tune on. She shuffles gracefully onto her stool. "Did you put this track on?"

"Yeah!" he confirms.

"I *love* Jackie Wilson! Actually, I love all the old soul singers!" she exclaims.

He nods and there's a short pause as he looks pensive, then he pipes up. "We could dance if you want!"

Lana looks shocked *and* confused. "What? Here? In the café?" she questions, astounded at such a suggestion.

His face lights up. "Why not?"

"Erm... Because it's a café! And there's *people*!" Lana quickly glances around apprehensively.

"Who?" Dean gazes around the room. "The two couples over there? that we'll probably never see again. Or Sam? Or Brad?"

Feeling way out of her depth now, she can only stutter, "well... yeah, *all* of them!"

He chuckles to himself and stands, then reaches out and grabs her hand.

"No, no, it's really not a good idea!" she squirms, pulling back her hand reluctantly and shaking her head, but he won't take no for an answer. He gently coaxes her up off her stool and pulls her close. As the song continues to play, Sam notices the spark between them so casually turns up the volume. Lana's so lost in the moment that she suddenly forgets all her inhibitions and any worries she had about the other people in the coffee house. All she sees is Dean. He twirls her around and pulls her close to him once more. They continue to dance and laugh until the song gradually fades and finishes. Upon realising there's no more music playing, they stop dancing, awkwardly smile at each other, and return to their seats.

Suddenly, Lana catches a glimpse of the clock and recognises that she's been so preoccupied chatting and laughing that she's lost all track of time and over an hour has passed. She quickly turns her head towards the door to check the weather and can see that the storm is finally faltering. It's only drizzling now, and sunlight is radiating through a vast, glorious double rainbow. She gasps and grabs her coat. "I've got to get going. I've got *so* much work to do at home and I've got a *really* early start as well." Lana's very conscious of the fact that she should have been home ages ago and that she needs to leave *now*, but she's secretly hoping that Dean won't let her go without asking her out on a date first.

Dean nods, now slightly unsure of her intentions. He smiles at her but at the same time seems discouraged and dejected.

Has she now made it awkward and blown her chance with him? Unclear whether she sounded too brash and if he's mistaken her words for rejection, she rapidly backtracks to try to rectify the situation. "But I'll be in here tomorrow evening, if you're here?"

Dean's whole demeanour immediately changes, he's entranced by Lana. He knows this is his chance and she's throwing him a line, so he takes it. "Yeah, I'll definitely be here, but maybe I could take you out one of the evenings for some dinner as well?"

Lana's stunned, but also delighted by his response and inwardly wants to jump up and down and scream with excitement. Her heart races as she intensely stares deeply into his eyes, but upon realising that she's standing there gawping at him like an amorous adolescent, she forces herself to quickly look away.

There's a mountain of takeaway leaflets on the side of the bar, so she grabs one and tears off a corner. She finishes putting her coat on then hurriedly searches through her cluttered bag for a ball-point pen. She starts to scribble down her phone number as she continues to speak. "So, this is my number and if you ring me later we can arrange something for tomorrow night, maybe?" she asks optimistically. She hands it to Dean; he takes it and pushes it deep into his back pocket.

"Yeah, I will *definitely* be ringing you later!" he replies assuredly.

Looking away shyly, she leans over the bar and shouts *bye* to Sam, thanking him once again for lending her the shoes, then on her way out smiles at Brad as she passes him. Upon reaching the doorway, she stops in her tracks and turns back to Dean, she puts her hand up to wave, he winks at her, she smiles reservedly and leaves.

Dean walks back to the table he was originally sharing with Brad and slides back into his seat. "Man! I was just about to go home! I think I've aged since I last saw you! I really feel like I'm starting to grow a beard!" Brad jokes whilst stroking his chin.

Dean stares him dead in the eyes as he pulls out the paper from his pocket, holding it up between his first two fingers. "Do you know what this is?" he asks.

Brad shakes his head. "A crappy, ripped takeaway flyer?" he replies sarcastically.

"Yes, but... with a phone number on it!" Dean flips the paper over to reveal Lana's handwritten phone number, then lifts his eyebrows up and down, coupled with an enormous grin.

"Well, although that took you a *lot* longer than I expected, it was still fast work my friend and for that I commend you!" quips Brad as Dean smirks back. "I also saw your dance moves, and I must say it was quite impressive! So, when are you seeing her?"

Dean smirks, "I've got to ring her later, but I'm hoping tomorrow night!" he replies excitedly, grinning from ear to ear like a Cheshire cat.

Brad nods multiple times, "Excellent!"

After dropping Brad off, Dean arrives home and warms himself some left over takeaway jerk chicken from his fridge. He pours himself half a glass of his favourite plum saké and turns on his television. As he sips his wine, he stares at the phone number Lana wrote on the flyer, he simply can't stop thinking about her. It's only been a couple of hours, but he can't wait a minute longer, he knows he needs to speak to her *now*. He *never* gets nervous around girls but for some reason he has butterflies in the pit of his stomach from the mere thought of calling her.

What he needs is some Dutch courage, so he fills up his glass again, this time to the brim and downs it in one, then breathes deeply. He checks the number from the flyer and starts to dial it, but before it even starts to ring, he ends the call. He has a lump in his throat, his hands are clammy and he's starting to break out in a cold sweat. He sighs, "This is *crazy*! What's wrong with me? Just ring her!" he mutters to himself.

He dials the number again and as it starts to ring his heart starts to pound triple time. "Hello?" Lana answers in a soft tone. There's a short pause as he wills the words to exit his mouth.

"Hi! It's Dean... from the café!"

"Oh, hi!" she replies enthusiastically. "I wasn't sure if you were gonna call!"

"Yeah, of course! I was just waiting a while in case you were eating your dinner or something!" He squints and shakes his head to himself, ashamed of his lame comment.

Lana feels so much more confident on the phone and less inhibited as Dean's not standing right in front of her. "Ah! Well I'm so glad you did."

"Yeah?" he queries, fishing for confirmation.

"Yes!" she reiterates clearly.

There's another moment of hesitation then Dean clears his throat. "So, do you erm... would you er..." He shakes his head again to himself for stuttering, then composes himself and perseveres, "like to come out with me tomorrow night for some dinner?"

Without a second of uncertainty she replies straight away, "Yeah, I'd love to!"

He is so relieved by her response, like a giant weight has been lifted from his shoulders. He's beginning to have excessively deep feelings for her and can feel the passion intensify even as he speaks to her on the phone. "Great! If you take my number and text me your address and I'll pick you up around seven if that's alright?"

"That's perfect!" she responds jubilantly. He reads out his cell phone number and Lana saves it to her phone.

"I'll text you that now and I'll see you tomorrow night then," she confirms, content with the outcome.

"I can't wait!" Dean blurts out, now uninhibitedly.

There's a brief silence, then to his delight Lana replies quietly, "Me neither!" Dean feels his stomach churn with exhilaration as they say goodbye and ring off.

He's ecstatic and excitedly he rings Brad to let him know he's set up the date. It rings. "B!"

"Hey, man!"

"So, I called her and we're *definitely* going out tomorrow night!"

"Yes! I think you might be punching a bit though, D!"

"Yeah, you're probably right for once!" he chuckles. They chat for a while longer then Dean ends the call and finishes his dinner. He can't stop grinning to himself for the rest of the evening. He's on cloud nine with Lana feeling exactly the same, they both continue to be overly energised for the remainder of the night.

Chapter 3

The First Date...

The following day all Lana and Dean can do is deliberate, wonder what the other is doing, and obsess about their forthcoming date. They both go to work but constantly check the time, their clocks, and watches. It's as though time is slowing down and coming to a complete stop; as Lana daydreams and continually stares at the clock without a single blink, she briefly snaps out of it and does a double-take. With a prolonged stare, it almost seems like the hands of time are actually moving backwards.

Dean's in an absolute daze as well. He and Brad are both called into a meeting to talk about company shares, and also to research prospective future land development sites for a new branch. The manager's voice starts to become second only to his own thoughts as he begins to drift off, gazing into thin air, distracted by his reflections and feelings for Lana.

He taps his pen on his pad several times preoccupied with his thoughts of her, but then gradually focuses his mind back into the meeting. He scrawls some notes on his jotter, but quickly scribbles them out realising his error. Turning to Brad who is seated next to him, he side whispers. "B? I need to get on this date! Instead of writing *land* I just wrote *Lana* on my pad! I'm losing it!"

Brad chortles. "You've got it bad my friend, and you haven't even been out with her yet!" Dean nods in agreement and tries his best to concentrate on the rest of his meeting.

Lana is simultaneously living out the exact same day and has been discussing Dean in depth with some of her colleagues. She's so excited and eager, it's impossible to concentrate on anything else. Although she's extremely busy working on some dress designs for a client, she can't seem to concentrate as her mind isn't on anything else but Dean. She continuously becomes distracted and can't stop glancing up at the clock. The day is dragging and after what seems like an eternity, the workday finally comes to an end and they both rush home.

Although there're still a few hours left to go before their date, Dean is unduly restless, so decides to start getting ready anyway. He pulls a crisp jet-black shirt from his closet and starts to steam iron it, then he hangs it up and begins to press his jeans. He polishes and shines his shoes, then buffs them until they're so shiny he can see his face in them. He places them on the floor next to his bedside table, then picks up his wallet and sorts out his notes, coins, and credit cards. Now just to shower and he'll be ready.

Even though he's elated to be going out with Lana, he still feels somewhat apprehensive so decides to call Brad for some support, encouragement, and words of wisdom. The phone rings and Brad picks up.

"Hi, Brad,"

"Hey, man. How's it goin'?"

"Just gettin' ready now, but I'm a little nervous to be honest!"

"Don't be ridiculous, D, you'll have her eating out the palm of your hand!"

"Well that's real nice!" Dean replies sarcastically, "But it's not like that, I really, *really* like this girl."

Brad chuckles, "I'm kidding! Just be yourself and everything will fall into place," he suggests reassuringly.

"Yeah, I hope so, I just don't know why she makes me so nervous!"

"Well it's obviously because you *like* her, so just be yourself and it'll work out, alright?"

"Alright, thanks man!" Dean pauses and exudes a puzzled look. "Hold on a second, I don't know why I'm even asking *you* for advice, you haven't exactly got a great track record with women!" he jokes.

"What! What do you mean? I'm *amazing* with the ladies!"

"Really? So, when was the last time *you* had a date?"

"I've had a lot of work on lately D, and you all of all people should know that!"   Dean laughs out loud, "Brad, I work *with* you! You have *no* work on!"

"Well, *actually* for your information, Jess said she has a friend who thinks I sound *extremely* funny and would *love* to meet me. She's gonna fix us up next week!"

Dean chuckles to himself, "Okay, well I'd love to see that!"

"Actually, thinking about it, why don't you just blow off Lana tonight and come out with me instead, and I'll show you how good I am with the ladies!"

"Hmm, however tempting that may sound, I'm gonna pass!" he replies sarcastically, smirking to himself. "Listen I'm gonna go finish getting ready, so I'll see you tomorrow B."

"Stay cool!" adds Brad. Dean rolls his eyes and simpers.

Attempting to get into a more relaxed state of mind, Dean loads some R&B music and takes a refreshing shower. As he dries off and starts to dress, he looks in the mirror and can see that the shirt he's chosen perfectly accentuates his tanned skin and emphasizes the green hue in his eyes. He's feeling fit, fresh, and handsome! He fastens his cufflinks, sprays on some cologne, and rubs a little gel in his hair. He is looking good and feeling confident.

Lana arrives home, throws her purse and coat onto her couch, sprints up the stairs and starts to rummage through all her clothes. She has absolutely *no* idea what she's going to wear and tries on at least *eight* different outfits consecutively. She doesn't want to wear anything *too* revealing, but at the same time still wants to look sexy. After much thought, deliberation, and *multiple* changes, and with now most of her wardrobe scattered on her bedroom floor, Lana settles for an off-the-shoulder sweetheart top with black lace choker, ripped jeans, and high heels.

She runs a bubble bath, throws in extra bath bombs and soaks, thinking about Dean and what the night ahead holds for them. Her mind starts to wander. What's he doing now? What will *he* be wearing? How should she wear her hair? Straight, curly, wavy? Red lipstick, pink? Where will they go? Will he hold her hand? Will he try to kiss her? There's just too much to think about!

The anticipation swells. She jumps out the bath, dries herself off, and gets dressed. As she gazes in the mirror adjusting her top, she suddenly remembers the Wonderbra she bought some time ago that she stashed in her bottom draw. She pulls it out and it's still in the pack on the hanger, so she rips it off and tries it on. She adjusts the straps and pushes everything together, her cleavage now abundantly bigger than a few moments ago. She raises her eyebrows, "Hmm, impressive!" she mumbles to herself.

She scatters *every* piece of make-up she owns over her king-sized bed, then fans it out and separates into different sections. Wrapping her hair tightly in a towel, she starts to perfect her face.

She decides that she's going to wear her hair down but wavy with a few curls sporadically placed, so she puts a few hair twists in her hair and dries it to set. She makes it slightly tousled and sprays with hairspray to hold it in place. She grabs some of her *Si* perfume from her bedside table and sprays it on liberally, as she recalls how much Dean said he liked it. She aligns her earrings, and she's finally ready! Now all she has to do is wait for him to arrive!

It's 6:45 p.m. and as Dean doesn't live far from Lana's house, he's nearly ready to leave out. He sprays on a little extra cologne and double checks himself in the mirror once more. He's excited yet still a little anxious. Clasping his keys, he gets in his car and drives the short journey to Lana's house. As he reaches a few doors away, he starts to slow down to check the house numbers, sees it and parks outside. He waits in the car for a few minutes more, making final adjustments. He runs his finger over his eyebrows, checking himself in his rear-view mirror and continues to psyche himself up. His heart starts to beat tenfold as he knows the moment has finally arrived. Tardily he walks to Lana's door, still feeling nervous. No woman has *ever* had this effect on him before.

As Dean rings the doorbell Lana's heart starts to flutter and her stomach stirs. She opens the door and there he stands before her, looking *extremely* handsome, effortlessly displaying his perfectly chiselled features. She knew he was good looking but didn't remember him being *this* gorgeous! Lana's spellbound and exhilarated, with a feeling of anticipation like fireworks on New Year's Eve!

He smiles fondly at her, "Hi!"

"Hi... Dean!" she splutters, trying hard to get her words out.

"You look beautiful!" he comments adoringly.

"So do you!" she blurts out, "I mean... erm," she stutters, "... You look *really* nice!"

He grins back, "You ready to go?"

"Yeah, I'll just grab my purse," she replies, her face now flushing a vibrant shade of pink. "I can't believe I just said that!" she mouths to herself as she picks up her purse and keys and locks her front door.

As they stroll to Dean's car, he gallantly holds the door open for her as she gracefully climbs in. He walks around to the driver's side and starts the engine. "So, is there anywhere you'd like to go in particular?" he asks attentively.

"If there's food, I'm there!" she jokes.

Already entranced and beguiled by her personality, he charmingly grins. "We could go to that new steakhouse, Beefsteak and Cheesecake. I pass it all the time on the way to work. It looks amazing inside if you want to try it?"

"Yeah, let's do that!" she replies excitedly in agreement.

He turns on the car stereo and they fluently chat and laugh throughout the entire journey.

A few moments later they arrive, and Dean pulls into the car park. Once more, he courteously opens the door for Lana, locks his car and then spontaneously reaches for her hand, much to her surprise, but also to her delight!

They approach the entrance of the steakhouse together and walk through the giant double glass doors. Although it's absolutely *packed* with people, the service is impeccable, and they are quickly greeted by the hostess. "Table for two, please!" requests Dean assertively.

"Follow me please, Sir," she replies politely.

They walk over to a lovely, secluded and intimate table in the corner. There's a single red rose placed intricately between two wine glasses, situated in the centre of the table, and a small scented candle encased in a glass jar, delicately flickering. The hostess leaves as a waitress walks over and hands them a menu each. "Would you like to order any drinks?" she asks enthusiastically.

Dean glances over at Lana. "What you having?"

"I'll have a coke please."

"Make that two cokes please," he tells the waitress.

"Two cokes," she repeats quietly to herself, whilst jotting down the order on her pad. "I'll be right back," she says, scurrying off to get the drinks.

They are both highly impressed with the service so far.

Dean scours the menu. Everything on the carte looks delectable. "Order anything you want!" he tells Lana generously.

"I hope you know I'm going to be paying my share!" she replies independently.

"No way!" he states with a defiant shake of his head. Lana squints and gives him a look in jest, he laughs. "Okay, how about I pay for tonight and then, you can pay for our *next* date?!" His suggestion is cheeky, and he *is* trying his luck, but at the same time is desperately hoping that Lana will say yes. Dean is *beyond* charming and charismatic and she just wants to throw her arms around his neck and kiss him passionately. As every moment passes, her feelings for him rapidly intensify.

She calms herself, "Agreed!" They look into each other's eyes endearingly and Dean gently nods, chuffed with himself that he's already secured another date with her.

"Well, that's *wonderful* news and also clearly means that you can't resist my charms!" he quips.

She smiles back at him bashfully. *Maybe I can't!* she thinks to herself.

They continue to peruse the menu, then Dean decides he's going to have steak and ribs and Lana's indicates that she'd like the same. He's impressed with her appetite and likes a girl who likes her food, and who doesn't feel uncomfortable to eat in front of him. The waitress returns with their drinks, and they place the order for their food. "Please help yourself to the salad bar while you wait," she informs them kindly. They walk over together, and Lana can feel the electricity in the atmosphere as she stands close to him. As they fill their plates, they sporadically glance and smile at one another.

As they return to their table, the waitress is already bringing over their food. "That was quick!" he acknowledges. The waitress smiles and places the food on the table, telling them that she hopes they enjoy their meals.

The food looks mouth-watering and delicious, but as Dean cuts into his steak, he realises that it hasn't been cooked to his specification. Instead of *well-done* it's *rare*, so he beckons the waitress back over and explains the error. She apologises copiously and tells him she'll get another one made up straight away, and also due to the inconvenience, his total bill will be discounted by twenty five percent.

The waitress takes the meal as Dean turns to Lana. "Well, that's nice of them to give us a discount, but obviously that's because they know they made a serious mis-*steak*!" he wisecracks. She chuckles and rolls her eyes. "What? You don't like my jokes?" he grins.

"Actually, it was pretty good; in fact, it was *well-done*!" she replies wittily.

Dean lifts his eyebrows in respect. "Well that's because I'm *rare*!" They both giggle at their bad jokes.

After receiving the correct food, they chat, laugh, and joke continuously throughout their meal. Soon after finishing their main courses, they decide to order the house speciality dessert, *double-bake chocolate chunk cheesecake* for two to share. The waitress brings it over in a monstrously large glass bowl with two long handled spoons. It's a massive, *colossal* slab of chocolate cheesecake, topped with fresh cream, drizzled with chocolate sauce, and sprinkled with humongous chocolate chunks. Dean stares at it, with a raised eyebrow. "It's almost the size of the table!" he quips. Lana cracks up as they attempt to devour as much of it as they possibly can. After several mammoth mouthfuls and much laughter, Dean sighs and places his hand on his stomach... "The food was *amazing*, but I'm out!"

"Me too!" she groans.

He beckons the waitress over and asks for a takeaway box so they can take the remainder of the cheesecake home and asks for the bill. After a couple of minutes, she returns with their receipt on a tray and also the perfectly packaged cheesecake, which he hands to Lana with a cheeky, "Good luck!"

Lana grins as Dean checks the amount payable, then puts the money and a *large* tip back onto the tray, then hands it back to the waitress. "Thank you *very* much Sir!" she says jubilantly, overwhelmed at noticing the considerable tip he has left her.

"No problem!" he replies respectfully. Lana's impressed by his generosity and kindness, especially since they messed up their order!

Grabbing Lana's jacket from the back of her chair, he holds it up gallantly for her to put her arms into. As he stands behind her, she can feel the chemistry radiating back from him. He picks up his coat and they leave, still engrossed in conversation.

The night is cool and peaceful as they walk hand in hand towards his car. "I can't remember the last time I ate that much food! It was delicious though!" she remarks. He starts to drive her back home but neither of them wants the night to be over. He purposely drives slower and goes around the long way to lengthen the journey. "Tonight's gone *so* fast!" she concludes.

"Yeah, it's flown by. It feels like I just picked you up five minutes ago!" he agrees.

Although he's taken an extended route, it's late and there's not much traffic so he's still arrives quicker than he would have liked to. He pulls up to Lana's house and graciously walks her to her door. She pushes the key in the lock, opens her front door then turns around to face him.

"Thanks for a lovely night, Dean," she remarks gratefully.

"Thank *you*, Lana. This has been, without a doubt, one of the *best* nights I've had in a *very* long time!" he states, gradually moving closer to her. They stare intently into each other's eyes until she shyly breaks his gaze. He grins.

"You're adorable!" Dean has such strong feelings for Lana, but he doesn't know whether to make his move and kiss her goodnight or not. He quickly contemplates the many outcomes in his mind, but the torrid passion he feels for her finally makes him lose his inhibitions and compels him to take her face in his hands and gently kiss her full, rosy, crimson lips. Lana feels lightheaded as though she's about to faint, but at the same time doesn't want him to stop. "You still want to meet in the café tomorrow?" he asks.

Still in a trance from his kiss and barely able to speak, all she can manage to utter is a faint "mm-hmm."

"What time?"

Lana tries hard to compose herself. "Erm... after work, around six, half six."

"I'll be there." Dean leans in and kisses her once more. He says *bye* in a whisper and walks back to his car. Lana's left there swooning like a love-sick teenager. She waves to him, closes the door then leans back on it, still entranced.

Feeling blissful and more content than she has ever felt in her entire life, all she can think about is Dean, how well their date went, how wonderfully they gel together, and how amazing he is. She tries to stop herself from smiling, but she can't.

She's *way* too excited to go to sleep so decides to try and subdue her mood by getting comfy and trying to unwind. She lights a macaroon scented candle and then re-lights her log fire. Although she's still full from their meal, she makes herself a small cup of hot cocoa to try and help her sleep, then plays some old soul tunes. She takes her oversized pyjamas out cupboard and pulls on her big squeaky duck slippers that she bought for herself in the Christmas sales. Finally, she removes all her make-up and applies a green avocado face mask. Placing cucumbers on her eyes, she's ready to relax for a while. She feels content, calm, and satisfied, immersed in her music and deep in her feelings and thoughts, reliving out her incredible date.

Dean arrives home. He has *three* messages on his answering machine which he presumes are no doubt are from Brad asking how his date went. It's late so he decides he'll talk to him tomorrow instead. He kicks off his shoes and turns his television on, then flicks through the channels and stops on the football. He throws the remote on his couch and heads into the kitchen. He takes a bottle of strawberry flavoured water from the fridge, breaks the seal, and starts to sip it. Feeling pensive, he gets comfortable on his couch and reflects on his date with Lana. As he starts to recall their marvellous, memorable night together, he suddenly realises how quiet it is in his apartment and exactly what he's been missing in his life. He smirks to himself as he recalls some of the things that they said to each other and their *very* weak jokes! Nearly an hour has passed, and he still can't stop thinking about her. As he closes his eyes, he envisages her face in his mind's eye. It's as though she's still there with him as he deeply inhales the remnants of her perfume embedded there on his shirt. He's restless and unsettled. He knows he can't wait until the next day to see her again, in fact he can't wait another single second. He turns the television off, puts his shoes back on, and grabs his car keys.

Dean jumps in his car and drives to his local all-night store where he stops off to buy Lana some flowers. He scours through several buckets until he spots a beautiful mixed bouquet of roses and peonies. He checks his watch several times as he knows how late it is, so hastily buys them, gets back in his car, and speedily drives back to her house.

A few minutes later, Lana's almost fallen asleep but jumps, startled to hear a knock at her door. She's not expecting anyone at this late hour. As she springs up, the cucumbers fling off her face. She rushes to see who it is, slippers squeaking with every step, and peers through the peephole situated in the middle of the door. Her eyes enlarge, she gasps, she can't believe Dean is standing there.

He hears the noise from her slippers, appearing confused he calls out, "Lana? You there? It's Dean!"

Lana's flustered. "Yeah, just a minute!" she shouts back, trying to muffle the despair in her voice. *Dean can't see me like this!* she thinks, consumed with desperation. She runs back and forth panicking and jumping around, anxiously wondering what she can do to remedy the situation. He calls out her name again and realising she has no time to take the face mask off or to get dressed, she decides that she's left with no other alternative but to reluctantly answer the door.

She very hesitantly opens the door and bashfully stands behind it, grimacing. "Hello?" calls out Dean curiously. Lana peeps her head around the doorway, unveiling her bright green face. He's stunned and dumbfounded, but then suddenly cracks up. His whole face lights up and he can't stop laughing.

"It's not funny!" Lana claps back, she is *so* embarrassed. "I wasn't meant to be seeing you 'til tomorrow!" she declares sternly.

"Well if I'd known you were going to look like that, I might have waited!" he jokes. She smiles awkwardly as Dean grins and hands her the flowers. Begrudgingly, she invites him in and closes the door behind him as he goes to sit down by the fire. Lana walks to him squeaking. He gazes down at her slippers and chuckles. She angrily pulls one off and throws it on the floor. "No! Leave them on, I like them! In fact, I might get a pair myself!" he quips.

Lana rolls her eyes and half smiles uncomfortably as she sits down next to him on the sofa, now just wearing the one slipper. "I thought we were meeting tomorrow?" she states defeatedly.

"Yeah, I know, but the problem with that is that you've cast some sort of spell on me and I just couldn't wait that long to see you again!" They profoundly hold each other's gaze. "I've been thinking about you ever since I dropped you off!" he proclaims.

Lana's mood starts to thaw. "I've been thinking about you too!" she admits shyly.

Dean casually moves closer to her and starts to gently twist and twirl her hair through his fingers as he continues to stare at her green face. "You *still* look beautiful!" he comments.

Lana knows he's joking, but still feels mortified and turns away. "I'm gonna go wash this off!" She starts to stand but Dean interrupts and grabs her hand.

"No, don't, it's late, I just wanted to see you for a few minutes."

Lana feels so much passion for Dean whenever he is close to her. "I'm gonna go and let you get some sleep and I'll see you tomorrow, hopefully not looking like Shrek!" he teases.

He pulls her close and kisses her lovingly. She sighs then notices he has some of her face mask transferred on to his cheek. "You have a bit of..." He stops her.

"It's fine, leave it. When I look in the mirror, it'll remind me of you! I better go, I'll see you in the café tomorrow."

"I'll be there!" she confirms.

She walks timidly with Dean to the door. "Thanks for the flowers," she murmurs adoringly. He winks, says bye, but then doubles back for one last kiss. Once she's closed the door, she can't contain her excitement any longer, she jumps up and down, with one slipper squeaking.

He gets in his car and punches the air with his fist "Yes!" he cheers to himself, bursting with happiness.

Chapter 4

Truly, Madly, Deeply...

It's the day after the *wondrous* night before, and Lana gets up extra early for work with a definitive spring in her step. Dean is the *only* thing on her mind and as she fills the water dispenser in her coffee machine, she can't help but daydream and drift off into a fantasy world where everything's Dean!

She opens her fridge door and glimpses at the cheesecake leftovers sitting there, smiling broadly to herself as thoughts come flooding back of their wonderful time together. She picks out a fork from the draw and starts to savour it straight from the box, slowly relishing every mouthful. With each bite she reminisces about their date and how she wishes she could be transported back in time and relive every single moment with him over and over again.

She pushes her kitchen window open and breathes in deeply, inhaling the clean, crisp, fresh air. She hears the harmonic sound of bluebirds chirping in unison and feels as though she's been sucked straight into a fairy tale. She just can't wait for the moment they're reunited again.

After what seems like another excruciatingly long day at work, she hurriedly starts her journey to the café. As she arrives, and on approaching the doorway, she lifts her head slightly to peer through the glass, like an inquisitive meerkat standing to attention. She bobs her head up and down a few times until she eventually notices him sitting there in the corner. Her stomach starts to stir a little, like a thousand butterflies are fluttering around inside her and apprehensively she breathes a sigh of relief. She's nervous but also extremely uplifted. Her nerves gradually dispel as she makes a beeline for him. Greeting her with a tender kiss on her cheek, they sit down. He's already ordered her favourite drink, so she gives thanks, unbuttons her jacket, and takes a sip.

In the background, the song *Rock Me Amadeus* randomly starts to play on the jukebox as Lana starts to burst into fits of giggles, concealing herself behind her coffee cup. "I didn't even know this track was on the list! Who put *this* on?" she jokes.

"I think *they* did!" Dean chuckles, motioning to a group of tattooed bikers sitting in the far corner booth. She casually peers over her shoulder and continues to quietly giggle to herself. He looks back to Lana and stares intensely at her for a moment. "I've been thinking about you *all* day!" he confidently blurts out. She was not expecting that kind of remark quite so soon but can't hide her joy as her face tells the story. She beams with delight and replies accordingly.

"I might have thought about you a couple of times!" she smirks. Dean's dimples make yet another appearance as he grins, delighted at her comeback.

"So, I see you managed to wash your face mask off!" he teases.

Lana shakes her head. "That was *so* embarrassing!"

He chortles to himself, but then his face changes as he becomes straight-faced and clears his throat a couple of times. "Lar? I wanted to ask you something." She's intrigued. "I know we haven't known each other for very long but, I'd really like to see you... I mean... on a regular."

Lana's astounded but thinks fast and in a flirtatious manner asks, "Are you asking me to be your girlfriend?" But Dean's serious about this, as she can tell from his calm demeanour and he simply nods his head gently, affirming his confirmation.

She thinks for a second then replies, "Well then in that case, I'd love to!" Her response is just what he was hoping to hear, and they fondly embrace, now officially a couple.

They unfailingly continue to meet in the café every day after work and *To Be Loved* by Jackie Wilson fatefully becomes *their* song. The coming weeks see them share several dates together. They take it in turns deciding what to do and where to go and one of Lana's choices is to take Dean roller skating. He squints. "Roller skating?" she giggles as he shakes his head negatively, "I'm not sure about that!"

"It's not just roller skating though," she adds, "it's *disco* roller skating!"

"Well, that's worse!" he jokes. Lana laughs as Dean rolls his head back with a humorous sigh. "Seriously though Lar, the thing is... I can't go!"

She looks concerned, "Oh! Why not?"

"Because... I don't want to!" he quips. She sighs at him and throws him a look. "I've *got* to go, haven't I?"

"Yep!" she answers positively, fastening her seat belt. "Drive on!" she indicates comically with an outstretched hand, as she then navigates him to the address.

A little while later they arrive at the site, and enter a vast car park in front of the well-lit building where there are several neon ice skating signs pointing the way, and much to his surprise, masses of people are walking in. "Who knew this many people liked this kinda thing?" he comments in amazement.

"Wait 'til you get inside!" she replies excitedly. Dean's genuinely feeling intrigued, this wasn't what he was expecting at all! As they approach the entrance, the music from inside is pumping out through the walls. They look at each other with heightened expectation. Lana hands their tickets to the doorman and they make their way in. The music's blaring and the atmosphere is excitable and addictive. Dean is flabbergasted that he actually likes it!

On another occasion they decide to catch a late-night movie. There's a cheesy romcom on that Lana's been wanting to watch for a while and although it's not really Dean's cup of tea he agrees to go because he knows it'll make her happy. As they arrive, he orders an XXL sweet and salted popcorn, drinks, sweets, and chocolate. "Don't you think we've got a bit too much?" she asks giggling to herself.

"If I'm going to have to endure this film, I'm going to need food to get me through it!" he jokes. Lana chuckles as she walks out in front.

As the film's about to start, the lights die down as they side shuffle through the rows of people. Dean can't see where he's going and nearly trips over and drops the popcorn everywhere. His eyes widen, as he gazes down at a few pieces that have fallen and are now scattered on the floor. "That was a close one!" he jests as Lana quietly titters to herself.

They locate their seats and the film begins. It's about twenty minutes in as Lana starts to giggle. Dean catches a glimpse of her out the corner of his eye and casually turns to look. He stares unwittingly, recognising just how naturally beautiful she is. He soaks up the serenity of the moment as he starts to comprehend that Lana could actually be *the one*.

Dean and Lana have been dating for nearly a month now. It's Saturday night and it's karaoke night at their favourite local Italian restaurant and bar, Bella's Restoranté Italiano. Dean's already been to Bella's a couple of times with Lana, but never for karaoke night! They noticed an advertisement for it the last time they went, so they asked Brad, and his sister Jess, if they'd like to join them this time round. Jess is already at Brad's house so Dean and Lana drive over to pick them both up. Everyone's in high spirits and looking forward to their night together. Brad sits in the passenger seat while Lana and Jess sit in the back gossiping. Although they haven't known each other for that long, they get on like a house on fire and are quickly becoming best friends.

They all arrive at Bella's and Dean takes Lana's hand as Brad walks in linking arms with Jess. They are seated straight away and order some beer, cocktails, pizza, and pasta sides to share. The guys are already eyeing-up the karaoke song list and talking about which songs everyone should sing, but now Lana's actually there, it's all becoming a bit too real and she's shy and reluctant to do it, so Jess tells them to leave her alone and *they* can sing together now instead. They write their names on the list and wait to be called up. Dean smiles lovingly at Lana, contemplating how her shyness is cute and endearing. He puts his arm around her shoulder reassuringly and kisses her gently on her cheek. "Don't worry, you don't have to sing if you don't want to, it's meant to be fun!" he chuckles. "I'll sing with Brad, okay?" Lana nods, feeling relieved. "It might be *really* bad, but we'll give it a go!" he jokes.

They're up next and Lana grins nervously as Dean walks with Brad over to the bar where the karaoke is set up. They tell the DJ what song they want and as he loads it up, they pick up their microphones. Dean gives her a little wink as the music starts, and she and Jess giggle to each other in anticipation.

Brad starts off in his extroverted, exuberant manner and everyone in the restaurant starts to cheer and clap. Lana bites her bottom lip bashfully, not knowing where to look as Jess laughs out loud. Dean takes his verse next and Lana's blown away by how good his voice is. He glances in her direction and she raises her eyebrows and gives him a complementary nod. He motions with his hands and shrugs his shoulders as if to say, *who knew*! Brad continues and by now all the customers in the restaurant are amused, entertained, and clapping along. The atmosphere is electric. After a few minutes, the song comes to an end as everyone applauds and cheers. Brad goes to sit back down, but Dean doesn't follow. He starts to whisper something to the DJ.

"What's Dean doing?" Lana quizzes Brad.

"I have no idea!" he replies, taking a sip of his ice-cold beer, also looking bemused.

Another song starts to play, It's Al Green, Let's Stay Together. Dean takes the microphone, and points directly at Lana. "I'd like to dedicate this song to my beautiful girlfriend, Lana." She feels her cheeks starting to redden as the music starts to play and he begins to sing. "I'm so in love with you, whatever you want to do is alright with me." Everyone is staring in Lana's direction; all eyes are on her and she feels so intimidated, yet still can't seem to take her eyes off him. "'Cause you make me feel so brand new, and I want to spend my life with you," he continues. Lana feels like she's been sucked into a movie and Dean is her leading man. She is *so* in love, but still feels quite shy around him and so proceeds to play it cool. He walks closer to her table. "Loving you forever is what I need." She smiles delicately but all she can think about is how much she wants to jump into his arms, wrap her legs around him, and kiss him all over his face!

The song finishes to raucous applause. Dean strolls back to their table, feeling decidedly pleased with himself.

Brad gawps at him and chuckles, "Man, I thought *I* had moves!"

As he turns to Lana, he has a twinkle in his eye. She sits there entranced, staring at his dimple-framed grin. "So, what did you think?" he smirks.

She feels flustered. "It was... *amazing!*" He nods as he strokes her hair. "Thanks! Y*ou're* amazing!" he replies in a soppy, sentimental manner.

With a shake of his head, Brad turns to Jess, "Oh man! I don't think I can take it! Shall *we* just go Jess!" Dean chuckles as Lana turns away timidly, but then he moves her face back towards him and gently kisses her on her soft, luscious lips.

The night is a resounding success! They haven't stopped chatting and laughing *all* night. So, after eating *way* too much food and downing a few too many drinks, they all decide to call it a night.

Dean only had two beers because he knew he'd have to drive, so he's still fully sober and Lana's only had a couple of cocktails, but Brad and Jess have had quite a few and are worse for wear. Dean starts the car and peers in his rear-view mirror. "You two alright?" he asks, tittering to himself. Brad nods drowsily in response and confirms in a slurred voice that Jess is stopping at his for the night, so not to worry about her. He drops them both off, then makes his way to Lana's.

By now it's almost two o'clock in the morning. Dean walks Lana to her door. "I had a wonderful time, D," she murmurs softly.

"I *always* have a wonderful time when I'm with you, Lar," he replies whole-heartedly. He grasps her face in his hands and kisses her tenderly, tells her he'll see her the next day and whispers goodnight.

Just as he's about to leave, she hesitates and clutches his arm, "Dean?"

He turns back around. "You okay?"

"Yeah, I was just wondering if you wanted to come in for a few minutes."

Dean is caught off-guard as he wasn't expecting the night to continue any further but is totally elated so goes with it.

"Oh! Yeah sure, I was going 'cause I thought it was getting late!"

Lana shrugs her shoulders. "It's Sunday tomorrow, so no work! You could come in for a night cap?" Their eyes lock and Dean motions his approval with a slight nod as she opens the door and invites him in.

She turns on the lights but dims them slightly and starts the fire as he walks over and sits on her sofa. "I've got coffee, tea, hot chocolate, juice?" she offers attentively.

"Hot chocolate please, Lar." She walks into the kitchen to make the drinks. As the time goes on and Lana's been gone a for quite a while, Dean decides to go and look for her, appearing at her kitchen door. "Everything alright? You want any help?"

She turns around, already holding the warm mugs of chocolate in her hands. "I was just coming in. Sorry it's took so long, I was heating the milk and I put the microwave on the wrong setting, so I had to start again. It took *forever!*" she rambles.

He doesn't say a word but instead just stands there looking her up and down. Lana blinks a few times, looking back perplexed. "What?" Dean walks over to her and without uttering a single word, takes the drinks from her hands and places them down on the side. He moves close to her and unreservedly takes control. He holds her face firmly in his hands and kisses her intensely but yet still with great tenderness. He takes her breath away with every kiss and every touch. She sighs.

He's totally besotted with her and can't hold back his feelings any longer. "I'm falling in love with you, Lar!" he declares in a whisper. Lana feels faint and giddy and realises she is powerless as passion takes over. She loses her inhibitions and pulls him nearer; he responds by picking her up and placing her on the kitchen table. She wraps her legs around him tightly and they finally, passionately make love.

He carries her to the bedroom where they drift off to sleep blanketed in each other's arms. A few hours later Lana is awoken by Dean stroking her hair and kissing and caressing her face and neck. Although half asleep, she reacts, she can't seem to resist him, and they make love *again*.

As morning breaks, they awake closely wrapped around each other. "Hi!" Dean murmurs, softly kissing her forehead.

"Hey!" she responds stirring, opening one eye only. This is the happiest she has ever been in her *entire* life, feeling peaceful and serene. They kiss for a little while longer, then she confidently leads him into the shower where they continue their affection and she can't help but be impressed by Dean's stamina as he initiates their passion and lovemaking once more.

Lana starts to dry her hair as Dean just sits there gazing at her. She catches his reflection in the mirror. "What?" she queries, her question accompanied with a little smirk.

"Nothin'! You're just *so* beautiful Larnie!" she grins back bashfully, puts down the hair dryer and jumps on the bed next to him. They kiss lovingly.

"You want some breakfast?" she giggles. Dean nods, so she runs jubilantly down the stairs and rushes into the kitchen to make them both some French toast, coffee, and juice as Dean gets himself dressed. She glances across to the table where the cups of cold cocoa sit from the night before, smiling contentedly to herself as she recalls their passionate rendezvous from a few hours earlier and everything that's happened since.

A few minutes pass and Dean arrives in the kitchen and as it's such a beautiful, tranquil morning they decide to take their food out into the garden. They sit closely side by side on the double seated swing whilst appreciating the beautiful chorus of harmonious, tweeting birds. "It's so peaceful out here!" he exclaims.

"Yeah, it's lovely isn't it? I spend quite a lot of time out here. If I'm not at work or in the café, I'm in this garden!" Lana has a vibrant rose bush at the bottom of her garden which is in full bloom.

"The flowers are *so* pretty!" he acknowledges.

"Roses are my favourite! Well roses *and* peonies since *you* introduced me to them!" she declares. Dean looks back fondly at her, positions his arm gently around her shoulder, and pulls her closer toward him. He kisses her cheek and then sips his juice. She beams, so satisfied and secure to be around him. They eat their food and chat, feeling blissful and blessed to be sharing each other's company on such a beautiful morning.

As the day progresses, Dean decides to take Lana into town for some lunch at a place he recently came across called Cha & Bix. It's a British tea and cookie lounge in the mall that's just opened, it's lovely inside and very stylish. Lana sits down and looks around as they order some tea, sandwiches, and cookies. "Mmm! Chocolate biscuits! This place *is* lovely but for some reason I feel like I'm betraying Sam by being in here!"

Dean grins as he nibbles on his chocolate chip shortbread. "I won't tell him if you don't!" he quips. They finish their tea and shop for a little while, then return to Lana's house.

They cuddle closely together in bed watching movies and thriving in the pleasure of each other's love, and both can feel the sexual chemistry radiating back from one another. Later in the evening they order a Chinese takeaway. Lana pulls two fortune cookies from the bag, taking one for herself and passing the other to Dean. She opens hers; it reads... *Someone you are thinking of is thinking of you!* Dean nods comically then opens his, it reads... *He who hesitates is lost*! He makes a face humorously, grabs her and nestles in her neck as she giggles.

The time soon passes, and after spending the *entire* day together, Dean *still* doesn't want to leave but knows he must as they both have work the following day. Lana desperately doesn't want him to go either. It's late in the evening by now and as he walks to the door, he has to force himself to go. "I'll see you tomorrow after work, okay?" he states softly, stroking her hand gently.

"Alright!" she replies subduedly, nuzzling her face into his chest as he cradles her in his arms. They kiss as she clings on to him and he gives her a little squeeze, then pulls himself away and reluctantly leaves.

As he gets in his car he texts her. *Thanks for a wonderful time, see you tomorrow. P.S. I love you, Lar.*

The message beeps through to Lana's phone and as she opens it and sees the words, her heart starts to melt. She reads it again and again, over and over, then puts a protection lock on it so it will always remain on her phone. She texts him back. *I had an amazing day Dean. P.S. I love you too*!

Lana crawls on to her bed and glances at the pillow Dean slept on. She pulls it close to her and hugs it as tightly as she can, like a snake constricting around its prey, breathing in the smell of his cologne still lingering there. She inhales it deeply, like it's the oxygen she needs to survive. She can't stop grinning to herself as she breathes in his scent, and re-reads his text message, over and over. Dean simultaneously reads his text then drives home feeling deliriously happy.

As soon as he reaches home, he has more messages from Brad on his answering machine so rings him back. Brad picks up. "Hello!"

"B!"

"You're alive! I've rang your phone *and* your house like a gazillion times!"

"I know, I know, I'm sorry, I was busy. I stopped over at Lana's last night!" he says modestly.

"*Yes*! You know, I think your little karaoke number really secured it for you, D!"

Dean shakes his head. "Will you stop? I'm really falling for this girl, she's special."

Brad laughs, "What's wrong with you? I ain't never seen you so caught up with a woman like this before!"

"That's 'cause she's different, I *really* like her B."

"Well, I'm sure she likes you, but you gotta take it easy, you've only known her a little while, you don't want to scare her off!" They continue to converse and Brad is genuinely happy for him, but he's never seen him act this way before and doesn't want to see him get hurt and, if he's being honest with himself, he feels a bit put out that someone else is spending so much time with him, and wonders if it will ultimately impact on their friendship.

At the exact same time Dean is speaking to Brad, Lana is ringing Jess. Jess picks up. "Dean stayed last night!" she blurts out without even saying hello.

Jess shrieks down the phone in elation. "Lar! I knew you two would get together!"

There's a brief pause. "I *really* like him, Jess!" she admits reservedly.

"Well, you know what? I think he *really* likes you too!" They chat for a while as she fills Jess in on all the juicy details.

The next day, Dean is pining for Lana in the café. She's later than usual and he's getting agitated and worked up waiting for her to arrive, as he wants to ask her to go to his place and it's getting late. He has her coffee ready and he's biting the inside of his mouth, checking his phone constantly and tapping his feet under the table, but he doesn't have to wait any longer as the door suddenly flings opens and there she is! Dean's expression alters positively as he walks over to her and she responds by affectionately wrapping her arms securely around his neck. They kiss as he picks her up and swirls her around. She giggles, then they walk back to their table hand in hand.

They sit down and Lana takes off her jacket. "Sorry I'm later than I said, D, my meeting ran over."

"It's alright, I missed you! I can't stop thinking about last night" he murmurs, gripping her hand and holding it snug in his.

She stares at him, "I missed you too! And yeah, me neither!" she responds quietly.

"Why don't you come to mine tonight and let me cook for you?" he asks.

Instantly, without a second thought she answers, "Yeah, I'd love that!" Although they've been dating for a while, Lana hasn't been to Dean's home yet, so she's excited to finally be going. They talk intently for a little while then she gets in her car and follows Dean back to his apartment.

As he places the key in his door, Lana starts to feel a little intimidated as this is the first time she's ever been there and doesn't know what to expect. He pushes the door open, clasps her hand in his and walks her in. She looks around and to her amazement everything is new, fresh, and clean. She frowns with a puzzled expression. "Well, this is *not* what I was expecting at all!" she jokes.

Dean grins as he pours her a glass of pop. "What *were* you expecting?" he asks curiously.

"A man cave!" she replies sarcastically.

He lifts his eyebrows, "And what's one of them?"

"You know, clothes everywhere, plates and rubbish left around the place, not the best smell!"

He grins again. "You're funny!"

Lana scans the room, then stops to admire a picture of Dean's parents and comments on how much he resembles his father. She then notices another picture of him sitting on a motorcycle. She picks it up. "Wow! Is this you?"

He turns to look. "Yeah, in my *very* young days! I used to ride a lot but I had a pretty bad accident so I gave it up, but it's not to say I wouldn't get another one someday."

She looks concerned. "What happened?"

"I stopped at some lights and I was waiting to turn, then this car tried to get around me but drove straight into me instead! I had a broken leg, a few cuts and bruises, but I was alright. I was more shook than anything, but... I've got this cool scar on my wrist!" He unbuttons his shirt and rolls up his sleeve to show Lana the heart shaped scar on his wrist. He smirks but she doesn't look impressed.

"My uncle got badly injured in a motorcycle accident a few years ago, he almost died!" she informs him gravely. Dean's face drops. "He loved that bike! He said it was the freedom of being able to move through the traffic that was the thrill and I even rode with him a few times, but they're too dangerous, D. Please promise me you won't get another one."

Dean understands her concern as he's had a few close calls himself and he isn't even that bothered about getting another one anyway so agrees to her wishes. "I promise!" he whispers, lightly kissing her on her nose.

He gives her a cuddle then places his arm around her waist assuringly and leads her into his kitchen. He opens his fridge and all the cupboard doors, then sits on his kitchen stool continually twisting back and forth, one way then the other, stretching out his arm, moving his hand across all the food.

"Now pick carefully." he jokes. "Choose some things you like, and I'll make us up something to eat." Lana looks impressed. Not only is Dean's place immaculate but now he's offering to cook her *anything* she wants from fresh! His fridge and cupboards are filled to the brim with healthy, nutritious food and everything is amazingly clean. Lana picks some chicken breast, and vegetables from the fridge and notices some large, juicy apples sitting on the side so jokingly asks Dean if he will also make her an apple pie for dessert, but to her astonishment he says he *loves* to cook and if that's what she wants, that's what he will do! She shimmies up onto a high stool next to his work surface then starts to flick through some of his old CD collection, as he grabs a bottle of wine from the fridge.

He notices her interest. "Wanna listen to some music?"

"Sure!" she answers, enthralled and compelled under the spell of his charm.

"I've got *old skool* R&B you know!" he says raising one eyebrow. He inserts a CD of R&B tracks into the stereo as he begins to prepare the food. Aaliyah, Ashanti, Jagged Edge, Sadé and other various artists blast out the speakers.

Lana's hypnotised by him and the variety of seductive music is only heightening her mood. She has to stop herself from staring directly in his direction. He glances at her periodically and smirks charismatically, which makes her heart miss a beat. They proceed to chat as he cooks, and she feels so content and satisfied. There's nowhere else she'd rather be. As one of Dean's favourite songs comes on, he walks over to her, softly pecks her cheek, then twirls her around as she giggles. She sits back down, and he continues to cook.

After about half an hour of cooking, chatting and laughter, the food is ready and the pie is baking in the oven, the smell wafting around the kitchen is divine. They sit down to eat and talk and laugh with each other throughout their meal. The food is sublime, and Lana finishes every last mouthful. He takes some Madagascar vanilla ice-cream from his freezer and carefully takes the hot apple pie out of the oven. He cuts a generous slice for Lana and piles a couple of scoops of ice-cream on top. "Wow, this looks delicious!" she comments, totally impressed by his culinary skills as she watches attentively at the ice cream starting to melt and trickle down the side of the crust.

"You better eat *all* of it, Lar," teases Dean.

"Somehow I don't think that's gonna be a problem!" she giggles.

He asks her to stay over to which she gladly agrees. They cuddle close together in his bed watching Netflix and talking for hours. He starts to kiss her seductively and once more their feelings of passion take over.

Chapter 5

Head Over Heels...

It's Saturday afternoon and Lana's packed a picnic basket full to the brim with drinks, a variety of sandwiches, chicken, potato salad, cupcakes, and fruit. It's considerably heavier than she anticipated, and she can just about lift it! Dean arrives to collect her as she struggles to pick up the basket. He takes it from her hand as she giggles and grabs a tartan blanket. "Lar, there's only the two of us, do think you might have gone slightly overboard?"

"We don't know how long we're gonna be out and I don't want you gettin' hungry!"

"I don't think there's any chance of that!" he quips, staring downward at the overflowing basket.

They decide to drive to a nearby forest and park. Dean merges on to a road of cascading trees which intertwine with each other to make an arched passage. Beams of sunlight burst through the branches and auburn autumn leaves, making the whole journey tranquil and picturesque. "D, this scenery's breathtaking!" Lana beams, he smiles back feeling content and delighted at her enthusiasm and blessed to be surrounded by this stunning scenery.

They come out the other side and arrive at the park, and before long uncover a lovely secluded location in a sheltered, wooded area. Dean treks over to a large weeping willow and arranges the blanket carefully on the grass underneath it, as Lana picks out some of the food from the basket. As she walks towards him, she notices an unusual shaped tree overlooking a rose bush and a beautiful array of flowers. "Wow Dean, come look at this!" He walks back over to her and notes the jubilation and joyfulness on her face. He's taken aback as he recognises how many of the things that most people take for granted Lana finds beautiful. Observing how enchanted she is with this undisturbed spot she's discovered; he decides to try and make the moment even more significant and unforgettable for her. He spontaneously pulls his keys from his pocket, to which he has attached several keyrings. One of them has a small penknife fastened to it, he takes it and flicks it open. He walks near to the tree and starts to carve a heart into it.

Lana looks on in awe as he carves *D & L, Always & Forever* inside the heart. He puts his arm around her neck and pulls her close. "Now this will *always* be our special place!" he whispers romantically. Lana can't contain her happiness or excitement. It evokes a feeling in her as she gazes up at him, kissing him impulsively, hard on his lips.

He takes her hand and guides her over to the picnic. As she sits on the blanket, he removes the rest of the items from the basket one by one and places them on the ground. Lana picks up the plates and serviettes as he glances at her pensively, then back down to the plates. Exuding a composed demeanour, he asks, "Do you believe in fate, Lar?" She seems a little perplexed at such a random question but is intrigued as to where he is going with this.

"Yeah, I guess I do!" she replies.

He nods and gazes at her. "So, do you think if there hadn't been that storm we'd still have met?"

She pauses. "I think our paths would have crossed, eventually." She adds "I think if it's meant to be it's meant to be!" he nods in agreement, realising that he can't even remember a time when he wasn't with her and how glad he is to have her in his life.

He wants to take Lana to meet his parents and after a beautiful day at the park he tells her they're having a barbecue at their house the next day and asks if she would like to go. He figures this would be a great opportunity for him to invite Lana round so he could introduce her to them and the rest of his family and friends.

The next day soon comes. He picks her up and stops off at a local store on the way to get a bottle of wine and some pop. "I can't believe I'm meeting your parents, D!"

He grins, then replies protectively, "Don't worry, they're gonna love you, Lar!" They arrive at his parent's house which is a lot larger and posher than she had imagined. The roads are lined with parked cars and she is feeling way out of her element.

"I didn't realise this many people would be here!" she states anxiously.

"Stop worrying, everything's gonna be fine, c'mon!" he says reassuringly clutching her hand and guiding her to the front door.

He rings the doorbell and is greeted by a feisty, highly spirited woman who shrieks, grabs him and pulls him in. "Dean!" she yells.

"Hi, Mom!" he grins.

"About time you made an appearance!" she scorns in a comical tone. "And you must be Lana?" But before Lana can respond, the woman embraces her with a giant bear hug as well. "I'm Phoebe, come in and make yourself at home sweetheart." Lana chuckles and gives Dean a humorous side glance as she walks in, through to the kitchen. Handing her a large glass of pop from the side table, he indicates that he'll be right back, walking over to the other side of the room. He shakes hands with a couple of people, and they converse for a moment, then they all start to walk back in Lana's direction.

"Lar, this is my dad, Chris. I'll be back in a minute." Before Lana has time to speak, she watches as Dean turns and walks out the room. She can't believe he has just left her there with his dad. Chris reaches out his hand.

"Hi, Lana! It's lovely to finally meet you. Dean has nothing but lovely things to say about you!" Lana smiles awkwardly, as her cheeks become wispy and start to flush.

"It's lovely to meet you too!" she replies, hoping she's making a good impression. Jess is also there with Brad; she sees Lana and rushes over.

"Lar! I'm so happy you made it! I'm usually left here on my own with all these old fogies!" she quips, sarcastically winking at Chris.

"Less of that young lady, or I'll be forced to withhold your succulent barbecued chicken!"

"You win Chris, please forgive me," she jokes. They smirk at each other then Jess walks Lana out into the expansive floral garden where the barbecue is in full swing.

Music is playing and everyone is joking, laughing, eating, and drinking. The atmosphere is relaxed and joyous. "Thanks for saving me Jess! Dean left me and I was feeling a bit in over my head!"

Just then Dean returns. "Hi Jess!"

Lana turns around. "D! Where did you go? How could you leave me with your dad like that?"

He chuckles, "Sorry honey, but I *really* needed the toilet, so it was either that or I'd have been the talk of the barbecue!" he quips. "How did you get on?"

"He was really nice. Both your parents are *really* lovely!"

"Yeah and *crazy!*" he grins. "C'mon, let's get some food," he says, confidently grabbing her hand and leading the way. They all walk over to the barbecue and he introduces Lana to all his other family members and friends then they line up for burgers. Although there are quite a few people there, she is made to feel at ease and she's astounded at how pleasant, kind, and welcoming everybody is. She's really enjoying herself, eating, drinking, and chatting with Jess and all the other guests.

Dean's mother pulls him to one side. "She's *very* nice, Dean. I've seen the way you look at her, it appears to me you that may be smitten!"

His face lights up with one of his huge magnetic smiles. "You might be right, mom. I think I might be!"

"Well you make sure you hold on to her now!"

"I'm trying my best, mom," he jokes.

The afternoon turns into the most beautiful evening, the garden now ringed in a rich sunset, with jollities and music, humorous conversation, and wonderful company. It is one of the best family events Dean's been to and he is so glad that Lana was able to be a part of it.

The next day he travels to the café after work to meet Lana as usual. She has his drink ready and is reading a newspaper column. "Hello beautiful!" he greets her with much affection, pressing his face onto hers and kissing her cheek.

"Hey!" she beams.

"What are you reading?" he queries, as he sips his piping hot latte.

"Cupid's Corner!" Dean puts his cup down and squints inquisitively.

"Hmm, that sounds interesting! What's that?"

Lana starts to rapidly ramble. "It's *really* romantic, I don't know if it's real or not, but I really hope it is! So, when people are on their way home, on the bus, the subway or whatever, they might notice someone, and then that person smiles back or waves but then they're getting off the next stop and you wonder if you'll ever see them again, there's a word for it." She looks away, clicking her fingers trying to think of the word she's looking for.

"Yeah, I think that word's *stalking*!" he jokes.

She rolls her eyes. "Intriguing! Intriguing was the word I was thinking of actually!" she replies sarcastically, Dean grins.

"Listen, I'll read you one. *To the beautiful brunette, wearing a pink sweater and carrying a butterfly shoulder bag. You smiled at me as I got off the bus in Herald Street just after five. After a hard day at work you're smile brightened my day and I would love to see you again. I'll be outside Tennessee's Bistro at 5:00 p.m. on Friday, hoping to see you there, from the shy guy.* How sweet is that D?" she swoons, "*and* it says that they place adverts the *same* day, so if you saw someone in the morning, it could be printed in that evening's paper!"

He chuckles under his breath at Lana's cuteness and romantic outlook. "I'm not too sure about all that Lar, but you are sweet! You wanna go for a drink later?" he asks, as she lightly nods her acceptance. They continue to chat and discuss other stories in the newspaper, then talk about the evening ahead. A little time later, they leave the cafe and go their separate ways to get ready.

Later that evening, Dean arrives to pick up Lana to go to their local bar for a couple of cocktails. The music is booming and they're thinking of leaving and going somewhere else because even though they're having a good time, the music is just too loud for conversation, they can't even hear themselves speak. Then Dean accidentally knocks over some of his drink, and this is definitely the signal for them to leave, but first he dips out for a minute to the toilet to wash his hands, sticky from the spilled beer.

He's literally only been gone a matter of minutes but on his return, he's faced with a situation that he could never have foreseen happening. A couple of guys are standing over Lana and she appears decidedly unsettled. He rushes to her aid telling them that she's with him and politely asks them to leave. The one man respectfully walks away and tells his buddy to go with him, but his friend is drunk and is not having any of it. "Let the lady tell me herself," he slurs, in a drunken and aggressive tone, looking Lana disrespectfully up and down.

Dean gets protective, moves closer to the man and reaffirms his position, "*I've* already told you!" But the man has had *way* too much to drink and is spoiling for a fight.

Lana tugs Dean's sleeve and implores, "just leave it, let's go," but the man laughs in her face and tries to provoke him further, it works! Dean doesn't listen to Lana's pleas and instead an argument ensues; he ends up having to duck as the man tries to throw a punch at him.

Lana moves out the way as Dean pushes him off, but the man comes for him again and this time the punch touches. Dean stumbles backwards against the bar, but then manages to regain his balance and floors the guy with one punch. The man's friend sees the commotion, runs back over and apologises for the guy's behaviour and drags him out. Dean is left nursing a black eye and bruised ego and Lana is upset and angered.

They leave the bar and Lana drives them back home. She's fuming and distressed, which leaves Dean feeling bewildered and flabbergasted. After all, he was only trying to protect her and defend her honour!

As they drive back to his place they argue in the car throughout the entire journey. "Why couldn't you just leave it? We could have just walked out of there; you didn't need to fight the guy!"

"Lar, are you serious? he argues defensively. "The guy was laughing in your face and you want me to just walk away from that?"

"Yes! That's *exactly* what I wanted you to do!" she states, furiously. "You should have listened to me. The guy was a drunken idiot, we could have just left, you didn't need to get involved. He could have done anything D; you could've got arrested and now you've got a black eye!" Dean is in total disagreement with her, and he doesn't care if he has an injury or not, because he's confident he did the right thing.

They arrive at his apartment and go in. Lana pulls out an ice pack from his freezer then rummages around the back of one of his cupboards for a first aid kit, finds it, then tends to his eye. "Ow!" he winces, as she presses the ice pack hard onto his face.

"It serves you right!" she says sassily, but upon seeing his sad reaction lowers her eyes, regretting her hurtful comment. She opens the medical kit and takes a fingertip full of antiseptic cream and gently rubs it into a small cut that has opened from where he was hit.

He grabs her hand. "Larnie?"

"Don't, D," she whispers, looking away. "You didn't listen to me; anything could have happened. There was *two* of them and they could have had weapons or anything."

"You're being silly; he was just some drunken idiot, and the other guy was cool."

Lana shakes her head, and looks away. "I'm gonna go."

"Lar, C'mon. Alright I'm sorry, I should've listened to you." He backtracks and tries to apologise and joke with her to lighten the mood, but she's having none of it.

"I'm going home D, I'll see you tomorrow," she expresses defiantly but with underlying sadness. Dean sighs and tries to get her to stay but she leaves, nonetheless.

After their argument, he feels uneasy, wounded by her reluctance to see his point of view and unsettled that they're not on speaking terms. He tries to ring her, but she won't answer. She texts him back, *I'll see you tomorrow, D. I don't want to talk tonight*. This is the first time since they've been together that they've fought and not spoken. He hates that they're arguing and racks his brains to find a way to reconcile with her.

He knows Lana's a hopeless romantic and recalls what she was telling him about Cupid's Corner, so he decides the next day he'll place an advert, knowing that she'll definitely read it. The next morning, he gets up early to ring the newspaper hotline and dictates the ad for that evening's paper. It reads, *To the beautiful blonde lady, who I've heard is called Lana and who always happens to be in my favourite café after work. No matter what kind of day I've had, knowing I will see you in the evening always makes every day better. I know fate crossed our paths for a reason and I hope you will join me for a cup of coffee at around 6pm. Your biggest admirer, D.*

Dean's been wishing the day away, persistently wondering about her and if she's thinking of him, if she's seen the advert and counting down the minutes until he can get to the café. The evening finally arrives and Lana's reading the *Cupid's Corner* column as Dean approaches, holding a vast, colourful spray of flowers, still sporting his black eye.

"Hi!" he mutters, sheepishly.

"Hello!" she replies distantly, momentarily glancing up at him then gazing back down at the newspaper again.

He sees the newspaper open in her hand, so continues unperturbed. "I hope you don't think I'm being too forward, but I see you in here quite a lot after work and you just being here always makes my day better, so I was wondering if I could buy you a drink?"

Lana stares at him with a stern, straight face, but upon noticing his injured eye and the beautiful bouquet of flowers, half smiles reluctantly, her heart defrosting, thawing only slightly. "This doesn't mean I've forgiven you, D." He looks down like a sad little puppy, she hesitates for a moment. "Okay, you broke me down, I forgive you!" she quips as her face breaks into a humongous grin. Dean grins back relieved, his smile encased in his huge dimples. He doesn't care who's wrong or right anymore, he just wants to be in her good books again.

"I don't want to argue with you, Lar... *ever!*"

"Me neither!" she agrees as he leans over her coffee cup kissing her peachy pink lips, but as their faces touch, her cheek accidently pushes against his eye.

"Ow!" he grimaces. She feels sorry for him and affectionately holds his face in her hands, gently planting a kiss onto his injured eye.

Smiling, he reaches into his pocket and pulls out on an envelope with Lana's name on it.

She frowns slightly. "What's this?" she asks curiously.

"Open it!" he teases.

She reaches into the envelope and pulls out a brochure. Her face erupts into a delighted expression. "New York!" she gasps.

"A weekend away for us! I've booked a hotel and spa and thought we could go shopping, if you're interested?" he teases.

She reaches out and takes hold of his collar, pulling him close and planting a seductive kiss on his lips.

Dean feels settled and at ease once more now they're back on speaking terms. "Our first fight! You know what that means, don't you?"

Lana shakes her head negatively, scrunching her face in uncertainty, "No, what?"

"You're gonna have to come back to mine so I can make it up to you!" he teases with a wink. She blushes concealing her timidness behind a few prolonged gulps of her coffee. They drive to Dean's and as soon as they enter, they can't keep their hands off one another. Desire takes over and they lustfully become intimate.

They've seen each other almost every day now for nearly six weeks solid. Dean's routinely waiting in the café for Lana and as soon as she walks in, he swiftly grips her hand, sits her down and starts speaking at a very accelerated pace. "Lar, I've been thinking about this *all* day and I know this might sound a little crazy, and I don't want to rush things and scare you off, but..." he pauses to catch his breath, "I think you should move in with me!" he impatiently blurts out. She looks overwhelmed and stunned. He notices her shocked expression; he gulps and continues to speak slower but a little more anxiously. "Alright, don't say no just yet, just hear me out. We live near to each other, we work close to one another, we see each other *every day* anyway and you know I'm in love with you. I'm pretty sure you like me a little bit too!" he reasons. Lana smiles coyly, "*And* when I'm not with you I'm counting down the minutes until I see you again, so what do you think?" There's dead silence and for a moment Lana doesn't utter a single word. He swallows hard, unsure if she's freaked out by his forwardness and if he's ruined everything or not, but to his amazement and sheer delight her face suddenly reacts.

"Actually, I'm stunned because *I* was going to ask if *you* wanted to come and move in with *me!*" she giggles.

"What?" Dean's eyes pop open, he can't believe his ears but is absolutely thrilled and over the moon at the outcome. They both laugh out loud, confirming how in sync they are with each other.

They hold hands across the table, blissfully in love, discussing their ideas in great detail. Dean says she can move in as soon as she wants, but Lana tells him she thinks it might be a much better idea if he moved in with her instead because she has a house and he only has an apartment which might be too crammed for them both. He tells her whatever she wants is fine with him. He really doesn't care where they live as long as they're together. They are totally engrossed in one another and every day are falling more deeply in love.

Everything starts to move rapidly, and that very same night Dean starts moving some of his belongings into Lana's house. Over the next few days things start to fall into place even faster as he makes the bold move of telling her that he's going to sell his apartment as he wants to be with her permanently. She has absolutely no doubts in her mind that this is exactly what she wants too, so he puts the wheels in motion and starts to organise the sale that very same day.

The next evening Brad arrives at Dean's home. "Yo, D! Did you see that big *For Sale* sign outside, they've put it really close to your door! You need to ask them to move it or people will start thinking it's your place that's up for sale!" he says chuckling to himself, presuming someone's placed it there in error.

Dean seems serious. "It *is* my place that's up for sale!" The atmosphere suddenly changes to dismal as Brad's face drops.

"What? But why?"

Dean sighs. "I was going to call you earlier, but I thought it might be better to tell you in person. B, don't freak out, just try and understand, okay? I know you said not to rush into anything with Lana, but, I'm moving in with her!" he explains.

Brad scoffs and becomes charged and animated. "What? Have you totally lost your mind? You've known this girl for what? Five weeks? *And* you're selling your apartment? Your home? D!" Brad shouts, incensed, shaking his head in disbelief. "Look, I know you're concerned and I get it, if it was the other way round I'd probably be saying the exact same thing to you, but I can't explain it, I *love* this girl, I'm *in love* with her and I want to *be* with her, *all* the time. It's just how I feel so *please* try and understand."

Brad rolls his eyes, he's overwrought. "D, it's too much, too soon. I mean why not just move in with her? Why sell your home? What if it all goes wrong? Then where you gonna live?"

Dean lowers his eyes, his voice quietens. "Remember Ben in sales, who used to live across the road? Well he's sorting it for me. He's already had some offers and I'll have the money from the sale. I could always buy somewhere else, but I know this is the right thing to do, I just know it is!"

Brad refuses to accept what he's hearing. "You're crazy man! You're not thinking straight," he scorns and storms out. Dean puts his hand to his head and sighs, feeling disheartened.

A few minutes pass and his phone rings, it's Lana. "Hello?" he answers despondently, whilst loosening his tie.

"Hi! Are you okay? You don't sound yourself."

"Yeah I'm fine, I just had a bit of an argument with Brad, that's all," he explains.

"Oh, what about?" she asks attentively.

"'Bout us." There's a pause and a few seconds of silence.

"About us moving in together?" she queries in a worried fashion.

"Yeah, he thinks we're moving too fast and I'm gonna get hurt along the way or something stupid like that, I dunno."

"So, what did *you* say?" Lana gulps, her stomach churning, her heart sinking, thinking that Dean's having second thoughts and is about to pull out. There's another pause.

"I told him that I love you and I'm following my heart." She breathes a sigh of relief, as he continues. "I've known Brad a *very* long time Lar, he's like a brother to me. I think he's just feeling a bit left out, but I know he's only got my best interests at heart. He just doesn't understand how I feel about you."

"I love you, Dean!" she divulges and as he feels her smiling at him down the phone, he laughs under his breath.

"I love you too, Lar!"

Lana begins to lighten the conversation. "Well if it's any consolation, I just told Jess and she had the exact *opposite* response! She said, you only live once and it's up to us, so if that's what we both want to do, then we should just go for it!"

Dean smirks. "Yeah, that sounds like Jess! Well hopefully she'll have a word with that stubborn brother of hers!"

"Don't worry about him, D, he'll come round."

"I hope so. I'll be over in about an hour with some more stuff alright?"

"Okay! I'll see you then."

"Alright, bye." Dean feels tense when he argues with Brad but knows in his heart that he's doing the right thing so finishes packing up some more of his things into boxes ready to take to Lana's.

An hour and a half later he arrives at Lana's house with his car packed to the brim with his belongings. He rings the doorbell and she appears. "Hi!" she greets him in an encouraging, optimistic tone.

He lifts his eyebrows with a big grin and embraces her. "I finally made it!"

She pushes the door fully open, but he only just narrowly squeezes past her as he's carrying such a vast amount of his things. He places them all on the floor. "Lar, I'll grab the other stuff in a minute, I really need to use your bathroom!" She giggles and Dean runs upstairs to use the toilet. After he's finished and starts to wash his hands, he looks behind his reflection in the mirror and realises that all of the bathroom is bright pink! There's even a pink frilly lace cover on the toilet seat! In fact, he becomes aware that a great deal of the house is extremely feminine. He walks down the stairs gingerly, reviewing all the paintings and décor as he goes.

Meanwhile, Lana's eagerly taken some more of Dean's possessions from his car and brought them inside. He tells her to stop then takes her hand in his.

"Lar, don't take this the wrong way, but I never really noticed before that a lot of your furnishings are very... feminine!"

Lana squints at him slightly puzzled. "Well that's 'cause... I'm a woman!"

He smiles and continues. "Yes, that is correct! But, maybe now I'm moving in we could re-decorate? I mean, I'll have the money from the sale so we could re-do the whole house if you want?" she frowns and looks offended, so Dean tries to backtrack, he stutters. "I mean obviously you've done an *amazing* job with everything; I just think it's all a bit *girly*, that's all."

A few seconds of awkward silence pass, then Lana breaks into uncontrollable laughter. "Of course we can re-decorate, it can be the first thing we can do as a couple!"

He sighs deeply with relief. "We'll make it into the house of our dreams!" he tells her as he clutches her tightly in his arms feeling satisfied and content. He daydreams for a minute, then his demeanour turns serious. "Lar, I know this is meant to be a special night for us, but I have to make things right with Brad." She scrunches up her nose lovingly and nods her approval. He pecks her on her nose, grins and takes his car keys out his pocket.

Dean sets off to the shop to buy some drinks, then heads straight around to Brad's house. He arrives carrying a pack of four beers, but Brad's still sulking as he opens the door. He throws Dean a look and marches off. "*Hello!*" Dean mimics sarcastically to himself, closing the door behind himself.

"You've known her a few weeks, D! A matter of *weeks*!" Brad scorns, continuing to escalate the argument from earlier.

Dean cracks open a beer and leaves it on the table for Brad. "I know this! I don't know what to tell you," he shrugs, "I just know she's the one for me!" he calmly states, then opens another beer for himself and takes a swig.

Brad's still in a vile mood and gives him daggers. "You're joking?" Dean retaliates. "Why can't you just be happy for me man?"

"Because it's ridiculous and everything's changing. I don't want things to change between us!" Brad retorts standing, his voice raised.

"What are you talkin' about?" Dean queries in total confusion.

"We've been best friends since we were kids, you've known this girl for five minutes and already everything's changing. It's always been me and you, D&B right?" he jeers. "But now you're gonna be holed up with this girl and where's that gonna leave us? Where's that gonna leave *me*? 'Cause if you ask me, three's a pretty crowded number!" Dean squints, sad that Brad's saying and thinking these things and that he's totally oblivious to his feelings.

He starts to reiterate his feelings in a quieter, calmer tone. "B, I've known you my *whole* life, you're like my brother! I see you nearly every day, you're *always* gonna be my best friend and I'm *always* gonna be yours, that ain't never gonna change, but we have to grow up sometime! Life changes, it's another chapter, but that doesn't mean you're not going to be in it! It'll be amazing, trust me. We'll get you a girl and we can all go on double-dates and everything'll be cool!" But this heartfelt statement does little to dispel Brad's insecurities.

Brad lowers his eyes and is silent for a moment. "A girl, huh? And how's that meant to happen without a wingman?"

Dean takes another gulp of beer and turns serious. "I get where you're comin' from, but you have to understand *my* point of view. I've spent every day with this girl since the moment I met her in the café. I love her! I *love* her, B!" he emphasizes strongly.

Brad turns away and doesn't speak for a minute. As he recognises how sincere Dean's being, he feels like he may have overreacted and misjudged the situation. He does like Lana a great deal and can see how much Dean genuinely cares for her. Ultimately he understands that he can't stand Dean's way and that he's fighting a losing battle so decides to admit defeat. "So, tell me more about this girl you're gonna find for me!" Dean's face cracks up. They finally get back on track and end up talking about old times and reminiscing for hours.

Chapter 6

The One...

Today is Lana's birthday and also *exactly* five months to the day since they met. Dean wants to make sure this is one birthday she won't forget in a hurry. Lana's sitting in the living room watching breakfast television and crunching her cereal. Dean's vanished into the other room to get her present that he's secretly stashed away. He pokes his head around the door radiating exuberance. "So, I've got a little something for you, but you've got to close your eyes first, alright?"

"Okay!" grins Lana gripped with expectancy, placing her breakfast bowl to one side. She closes her eyes, squeezing them tightly, but then slightly opens one of them.

"No peeking, Lar, I'm not joking! I *will* take this back!" he quips.

She can feel Dean moving away and is intrigued to know what he's up to. "D!" she calls out impatiently.

"I'm comin' back!" he chuckles.

She hears some rustling and whispering. "D, if you don't hurry up I'm opening my eyes, 'cause I can't take the suspense anymore!"

"Well you don't have to because you can open your eyes now!"

Lana opens her eyes and sits there open-mouthed as Dean perches on the edge of the sofa holding the cutest, most adorable little puppy she has ever laid her eyes on. It's a tiny eight-week-old Yorkshire Terrier pup, snuggled up cosily in a soft blanket. "Dean!!!" she shrieks. The puppy is jet black with streaks of golden tan running throughout his fine soft fur. She picks it up and snuggles it close to her face. "Oh, he's so cute!" She puts the puppy down on the rug next to her, jumps on top of Dean and flings her arms around his neck, kissing his face over and over.

Laughing he ask, "but, did you notice anything else?"

Lana looks down and around and then picks up the puppy again. It licks her chin over and over, then gives out a little bark as she chuckles. She gazes down at the blanket. "Aah! It has coffee cups on it!"

"Yes! But, did you notice anything *else*?" he queries once more.

She squints and smiles, intrigued as to what mischievousness Dean is up to now. She lifts the puppy and gently shakes the blanket, where she spots a tiny little gift bag that's been tied onto the label. He gently detaches it and hands it to her. She places the puppy gently back down onto the blanket and reaches into the bag. Her expression suddenly changes as she lifts out a little box. She turns to Dean. "Open it!" he whispers. Cautiously, she flicks open the catch and inside appears the most beautiful ring she has ever laid her eyes on. It's a heart shaped chocolate diamond, set in a rose gold band, with individual diamonds delicately placed upon either side of it. She sits there staring at it in disbelief.

Dean takes the ring from her and holds her hand in his. He gets down on one knee with the puppy barking and jumping all over him energetically. The nerves start to kick in, but he manages to stay calm. "Lana, since the very first moment I laid my eyes on you, I've never felt happier. You make *everything* amazing. I know as long as I have you in my life everything will always be alright, and anything is possible. You are the most beautiful, kindest, *craziest* woman I have ever met, and I don't want to be away from you for one second. I want to grow old with you, Lar! Would you do me the honour of becoming my wife?"

She sits there, gob-smacked, dazed, and in shock and for a moment in complete silence. "Lana? Please say something, I'm losing all feeling in my leg!"

Her whole face suddenly breaks into the most ginormous smile, she's elated. "Yes! Yes! Yes!" she shrieks, "Dean, I love you *so* much."

He is totally overwhelmed by her response and attentively places the ring on her finger, it fits like a dream! "I love *you* Lar!" he whispers softly. "You've made me the happiest man alive!" They kiss passionately and embrace as the puppy jumps and leaps all around them.

Lana is beyond ecstatic; she can't stop staring at the ring. "Do you like it" he queries in a whisper.

"It's perfect!" she replies, grinning from ear to ear. She scoops up the puppy in her arms and cuddles and cradles it in her neck. "This is the happiest day of my life, D! I can't believe you did all this! We're going to get married; we've got this beautiful little puppy *and* it's my birthday!"

Lana cups the tiny puppy's face in between her hands, gazing at him lovingly, stroking the fur between his nose and forehead. "What shall we call him, D?" They muse over several ideas as to what they should name the dog.

"What about Max?" he asks.

"Hmm, nope, what else?"

Dean reels off a list but after each suggestion Lana shakes her head. "Snuggles? Fluffy? Buster? Buddy? Tramp? Rocky? Milo?" He's starting to give up as she can't make up her mind. "Harold!"

Lana giggles, "I just want a strong name, something unique and different!" They sit there pondering and contemplating different ideas, but there's nothing that springs to mind or that they're completely happy with.

"You know Lar, we don't have to name him *right* now, we can think about it for a few days." She nods in agreement and they sit back to watch some T.V.

A film is just about to start, a biopic retelling the story of Wolfgang Amadeus Mozart, called *Amadeus*. The puppy runs over to the television and starts barking and excitedly. Lana and Dean look at each other at the *exact* same time, laughing as they recall their time in the cafe when the song *Amadeus* was randomly playing and they both think that this must be a sign. "Amadeus!" They both shout jubilantly in unison.

"Amadeus it is!" he concurs, relieved that they've finally found a name they both like and are content with. Turning his head sideways, Dean remarks, "I really think it suits him you know, Lar!"

"Well, that's 'cause... that's his name!" Dean smirks and Lana is over the moon.

She rushes to get her phone to ring her parents and family to inform them of all the good news and Dean decides to go and ring Brad first.

"Hey, B!"

"How's it goin'?"

"I need you to do me a favour."

"What's up?"

"I need you to be my best man!" he reveals. There's an extended silence. "Hello?"

"Yeah, I'm still here."

"I'm getting married, B, and there's no-one else I'd rather have by my side when Lana's walking down that aisle! So, what do you say?"

Brad is speechless, which doesn't happen very often, but truth be told he is actually dumbstruck, trying to catch his breath and channel his thoughts. Although Brad always puts on a witty persona and cool exterior, deep inside he's just a sensitive soul. Dean waits patiently for his response as Brad's voice starts to break. He tries to keep it together. "Yeah I'd... Yeah that'd be... I'd be honoured Dean."

Dean grins down the phone. "Well, so would I!" he replies respectfully. He rings the rest of his family who are over the moon and congratulatory.

Lana is in a tremendously beneficial position to organise her wedding, as this is what she does every day for a living. She has countless contacts and will undoubtedly be able to get many free items and huge generalised discounts.

Brad is aware of this and knows they already have pretty much everything they will ever need, because they live together, but still wants to get them something extra special. He has heard them chat before about how much they wanted to go to Nice in France, so he discusses it with Jess, and they agree that they'll buy their honeymoon for them and split the cost. He decides to book it straight away before Lana arranges anything, so visits the travel agent with Jess and they arrange for the flights and a deluxe suite overlooking the ocean. They decide to take the tickets and brochures to them the same day to surprise them.

Lana and Dean are snuggled up watching a movie and aren't expecting any visitors. but then there's a loud knock at the door. Dean answers it and welcomes them in. "We're watching a movie, what d'ya want?" he wisecracks.

They all sit on the sofa together and Brad pulls an envelope from his breast pocket. "We know it early, but we thought we'd bring our wedding gift for you both today, before you start arranging anything!"

Dean squints at Lana, still unsure what they're talking about, as Brad passes him the envelope. "Oh, you didn't have to do that, but what is it?" he jokes.

"Open it!"

Lana moves close to Dean, resting her chin against his neck and peers over his shoulder as he rips open the envelope and starts reading the ticket information. He pulls out the brochure revealing the amazing pictures and detailed itinerary, they both look flabbergasted. "France!" Lana cries out, thrilled and delighted, "Dean, it's Nice!" she shouts in disbelief. Everyone is over the moon at the pleasurable outcome. Dean and Lana thank them profusely for their thoughtful, kind, and expensive gift.

Things start to move quickly, as the arrangements for the wedding start to get under way. A couple of months pass, and things are coming along swimmingly. They both decide to hold their bachelor and bachelorette parties on the same night, as neither are really interested in attending but their friends have persuaded them that it's all part of the whole wedding experience, so they conclude that if they hold both parties on the same night, it will be less harrowing for both of them!

Although Lana's a little reluctant, Jess is excited enough for the both of them as she arrives at her house with all their friends. Lana welcomes them in and has an abundance of assorted cocktails ready and waiting, already perfectly prepared. Everyone greets each other with positive energy, enthusiasm, and amusement as the night's frivolities commence. Everyone is dressed in fancy dress and they've bought Lana a *learner* outfit, a feather boa and headband with flashing lights, much to her hilarity.

Jess has organised their event to be held at their local cocktail bar, complete with full stage, restaurant, and incorporating an extra-large VIP booth. Dean is getting ready in the bedroom as Lana runs upstairs to say goodbye. He's adjusting his tie in the mirror. "D, everyone's here now so I'm leaving, I'll see you later, honey."

He looks her up and down, amused by her outfit, "good luck!" he jokes.

"Good luck to you too, Sir!" she quips back.

"And remember if Jess has got you a stripper, no peeking!"

Lana rolls her head back and laughs. "Yeah the same to you, but I've already told her I don't want one, so it'll be cool!" He kisses her, then she runs back down the stairs. Just as she's going out the door, Brad is arriving with their male friends. Everyone jokes around for a minute, then Lana shouts up the stairway, "Dean? Brad's here!" He rushes down the stairs to greet his pals as Lana finally leaves. Brad has arranged to take Dean and their mates to a nearby night club. They all drink cold beers, and there's much laughter and banter as they all chat about their expectation for the night ahead.

Lana is dressed in her full *bride-to-be* attire, including the famous *L* sash as she and her friends arrive at the bar. They are already a little worse for wear from the drinks that Lana made them earlier. They sit in their reserved booth and consume even more cocktails, then nibbles are brought over to their table. They dance to their favourite songs and Lana doesn't want to admit it, but she's actually having a ball!

Just as the night is in full swing, the hostess grabs the microphone and makes a surprise announcement, "Ladies and Gentlemen, please welcome our very special guest, let me hear your appreciation, please give it up for... The Big Purple One!"

All of a sudden, Jess leans over and whispers in Lana's ear. "Lar? I know you said you didn't want a stripper, but what's a bachelorette party without a stripper, right?"

Lana starts to feel panicked. The hairs on the back of her neck start to stand, "Jess, what did you do?" she asks nervously, squinting her eyes suspiciously. The music begins and the lights dim as the song *Kiss* starts to play, blasting from the speakers, Lana turns her head. A man dressed in a Prince outfit starts dancing and prancing around provocatively and singing outrageously. Her jaw drops, she's aghast. "Oh... My..." But before she can finish her sentence, he notices she's the bride-to-be and starts to walk across the room straight in her direction, thrusting and gyrating as he goes. He swaggers and struts around her, Jess, and their friends. "And now is the point where I kill you!" Lana tells Jess, smiling through gritted teeth. Jess bites her lower lip, attempting to conceal her laughter as Lana dramatically swerves like she's in the *Matrix*, trying hard to avoid his advances, and instead guides him in the direction of her friends.

After much awkwardness and as the song nears the end, he abruptly and unexpectedly rips off the bottom half of his Prince outfit to reveal a huge purple thong. Lana's eyes nearly pop out of her head as he starts slapping his own bottom whilst gyrating to the music, moving extremely close to her again. With a start, she quickly stands up, ensuring her eyes don't glance downward.

"Lovely! Thank you!" she stammers to the stripper, in a high-pitched voice, grimacing as she turns to Jess. "So, anyway, I'm ready to go!" Jess laughs rowdily, slips some money into his thong and gives him a cheeky wink, to which he winks back, much to Lana's horror. Lana shakes her head, takes Jess by the hand and pulls her away. Everyone applauds him and cheers as he backs up off the stage and leaves.

"I can't believe you did that to me, Jess!"

"Well, as you didn't want a normal stripper, I thought a novelty one would be better! There were others you could choose from as well, but *he* was definitely the best option available."

"*He* was the best option available?"

"Mm-hmm," Jess nods in confirmation.

"Dare I ask, but what were the *other* options?"

Jess ponders for a second, then starts to count them on her fingers. "Well, let me see. There was Gramp-A-Gram, but nobody wants that! Then there was a Do-It-Yourself Dumbledore, and God only knows what that means so he was a no-go and their main attraction was a large tribute act called Magic Mikey and the Seven Dwarfs, and that didn't even bare thinking about!"

Lana pipes up, "Hmm, well that's just conjured up a whole heap of weird thoughts for me!"

Jess agrees, "Yeah! So that just left The Big Purple One! And I know what a big fan of Prince you are, so it was a no-brainer, it *had* to be him!"

"Why did it have to be *anybody*?!" Lana wisecracks. "And yeah I am a fan, but now I'm looking at Prince in a totally different light, thanks to you! You know, I would have been happy to just go and get some pizza, Jess!" They both laugh and giggle as they move to the restaurant area with the rest of their friends.

Dean is simultaneously experiencing the exact same night, well sort of! His stripper is a *normal* one, but he doesn't want to be there either. His thoughts are consumed with Lana and he's not remotely interested in the things that he once was. He's ready to settle down and he's just going through the motions of the night to humour Brad as he's gone to so much trouble to organise it for him.

As the stripper writhes around him, he actually starts to feel uncomfortable, and even though Brad is egging him on, he declines to participate and pushes the girl away. He's not interested in the slightest in anyone else and tells Brad to entertain her. Brad can see his genuine discontent and wants to ensure they have a good time, so they agree to go to another club much to Dean's relief. After a reasonably entertaining evening, they both arrive home, both a little worse for wear. They discuss their evenings, how they're both content now that they're back in each other's arms, and how they can't wait until the day comes when they're married.

Chapter 7

For Better or For Worse...

Just over a month later, and their wedding day finally arrives. Both Lana and Dean are completely ecstatic, but a shade overwhelmed with nervous energy. Lana sits in her bedroom gazing into her oversized mirror as Jess helps her with the last finishing touches to her hair. "Can you believe it, Jess? Can you believe this day is finally here and I'm going to marry Dean?"

Jess smiles sweetly. "It's going to be an *amazing* day, Lar!" Lana just can't stop smiling.

Dean's getting ready at Brad's house. Brad's not taking his *best man duties* very seriously as he's admiring himself in the mirror and adjusting his *own* tie. "How do I look, D?" he asks.

Dean looks up, "Great, but do you wanna give *me* a hand maybe?"

Brad smirks, walks over to him and helps him fix his cravat. He steps back and fondly looks him up and down, "Looking gooood!" Dean rolls his eyes and finishes tying his shoes.

"How long we got?" he asks feeling slightly nervous whilst fastening his cufflinks.

Brad checks his watch. "About half an hour."

Dean sighs. "I wonder what Lana's doing right now."

"She's probably already there waiting, knowing her!" Brad jokes. He smirks then adds, "I'm kidding, I just spoke to Jess and they're still getting ready. She said they're leaving in twenty minutes. It's not too late to run you know, D!" he teases.

Dean grins back, "Nah, I think I'll give it a go! Let's take a slow drive down!"

"You don't want to wait for the cars?" Brad enquires.

"We'll take my car. I want to make sure I'm there waiting for her when she arrives!"

Brad smiles proudly, with an acknowledging nod, "Alright! Let's go then!"

Meanwhile, the song *Bonnie and Clyde* starts to play on the alarm Jess has set on her phone, Lana chuckles. It's time to leave. Lana stands and takes one more look in the mirror. Jess gently lifts the delicate lace veil over her head and gushes, "You look *stunning*, Lar. Dean's gonna lose his mind!" Lana bites her lip as Jess looks on with pride, "You ready?"

She nods enthusiastically, "Let's do it!" She feels completely exhilarated. This is the day she's been waiting for her *entire* life. She picks up her ivory embroidered purse as Jess gently gathers the fragile train of her dress and follows her closely down the stairs.

As she reaches the bottom, her parents and bridesmaids are waiting there to greet her. Her mother pulls tissue after tissue from several boxes scattered around the room and dabs the corner of her eyes, as emotion overtakes her. Her father notes her entrance, stops pacing, and gasps, overflowing with love and pride. "Lana, you're a vision! You look absolutely beautiful!" He states proudly. All her bridesmaids rally round, complementing her dress and beauty. They take numerous pictures then her father walks to her side and links her arm in his. "Ready?" he asks, thrilled and delighted to be sharing this special moment with his daughter. Lana nods and they all walk outside to their awaiting cars. Due to her links, she's managed to negotiate a brand-new, top of the range, white stretch Chrysler 300 limousine and another three prestigious wedding cars on free hire for the *whole* day. Lana has the limo and one of the cars, and the other two remaining cars have been sent to pick up Dean's side of the family.

Lana clambers carefully into the limousine with her father seated beside her, and they begin their journey to the church as Jess and the rest of her entourage pour into the other car and closely follow behind. As she gazes out the window and they start to get nearer and nearer to the church, she begins to have heart palpitations and experiences the sensation of butterflies. Although she loves Dean more than anything and truly wants to marry him, the realisation and nerves are kicking in that this day has finally arrived, and that the moment is almost here!

After ten minutes or so, they arrive at the church and the car pulls in. Lana's father gets out, opens the door and holds out his hand. She takes it and carefully climbs out. The other car speedily pulls up right behind her. Her mother and bridesmaids stay close as Jess gets out and quickly rushes to gather up all the lace from the back of Lana's dress again. Everyone follows suit and make their way down to the church entrance.

As she approaches the church, she glances over to the other cars parked outside. Noticing Dean's car, she realises that he must already be inside waiting for her. Her father recognises her nerves are growing, so gives her hand a little reassuring squeeze, which automatically puts her at ease. "They're waiting for you, Lana!" he tells her in a comforting manner, she sighs and nods back. Her father takes her arm as she grasps her bouquet tightly. Her floral arrangement is made up off vintage roses and peonies. They're a selection of creams and pink pastels tinged with darker pink edges, her favourites since Dean bought them for her when they first met.

Making their way into the church, her father gives the priest the *thumbs up*, who in turn nods to his assistant priest to start the musical pre-recording. They've chosen s*teel drums* for the church entry music and as the music begins to play Dean can feel his stomach starting to churn with nervous excitement. He turns and raises his eyebrows to Brad, who in turn nods back encouragingly. Jess and the other bridesmaids start to make their way down the aisle. Dean smiles, appreciating how wonderful everyone looks, but there's only *one* person he's ultimately waiting for and then, there she is, a beautiful vision of perfection standing before him. Dean's focus is now entirely on Lana. As he hones in on her, he can't believe how stunningly beautiful she is. As soon as Lana sees Dean standing there waiting at the end of the aisle, her nerves instantaneously dispel. All eyes are on her now and with her every approaching footstep Dean is overwhelmed with a feeling of love and is completely entranced and mesmerized by her angelic presence.

Her hair is gently tousled into soft waves, which sits just below her shoulders, with a single cream rose delicately clipped into one side, just above her ear. She's chosen the most elegant, stunning dress, which is an ivory, off the shoulder design, that comes in at the waist but has a full skirt. It is layered in delicate lace and Dean notices her full red lips peeping through her exquisite veil as she gracefully floats nearer.

As she finally reaches him, Lana kisses her father's cheek which leaves a faint lipstick imprint, then Dean shakes his hand and turns towards her. He slowly lifts her veil and gently takes it over her head to reveal her beautiful face and radiant smile. "Lar, I've never seen you looking so beautiful!" Her cheeks turn rosé as she hands her bouquet to Jess. She takes Dean's hand and they both turn to face the priest.

The music lowers and fades as the priest begins to speak. "May everyone please be seated!" he requests. Dean side-glances at Lana and gives her a little wink as she smiles back modestly. There is now complete silence in the church. You could hear a pin drop.

Priest, Father Patrick Hannigan is governing the service, although he isn't your stereotypical priest. He's very witty and quirky and always tells it exactly how it is. He has a highly mischievous sense of humour and is of very unique character. Quietly, in his very strong Irish accent he whispers, "You look very beautiful, Lana, you're a very lucky man, Dean!" Dean turns to Lana and raises an eyebrow is jest, she lowers her eyes trying hard not to snigger.

Priest Hannigan looks out towards the congregation and the nuptials begin. "We are gathered here today in the presence of God, angels, family, and friends to celebrate one of life's greatest moments, to give recognition to the blessing, worth, and beauty of love and to unite these two *lovely* people, Lana and Dean, in holy matrimony. I have known Lana and Dean for a while now, and I must say that I cannot recall ever witnessing a couple more in love or more perfectly suited than these two, so I would like to take a moment to talk about the unity and blessing of love itself. Love should always be the primary factor of any marriage. Everyone should live with faith, hope, and love but the greatest of these is love. Love must *always* be the most important thing in life. Some people are fortunate enough to experience many wonderful things in their lifetime, but nothing will ever surpass love. If you have genuine love in your life, you have surely been blessed, as there are no greater riches. In a good situation you have a life partner to share life's joys with and if a bad situation should arise, you have a loyal friend, confidante and loving partner to help you through those troubled times. Love really is everything, and so with that being said, let us begin!

If there is any person here present, who knows of any lawful impediment why these two people should not be joined together in holy matrimony, please speak now or forever hold your peace". Dean turns his head suspiciously looking into the crowd with a comical stare as everyone chuckles under their breath, then he looks back to Lana with a cheeky wink. The priest smirks and continues. "If you would please both face each other. Now it would be grand if we could have the rings!" Brad pats down his pockets pretending to have lost the rings, then raises an eyebrow as he slowly passes them to Dean. "There's always one bright spark isn't there, Dean! There's *two* in my family!" jokes the priest, as everyone giggles. Dean takes Lana's ring and hovers it over her third finger, as the priest continues. "Please repeat after me," Dean repeats the vows, then the priest turns to Lana and asks her to do the same.

After they have exchanged rings and vows, proving their love and commitment, a hymn is played and a biblical verse is read, then the priest lights a candle. "May the bond between husband and wife never be broken, those whom God has joined together, let no man put asunder." Another couple of verses are read, full of meaning and thought-provoking wisdom.

"In so much as Dean and Lana have consented together in holy wedlock and have witnessed the same before God, having pledged their love and commitment to one another and having declared the same by the giving and receiving of a ring, by the power vested in me by God, it is with the greatest of pleasure that I now pronounce you husband and wife. You may kiss your beautiful bride, Dean."

Dean takes Lana's face in his hands as she closes her eyes and he softly kisses her lips. She starts to smile mid-kiss as everyone starts to cheer and applaud. Dean grins widely and turns to Priest Hannigan to shake his hand and thank him for such an amazing eulogy and service. "Thank you so much, it was perfect!"

"You're very welcome, Dean," replies the priest proudly.

Dean turns back around to Lana. "Well, you've gone and done it now, we're bound together *forever*!"

"I think I can deal with that!" she giggles, feeling content and over the moon.

They make their way back down the aisle and as they walk outside, they're showered in an avalanche of confetti. Everyone takes pictures, videos and rush over to congratulate the happy couple. Priest Hannigan joins them outside, as they walk over to the adjacent scenic floral garden for even more pictures with their families and friends.

Dean, Lana and all the guests depart in their deluxe cars and head to the magnificent hotel where the reception is being held. Lana has pulled out all the stops for their reception and her contacts have not failed her. As they drive into the entrance, the whole place has been adorned with tranquil lights, trimmings, and beautiful decorations. Before getting out the car, they chat on their own for a few stolen moments. "We finally did it, Lar! You're my wife!" Lana can't stop grinning. They embrace then make their way into the reception.

After elated cheers from all the guests, everyone is seated in their allocated places and the reception begins. Champagne is offered all around and the wedding breakfast takes place. They begin to tuck into their deluxe three course meal and chatter and laughter can be heard throughout.

Roughly an hour passes then Brad stands, picks up his table knife, and strikes the side of his champagne glass a couple of times to attract everyone's attention. "Hello, everyone! Can I have your attention, please?" The mumble of voices lower and fade as everyone turns to focus on Brad. "Yes, that's right, it's the reason you all came here today, to hear the best man's speech!" he quips. All the guests turn and smile at one another.

Dean turns to Lana. "Here we go!" he mumbles in jest.

"Firstly, can I say thank you to all the bridesmaids, looking lovely ladies! The groomsmen, not so much!" Everyone quietly sniggers. "You know, a lot of people think that being asked to be the best man is a great honour. Well let me tell you, it's not! It's a bit like dragging yourself out of bed for work on a Monday morning, you don't really want to do it, but you know you have no choice!" Chattering and giggling continue in the background. "Now as a lot of you know, there are many rules and regulations as to what you can and can't do at weddings. Probably the best-known rule would be that no-one, apart from the bride, should wear white... Lois!" He looks over to a lady at another table wearing white, as she starts to blush a bright crimson red. "*And* another is that no-one should look more beautiful than the bride or more handsome than the groom and so I'd like to thank everyone on table five for sticking stringently to that code!" Everyone looks over to table five and giggles. Dean closes his eyes and shakes his head as Lana laughs raucously.

"So, what can I say about my lifelong, best friend, Dean?"

"Nothing!" Dean shouts back sarcastically, as everyone titters. Brad scoffs.

"We are *so* close that for a while, I did consider branding our bromance by making a logo for our clothing. I was thinking of making some B and D t-shirts and calling them BAD, but unfortunately, for some reason, Dean was against it. It was good enough for Michael Jackson D!" he shouts in jest. Dean shakes his head again, whilst muttering *good Lord* under his breath.

"As many of you know, Dean and I have been friends since we were young, and so I think it only right that I share a few stories with you all today!" Dean squints suspiciously.

"Now, some of you might be surprised to hear this, but he wasn't always as good looking as he is today. When I first met him, he used to wear three-inch-thick glasses, he had a unibrow and walked with a limp, I felt sorry for him and so decided to take him under my wing." There's a low level of sniggering and a slight pause, Brad shakes his head.

"Okay, none of that's true. Yes, Dean *has* always been this stunningly good looking and standing next to him sometimes makes you feel like you've been hit by the ugly stick!" Low level chuckling ensues.

"I remember from way back when we were kids, Dean always had *all* the girls rallying around him." Lana glances at Dean, one eyebrow raised then breaks into laughter. "One girl in particular from the corner store, Stacey Fishburne! Remember her, D?"

"I'd rather not, thanks!" Dean retorts. There's another wave of laughter from everyone in the room.

"Well, let's just says she'd visited that sweet shop a few too many times and she was *very* sweet on him!"

Dean puts his hand over his face, "I knew this was a bad idea!" he jokes to Lana as Brad continues.

"As we grew older, and more experienced," he jokes with a wink, "it became apparent that being Dean's wing man would not be bad at all! There were a lot of situations when having a friend like him came in very handy. Many a fake call saved me from many a sticky situation! I remember one night we went to this club and I noticed a *very* attractive woman leaning up against the bar. So, I'm staring at her thinking this could actually be my lucky night! She had the most luscious blonde hair, the longest legs I've *ever* seen, and she was wearing this amazing little red number, I couldn't believe my luck! She was exactly my type, as though someone had made her just for me and placed her there at the bar! Dean spurred me on to go over and speak to her, so I downed a couple of shots, and when I say a *couple* by that I mean probably six or seven, then got ready to make my move. I plucked up the courage I needed and casually walked over to her. So, I take a deep breath, I tap her on the shoulder, she turns around and... she's a man!" Everyone is in stitches. "I was so drunk that night that I still might have! But luckily for me, Dean was there to pull me away so I could see the light of another day!" Continued howls of laughter fill the room.

"So, Lana, since the Stacey Fishburne incident, there have been quite a few ladies who've been sweet on Dean, but none of them ever came close to having the impact on him you have."

"Lar, until you came into Dean's life he was lost. He was a wreck, a loser, roaming aimlessly in life from one girl to the next!"

Dean cuts him off. "No, that's you, B!" Brad rolls his eyes, unimpressed and stares sarcastically.

"*Anyway*, I will be the first to admit, that when the two of you first got together I had my doubts. I was hesitant. I thought it was all moving a bit too fast, but I was wrong." Brad starts to get serious. "I've never seen Dean this happy in his whole life and that's all because of *you*, Lar! You're an *unbelievably* amazing woman and you're *definitely* the best thing that could ever have happened to Dean, and I'm certain he thinks the world of you." Dean gently squeezes Lana's hand as they smile adoringly at one another.

"If two people were ever meant to be together it's you two, and I truly couldn't be happier for you both. So, if everyone could please raise their glass and join me in wishing this lovely couple a *lifetime* of happiness." Brad holds up his glass in the air. "To my *best* friend and his *beautiful* bride. To Dean and Lana!"

Everybody raises a drink and repeats. "To Dean and Lana!" The whole room ignites with almighty applause as Dean lifts his glass and gives Brad a proud nod. Brad downs his champagne in one, holds up his glass to Dean and nods back. Dean and Lana share a lingering, tender kiss.

Dean stands. "Thanks for that, B. Well, for most of it, I think!" Everyone quietly chuckles as he glances down at Lana with pride, then back up to his guests. "Firstly, I'd like to say a *huge* thank you to everybody for coming out today to celebrate this glorious day with us. This is without a doubt, the happiest day of my life." He turns to Lana, who gazes up at him with adoration. "Lar, I am *so* blessed to have you in my life, and I know Brad's was joking, but he was right! I didn't know it, but I *was* lost 'til I met you. I wasn't looking for anybody, but somehow you fell into my life, literally!" Lana smirks. "And well, since that day, you've made *every* moment better and I could never imagine my life without you now." A prolonged ripple of *aww* echoes around the room, from the murmur of the sentimental crowd. Dean raises his glass to Lana, "So I'd like to propose a toast, to my stunning wife, the woman who found me and made me complete. Here's to a long and happy marriage. I love you!" he gushes. Lana raises her champagne glass and clinks it on Dean's. Everyone's feeling emotional and extend their applause.

It's time for their first dance and unsurprisingly it's their song, Jackie Wilson's, To Be Loved. Everything seems surreal and Lana feels like she's having an out of body experience, as if she's watching herself dancing with Dean from afar. She recalls how she danced with him for the first time when they met in the cafe and remembers how he twirled her around. She giggles as they dance and the love she feels for him is indescribable.

The party continues in full force, until early evening when it's time to cut the cake. They make their way to the events table where it is elegantly situated. Rose petals are scattered liberally on the table surrounding the cake stand, and the cake itself is an ivory three-tiered strawberry, lemon drizzle and chocolate cake, decorated with cascading pink tinged edible roses, diagonally placed down the three cakes. Sitting on top is an ivory porcelain cake topper twisted into the shape of a heart with a couple dancing inside. The atmosphere is highly romantic and as Lana picks up the cake knife, Dean stands behind her and places his hand on top of hers as they slice into it together. They feed each other a few spoonful's and the guests take photos, clap and cheer. The love Dean feels for Lana is immeasurable.

More dancing, singing, and laughter follow but as Dean is entertaining everyone with his moves, he spots Brad out the corner of his eye, sitting at the bar seemingly depressed and dispirited, so pulls himself off the dance floor and makes his way over.

"What's up, B?"

"Nothing!" he replies unconvincingly.

Dean senses something's wrong so calls him to take a moment out, and they walk outside together. "What's wrong?"

"It's nothing, I was just thinking when I was watching you and Lar on the dance floor, I just don't think I'm ever gonna have that, D," he remarks, shaking his head unhappily.

Brad is *so* happy for them both, but not only has this day made him question himself, but he is also in a way envious of their connection, as he's never even had a proper relationship, let alone been in love! Brad's had a little too much champagne and is starting to overthink the situation and become reflective. "But seriously Dean, what's it like to be in love?"

Dean half smiles. He feels sorry that Brad hasn't found the right woman yet. He sighs. "It's a feeling, the most *amazing* feeling, and I just want to be with her, like *all* the time, and when I'm not with her she never leaves my thoughts. We just want the best for each other, that's all I can tell you. I know that one day you're gonna find a beautiful, loving, *crazy* woman to take you on, I mean to spend your life with!" he jokes diplomatically. They both laugh, "And then you'll understand and be as happy as I am! It'll definitely happen one day, B."

Brad looks a little downcast, "I hope so, man."

"It will!" Dean replies assuredly. "Now come on, let's get back to the party, it's not every day I get married!" Brad's aura changes as Dean hooks his arm round his neck and they make their way back inside.

The night continues with dancing, laughter, gleeful conversation and a delicious Caribbean buffet is served. Lana is swept up in a magical whirlwind of love, the most perfect wedding she could ever have dreamed of.

As the evening draws to a close, an elaborate firework display completes their magical, special day. They thank their guests and arrange for their wedding gifts and remainders of their cake to be taken back to their house, then take a short walk upstairs to their honeymoon suite.

Dean takes his key card and swipes it to open the door, then picks Lana up and carries her across the threshold, much to her amusement. He places her gently on the bed, as she giggles then looks intensely and profoundly into her eyes, "I can't believe you're my wife! We actually did it!"

She grins. "I'm officially Mrs Smith!" she replies, her heart all aflutter.

"You know what we could do? We could make our own film. We could call it *Mr and Mrs Smith 2*," he quips. They laugh and talk deeply, then consummate their love for one another.

The next day they return home to pick up their luggage, then fly out to France. After a long flight, they finally arrive and as they enter their room, Lana pushes open the adjoining balcony doors of their bedroom windows synchronously, breathing in the warm, pure air. The view is breathtaking, she can't quite believe her eyes, dumbfounded at the beauty of everything. Dean's in the bathroom, so she calls out to him. "D? It feels like I've fallen into an oil painting! It's like everything's in Technicolor!" she expresses over-excitedly. "You've gotta come see this!" She stands there in awe, gawping at the stunning scenery. Their room overlooks the striking turquoise blue waters of the Mediterranean Sea and she continues to stare in wonder, feeling like she's been sucked straight into her computer's screen saver! Dean walks out the bathroom and goes to investigate. They stand there wrapped in each other's arms, looking out into the glorious horizon, feeling fortunate and blessed.

Their honeymoon is filled with much love and laughter, numerous shopping trips to the unique, vibrantly colourful streets. consisting of outdoor coffee shops and patisseries. They visit the famous markets which line the roads, made up of stalls filled with organic fruit and vegetables, perfumes, and handmade soap to name but a few. Local artists paint the picturesque scenery and beautiful flowers fill the streets. They visit the harbour and make wonderful happy memories.

Chapter 8

I'll Only Be A Few Hours...

Four and a half years later...

It's a beautiful, glorious day. Rays of sunshine stream through the crack of the slightly open curtain and the alarm starts to beep. Lana hits the top of the clock to turn it off whilst her eyes remain tightly shut.

Dean grabs her and pulls her toward him, placing a gentle kiss on her forehead. "Hey baby, you know what day it is?"

"Sunday?" murmurs Lana, slumberous with her eyes still closed.

"Yeah, but also, it's the day of *love!*" The corners of her mouth start to upturn slightly. He kisses her again on the curve where her lips align and implores, "Don't go out today, let's just stay in bed."

She yawns and opens her eyes. "I can't, D, Jess is coming over. I've promised I'd take her to the office and go through all that stuff with her today. I'll only be a few hours, I promise!" Dean half smiles but looks rejected and dejected. Lana feels bad, she doesn't even really want to go, but she's already promised Jess and she only intends to go for a little while anyway. She sits up, takes Dean's face in her hands and continues, "So, *you* need to get up and make me some breakfast!"

His magnetic smile emerges once more as his good mood returns, and he nests his face into her neck. Lana laughs uncontrollably as his nose touches the funny bone on her jawline and goose bumps travel down her arm. They play fight then she hesitates and gazes up at him seductively, his alluring charm luring her in once more.

With desire taking over and unable to resist the magnitude of his charisma, once more she falls under the spell he has cast and zealously they make love.

He jumps off the bed as she smiles back at him. "And that's why *I* am the King!" he wisecracks, with a cheeky wink.

Laughing, she shakes her head. "I don't believe you just said that!"

"Oh yeah!" he replies with a brash grin and knowing nod. He starts to run a shower, as Lana is left there giggling to herself. He scrolls through his phone and loads his song list. As reggae music starts to play, he jumps in the shower and starts singing along to the songs. He calls out over the noise of the streaming water, "So angel, that reminds me, do you fancy going to that Caribbean place that opened in town? The food and cocktails are meant to be *amazing*, and I heard they play R&B and reggae music... *all* night!"

"Yeah! That sounds great!" she calls back enthusiastically.

"Alright, I hope they're not fully booked! I'll try and book it for around seven okay?"

But this time she doesn't respond, instead she abruptly pulls open the shower door and looks Dean up and down flirtatiously.

"Wit Woo!" she whistles. Dean grins, wittily nodding in recognition of himself, takes her hand and pulls her in. They laugh, kiss and embrace.

As they emerge from the shower, Dean dries off and Lana starts to diffuse her damp hair.

"I'm gonna make some breakfast Lar."

"Okay, I'll be down in a minute."

Dean winks at her and rushes down the stairs. He makes a hearty breakfast of croissants, eggs, juice, coffee, berries and yoghurt. A few moments later Lana arrives in the kitchen, her face lights up. "D! You didn't have to do all this!" He hands her a large card, a massive box of assorted

Belgian chocolates, a colourful assorted bouquet of exquisite flowers, and a small rectangular gift box. Lana chews on her lip and reaches her arms around his neck. "Thanks D!" she says bashfully and pecks him on his cheek. She sits down and carefully opens the box. Inside sits a stunning 24 carat gold necklace with their initials D and S intertwined. A massive grin appears on her face, she's overjoyed. "Oh, Dean, it's so beautiful! Thank you!" He loves doting on her and is *so* happy when he can see she's happy. He takes it from her, lifts her hair and fastens it gently around her neck. She walks to the mirror and touches it, gazing at it admiringly. "Wait there!" she points at Dean, instructing him not to move. She runs into the living room to the secret place where she's stashed his gift.

Lana hands him the card and gift. It's quite a small square box roughly the size of his palm. "Is it a basketball?" he jokes.

She giggles. "Nope!"

"A pair of slippers?" he quips,

"No! Wrong again" giggles Lana,

"I give up! I'm gonna have to open it!" He unwraps the gift paper and opens the box. Sitting inside is a *very* expensive designer watch. "Larnie!" he gasps, completely astonished. "I love it!" He takes it out the box and straps it on his wrist. "Thank you, baby," he remarks gratefully, twisting his wrist around to admire it. He pulls her close, grabbing her waist and passionately kissing her lips.

"Let's keep the cards until later when I get back and then we can read them in bed together," she says flirting with him.

Dean raises his eyebrows. "That's a *very* good idea!" He hugs her and kisses her cheek softly. Lana is still only wearing her bathrobe so hurries back upstairs to get dressed as Dean admires his watch.

A few moments later she shouts down to him. "Baby? Have you seen my diary anywhere?"

"Nah, Lar, I haven't, but I'll have a look."

"Alright, thanks!" she replies. A couple of minutes later, she hurries down the stairs. "Did you find it?"

"No, I couldn't see it anywhere, but don't worry, it'll turn up."

"Hmm, I just really needed it for today, I'll have a look in the living room." Lana goes to search as Dean calls the restaurant to book the table for that evening.

Meanwhile, Brad and Jess are just arriving. Brad locks his car as Jess walks up the driveway to the house and knocks on the door. Dean greets her and lets her in. "Hi Jess!" shouts Lana from the other room.

"Hey, Lar!" Jess heads straight to the kitchen, picks up a plate and helps herself to some croissants and berries, then pours herself a large glass of fruit juice.

"Help yourself, Jess!" jokes Dean.

Brad comes in and sits down at the breakfast bar. Jess doesn't stop talking as Lana's rushing around, trying to get ready. She goes into the other room to get her shoes. "Lar you ready yet?" shouts Jess impatiently.

"Yeah, just a second, I can't find my diary." Lana emerges looking flustered, "Maybe I left it in the car," she sighs. "Oh, it doesn't matter, I'll look for it later or we'll be here all day."

She grabs her purse and is just about to leave but Dean stops her. "You need something to eat, honey," he tells her.

Lana picks up a croissant and takes a bite then sips half a cup of juice. "I really want to rush, D, so I can get back. I'll get something at lunchtime." Dean's not impressed but knows the sooner she goes, the quicker she'll be back, so agrees. Lana says bye to Brad and kisses Dean, *intensely*.

"Oh my God, you guys, four years and you still act like newly-weds, it's disgusting!" teases Jess, rolling her eyes. Dean grins and raises an eyebrow to Lana.

She reaches for the handle of the front door but just as she's about to open it, Dean sprints to her and grasps her hand. "The table's booked, and we need to do that *card thing*, so hurry up, alright?" Lana nods, smiles shyly and kisses him once again.

Jess flings her head and roll her eyes at Lana then hurries her out. "Just get in the car!" Lana jokes as Dean smirks to himself and shuts the door.

Lana starts the engine as Jess is talking non-stop about a guy she's seeing and tells Lana that they're going on a date that evening. "Who? That Wayne guy?" asks Lana.

"No! Not Wayne, its *Dwayne!*" Lana shakes her head and exhales.

"You know, Jess, I just can't keep up with you anymore!" Lana puts the car into gear and starts to drive, but she's distracted. Her mind is wandering, still curious as to where her diary could be, as Jess continues to chat incessantly.

She reaches for the glove compartment to see if it's in there whilst trying to drive at the same time. Jess pushes her hand away, "*I'll* look, *you* just need to concentrate on the road, Lar!"

"You're right, sorry, it's just been bugging the hell out of me!" she replies, feeling overly frustrated.

Jess rummages around in the side of the door and pushes her seat back to look underneath it. She turns around and peers over the back seats. "It's definitely not in here. It must be at yours; I'll help you look for it when we get back, okay?" Lana nods despondently.

Although it's a Sunday morning, it seems exceedingly busy for the time of day. "There's a lot of traffic today, Jess. Don't you think?"

"Yeah, there really is! It must be because it's Valentine's Day and all the guys just remembered, and now they're having to rush around at the last minute to get their girlfriends gifts!" They both smirk. "But talking of that, I don't want to be too late 'cause I wanna get back to Dean. We're going out for a meal later!" Lana states jubilantly as Jess smiles back kindly.

The traffic somehow seems to be worsening, so Lana decides to deviate to the highway. Spotting the signs, she accelerates to join. There's only a handful of vehicles in front of her now, "Yes!" she beams. "There's hardly any traffic on here, and if I get in the fast lane, we'll be there in no time!" Jess nods several times in agreement. Lana changes lanes as Jess turns the radio up and starts singing, lip syncing and bobbing her head to the track.

A few minutes pass and Jess glances up the highway. She observes a logging truck just a little way in front of them in the next lane, packed to the brim with timber. The enormous tree logs are strapped down with rope and leather straps, but Jess notices that one of them is starting to come loose, and immediately becomes alarmed. "Lar? Is that meant to be shaking like that?"

Lana glances over. Appearing fearful, her pupils dilate. "*No!*" she replies undoubtedly. They're both feeling extremely concerned and uneasy. "I'm gonna put my foot down and get around it." Jess nods several times in agreement.

Meanwhile, Dean's in the kitchen making himself a coffee and coincidently, notices Lana's diary out of the corner of his eye. It's poking out from the side of the kitchen worktop! He flips up the side and carefully pulls it out. He knows she's probably still looking for it, so rings her. Lana's cell phone starts to vibrate. She sees it's Dean and reaches out to grab it, but it falls out her hand and drops to the floor.

Lana leaves it there as she hastily and forcefully pushes her foot to the floor to accelerate to get past the truck, but she's in his blind spot and is unaware that he's about to change lanes too. As they change lanes simultaneously, the vibration agitates the logs even more, which in turn push against the ropes and loosens them. The back-rope snaps. The logs rapidly break free and start bounding at speed towards Lana's car. Lana quickly reacts and tries her best to swerve out of the way, but she can't make it in time. Jess starts to scream. The driver of the truck suddenly notices them in his mirror and tries his hardest to move, but he doesn't have time either as Lana's car is now moving at considerable speed. She loses control. The lorry and countless logs end up careering into the side of her. More timber starts to fall and there's nothing either of them can do to avoid the collision. Jess and Lana lock eyes as everything feels like it's playing out in slow motion and they're completely powerless to escape it.

The thunderous roar from the initial impact echoes across the highway and after what seems like an eternity, the car finally slows and comes to a standstill. Jess is violently flung out the door, while Lana remains trapped inside. The wheels on the lorry screech and come to a deafening, dramatic halt. The driver breathes heavily as he sits in stillness and silence for a moment, his hands glued to the steering wheel, his body locked in shock. He stares into his rear-view mirror as the enormity of what has just occurred suddenly hits him. He leaps from his vehicle and calls emergency services whilst at the same time sprinting down the highway towards Lana's car.

Several other vehicles are sporadically scattered along the highway, many with hazard lights now flashing. The whole scene is horrendous and horrifying.

Lana's cell phone clicks to voicemail, Dean leaves a message on her phone. "Hi, baby! Guess What? I found your diary if you were still wondering where it was. I'll see you in a little while, don't be too long or I'm comin' down there to get you! Alright, bye." He rings off but as he does, he feels a strange, painful burning sensation in his chest. Thinking he has indigestion, he ignores it and pours himself a glass of water.

Silence.

Chapter 9

Devastation...

Jess is lying on the ground, slipping in and out of consciousness, surrounded by a plethora of scattered glass and debris. There are logs, broken pieces of wood, and timber scattered everywhere down the highway, as far as the eye can see. Jess begins to blink a couple of times as she starts to come around and can just about make out the faint sound of sirens approaching in the distance. Gradually, with every passing blink she starts to realise the magnitude of the situation and as she reflects, she relives the events that have just unfolded.

The adrenaline begins to wear off and the pain and panic instantly start to kick in, as it dawns on her how severely hurt she is and that she's lying there sprawled in the middle of the highway. She gradually raises her hand to her cheek and holds her jaw, she opens and closes her mouth a few times. She manages to lift her head off the ground, just enough to enable her to see the car lying there on its side. She can't believe what a terrible state it's in and knows that Lana must still be inside. Jess attempts to drag herself along the road towards the car, but she's in excruciating pain and must stop. She calls out hysterically for Lana, but there's no response.

The sirens get nearer and as the police arrive, they begin to cordon off the road. The driver of the truck rushes frantically towards Lana's car. He peers through the window and shakes his head, "*Oh my God!*" he yells over and over. He notices Jess and rushes over to her. "Are you alright?" He's extremely concerned, out of breath, and panic-stricken.

"I can't move... the pain! I can't move my leg!" weeps Jess.

"It's alright. Just stay still. An ambulance is on its way," he tells her softly as he places his hand on her arm, patting it gently to try and comfort her.

"I can't, I need to get to my friend!"

"No! You mustn't move, you're injured, just keep still!"

As she stares at him, all of a sudden it becomes clear to her that this is the truck driver, and *he* is responsible for all this. She glares at him and forcefully shoves his hand away. "This is *your* fault! Those logs fell off *your* truck! It's *all* your fault! Get away from me!" she screams at him hysterically, her voice breaking with emotion.

The driver falls back on the road and sobs, "I'm sorry. I'm so sorry," he cries over and over. They're both in shock as the emergency services begin to arrive.

The paramedics are now on the scene and rush to tend to Jess. "What's your name, love?" he asks as he speedily removes medical equipment from his bag. "Jessica," she stammers, writhing in pain.

"Okay Jessica. We're going to give you some oxygen and I'm going to put this brace around your neck for precaution. I know it's difficult, but just try to stay calm."

"My leg, I can't move my leg," she sobs uncontrollably.

"Okay, try not to move." He holds the oxygen mask over her face and straps it around the back of her head, then gently moves the neck brace into place. Another couple of paramedics take a stretcher and place it on the floor next to her. "Alright Jessica, we're gonna have to move you onto this sheet now so we can get you on the stretcher," he explains. He takes the sheet and starts to gently push it under her then tries to roll her slightly to pull it through, she screams with the excruciating pain. "Alright love, we've done it now, I know you're in a lot of pain, but we have to get you to the hospital as soon as we can so on the count of three we're going to lift you onto the stretcher."

"You need to get my friend; I think she's still in the car!" The paramedic looks over his shoulder towards the direction of the car and can see what a bad state it's in. He looks back to his colleague with a very worrying look but smiles reassuringly at Jess.

"Don't worry, there's people here to tend to her now." Another ambulance quickly pulls around and several fire engines are also following closely behind. The Chief Fire Officer jumps out and runs over to Lana's car with another fireman. Jess is securely strapped onto the stretcher and placed into back of the ambulance, while she continues to cry out in pain and scream for Lana. They put on the sirens and race her to the hospital.

Lana's car is now completely on its side and partially crushed. The emergency services have to try and tend to her through the broken door and carnage while the firemen start to cut it away. They very quickly manage to pull Lana out and place her onto a stretcher. She is unconscious and her life is now hanging by a thread. She has severe cuts, gashes, and deep wounds, multiple bruises, and several broken bones. Her pulse is drastically low, and she is desperately fighting for her life. They all run with the stretcher and wheel her into the ambulance then quickly hook her up to the monitor, but as they do she flat-lines, so the medics frantically commence CPR. They manage to bring her back, but her pulse is still dangerously low, so they continue compressions en route, whilst one of the other medics starts to bandage her wounds. They rush her to the nearest hospital with sirens blaring.

A few minutes later, Lana arrives, and they rapidly run her through to the emergency room. She is in a *critical* condition. Numerous monitors, respirators, and tubes are attached, and a cannula hastily inserted into her hand. She's placed on a drip whilst several doctors and physicians monitor her and try to stem the bleeding from her leg wound.

All of a sudden, she flat-lines as her heart abruptly stops again. There is no pulse at all now. Everyone manically starts to run around the room, as the doctor begins chest compressions and Lana is injected with drugs to try to cause her heart to react. There's no response, so he decides to try to resuscitate her with defibrillator pads. "Clear!" he shouts. At least ten medics are in the emergency room with Lana now trying everything they can to save her life. They inject her again and desperately continue with heart compressions.

They try continuously for nearly *fifty* minutes to bring her back to life, but it soon becomes apparent that everything they've tried has been ineffective and that their efforts are futile and hopeless. The doctor shakes his head and glances up. "Enough! It's been too long; the injuries are too severe. We need to stop." There's an air of silence in the emergency room as everyone feels discouraged and sorrowful.

"Call it!" says the doctor defeated and downcast.

The nurse checks her watch. "Time of death, 9.59am," she states demurely, as the sheet is slowly pulled up over Lana's face.

Meanwhile, the guys are watching football as the police pull up outside. "What kind of pass was that? My grandma plays better than this!" Brad argues. Just then, there's an incessant knock at the door.

Dean grins and grabs Lana's diary from the side. "I told you they'd be back, there's only so much of Jess one person can take!" he jokes.

"That's my sister you're talking about!" Brad calls out with a raised eyebrow, Dean chuckles and opens the door thinking that Lana's come back for her diary.

"I knew you'd be bac..." Dean doesn't finish his sentence as two police officers are standing there before him. His face drops as he notes their serious demeanour and a lump steadily starts to form in his throat.

"Hello. Are you the husband of Lana Smith?" one of the officers asks gravely, Dean nods silently. "Can we come in, Sir?"

"Why? What's happened?" he asks anxiously.

"We really need to come in, Sir."

He lets them in still clutching the diary. Brad sees the police officers and quickly jumps up off his chair. "What is it? What's wrong?"

"Please sit down. I'm very sorry to have to tell you this, but there's been a *very* serious traffic accident." The police officers begin to explain the situation. Although information is still coming in and it's limited, they've been briefed that Lana didn't make it and Jess is in an extremely serious condition. They tell Dean and Brad that that the driver of the truck has been arrested and both women have been taken to the same local hospital. Dean shakes his head in disbelief. He drops the diary to the floor, takes his car keys and sprints to his car faster than he has ever ran in his life. Brad ushers the police out and runs after him, dives into his car and they speed to the hospital together.

Dean's mind is a blur. He's distraught and driving like a lunatic, and in his rush to get to Lana runs a red light. He swerves out the way of the oncoming traffic and carries on regardless. "It must be a mistake; they've got it wrong. She's fine... she's fine!" he mumbles to himself repeatedly. Brad side glances at him but doesn't say a word. He just sits there dumbfounded, in total shock himself.

As they arrive Dean's heart is racing, his hands are trembling, he's severely shaken and disturbed. *Please God, please let Lana be alright,* he thinks to himself continuously. He parks the car as close as he can to the main entrance and jumps out, oblivious to whether he's blocking the entrance or if he'll incur a parking fine. Brad follows closely behind, and they sprint together, barging past people in their hurry.

Brad stops a nurse to ask if she knows where Jess is as Dean pushes past the people in the queue to frantically ask the receptionist where Lana is. "Lana Smith. My wife, Lana Smith. Where is she? What room is she in?"

"Sir, there's a queue!" she responds blankly and snootily.

"The police sent me. It's my wife, she's been in an accident and she's badly hurt, please, I need to get to her!"

Another receptionist can see Dean's sheer panic and despair and tells the other woman to deal with the queue and she'll deal with him. "What's her date of birth, Sir?" He gives the details and she checks her computer.

"Please hurry!" he pleads.

"She's in Room 31, on the first floor." But before she can continue with what she's saying, Dean starts to run. "But you can't go up there, Sir!" The receptionist stands up and calls out after him, but he ignores her pleas and races down the corridor irrelevantly. He dashes up the flight of stairs leading to the first floor and bursts through the double doors, then desperately starts searching for the room numbers.

As the numbers get closer to 31 he slows down. Then he sees it. He feels as though his heart's fallen into his stomach; he stops to take a breath. He gradually walks towards the door, then slowly peers through the glass. He can see a body lying there covered by a sheet. Dean starts to breathe heavily; his heart is pounding out of his chest. He's frozen, unable to move.

There's no-one else around apart from the doctor who tried to save Lana who's still in the corridor, waiting for the porters to take her downstairs to the hospital morgue. He notices Dean. He can see how distressed he is, so approaches him. "Excuse me, are you a relative of Mrs Smith?" he asks quietly with concern, Dean nods despondently.

"I'm her husband," he mumbles almost silently.

The doctor clears his throat. "Unfortunately, Sir your wife suffered internal injuries that were *very* serious. We tried everything we could to revive her. We tried to resuscitate her for nearly an hour, but she didn't respond; even if we had found a rhythm, there's an extremely high chance she would have suffered brain damage due to the length of time her heart had stopped beating. I'm very sorry for your loss, Sir. We honestly tried everything we could to save her." Dean doesn't take his eyes off Lana for a one second or even blink the whole time the doctor is talking.

Dean can't believe what he's hearing, everything feels so surreal, he just saw Lana an hour and half ago! It's Valentine's Day! They have plans for tonight! How can all this be happening? It *must* be a bad dream!

Very gently, he pushes the door open. Still not taking his eyes off Lana, he warily walks over to the bed. The doctor accompanies him as Dean shakes his head in disbelief and horror, suppressing his every tear. He takes a gulp as he guardedly sits down beside her. He knows he has to look under the sheet and is praying to God that somehow they've got it wrong and this is someone else.

He feels as though he's about to have a panic attack as he takes a corner of the sheet in both hands then slowly lowers it from her face and folds it down to her chest.

But his worst nightmare is confirmed. It's her! It's Lana! As he recognises how many injuries she's suffered, his breathing grows more and more shallow. He takes her lifeless hand in his, its stone cold. He stares at the necklace he placed around her neck just a short while ago. As he finally blinks, a pearl of a tear rolls down his cheek and meets the corner of his lips. He gently rests his head on her chest, closes his eyes and whispers. "Lar, I found your diary, it was in the kitchen. You have to wake up, I booked us a table for tonight. We've got to go home and get ready!"

He lifts his head to look at her once more. All the colour has drained from her face. Dean moves the sheet slightly from her arm and observes the multiple bruises, cuts, and wounds that she sustained. He can't stop himself from hyperventilating and goes into shock. The doctor has to intervene, so leads him out the room to sedate him. Dean is *beyond* devastated.

After having been administered the medication, Dean is escorted to a separate room and sits on the bed in silence, staring out into the clouds through the open blind. A few minutes pass and Brad rushes into him, overpowered by emotion, tears streaming down his face. "D! The doctor told me what happened to Lana. I can't believe it, I can't..." he stops in mid-sentence and grabs Dean. He hugs him tightly, but Dean doesn't respond, he just gazes out into thin air. "I'm so, *so* sorry Dean, I don't even have any words!" he blubbers. They sit together for a while in silence while the enormity and magnitude of events whirl around their minds.

Sometime later, Dean suddenly reacts. "Where's Jess?" he asks solemnly, still staring straight ahead.

"They've put her in a room downstairs, she's got some *bad* injuries, but thank God she's gonna make it!"

Dean nods several times over and over. "That's good, that's good," he murmurs. "Does she know?"

"Yeah, I went to see her a few minutes before I came to you. I wanted it to come from me!"

"I need to see her; I need to know *exactly* what happened!"

Brad looks alarmed. "She's not in any state for questions, D. She's in a lot of pain, still in shock and pretty drugged up man."

Dean looks stern. "Lana's not here anymore and I need to know why that is!" he states in a slightly raised tone.

Brad nods calmly, "Okay, we'll go down there, but just take it easy on her, alright?"

The hospital has recommended that Dean stay overnight so they can monitor him, but he refuses. Instead he walks with Brad to the room where Jess is being treated. Dean lightly pushes the door open and sees her lying there covered in gashes and bruises, her arm and leg wrapped in fresh plaster and her neck encased in a brace. Brad kisses her forehead, then sits on a chair in the corner by the window. Dean greets her and kisses her on the cheek. "Hi, Jess!" he says softly.

"Dean!" she whimpers woefully, groggy from all the medication. Individual tears stream down her face as she painfully holds open her arms beckoning him to embrace her. He gulps, walks closer to gently hug her, then sits on the side of her bed. She trembles and sobs as Dean holds her hand in is. "I can't believe what happened, I can't believe Lana's gone." she splutters. "I wish we could all go back to this morning, it's a nightmare."

Dean cuts in. "You're alright, though?" he whispers.

"I'm gonna be alright." she weeps, wiping the cascading tears from her cheek. Dean sighs deeply.

"Jess, I know you've been through a lot and you're not feeling good, but I need to know *exactly* what happened."

She nods. "Yeah, of course! But I thought the police already talked to you!" she sniffles.

"They did, but I wanna hear it from you!" he replies unrelenting, as Brad throws him a look.

She tries to shuffle up the bed a little. "Well, when we left your house, Lar was driving and she decided to get on to the highway so we could get to work quicker, but when we got on, there was this truck way out in front of us that had all these logs on the back that weren't tied on properly. We saw it and Lana switched lanes, but one of the logs fell and it came tumbling towards us and she tried to swerve but lost control of the car. It all happened so fast D, one minute we were talking, then the next..." She shakes her head and starts to weep as Brad rushes over to console her. He puts his arm around her shoulder.

"It's alright, Jess."

Dean stands, aggravated and stares at her. "So, *you* were talking, Jess!" Jess frowns, confused at his tone, as Brad glares at him.

"Well, yeah. I was telling her about my date, and she was talking about yours, but it just happened, D!" she stutters anxiously.

Dean stares at her dead in the face and abruptly stands up. "I gotta go!" he declares sternly and storms out. Jess looks to Brad with trepidation.

"I'll be back in a minute." Brad tells her softly and runs out after Dean. "Dean!" he yells.

"What?" Dean angrily snaps back.

"What you doing, man? You know what Jess has just been through!"

"Well, at least *she's* alive!" he replies bitterly.

Brad is angered. "That's not fair, Dean. None of this is Jessica's fault!"

Dean squints and scoffs. "Not her fault? Lana didn't even *need* to go anywhere today, Jess just probably just *nagged* her into it. All I know is that if Lana didn't go to work today, she would still be here now. Jess was probably talking to her so much she distracted her from the road. She's *always* talking, she don't stop talking, B!"

Brad can't believe what he's hearing. "That's *Jess* you're talking about!" he declares earnestly.

Dean shakes his head, nostrils flaring, "Yeah, and *she* is still alive, and Lana isn't!" They hold each other's stare for a moment then Dean breaks eye contact, turns and storms off.

He struts back to his car, opens his window, and sits there in shock, feeling numb and dazed. He lights a cigarette and inhales several times as Brad follows behind, jumps in the passenger seat and slams the door. They stare at each other but don't speak a word. Dean sighs, throws his cigarette out the window and with tears welling in his eyes, places his hands against his forehead. "I didn't mean any of it." he whispers. "This can't be happening, B, it *can't* be real! It's gotta all be a bad dream or something." Brad's whole demeanour changes to sadness. He can't find any words and starts to quietly sob as he becomes engulfed in Dean's despair and agony, and the severity of the situation fully takes hold of him.

Dean glances at him then bows his head. "I need to go back in, I need to be with her," he states gravely. Brad agrees and they sombrely walk back towards the hospital. Dean raises his head to the sky, there's not a single cloud in sight. They walk back to the room together in complete silence.

Dean reaches for the door handle, but just as he's about to turn it, a nurse calls out. "Excuse me, Sir?" he turns to look. "The lady who was in here, she's just been moved, I'm afraid."

"Where is she?" he asks in a serious but anxious manner.

"They've taken her downstairs. Are you a relative?"

"Her husband." Dean whispers feeling faint and nauseous. He steadies himself against the wall and falls onto a chair situated outside the room.

The doctor is still on the wing and notices Dean again, he interrupts. "I thought you were being treated downstairs Sir?"

Dean doesn't respond but just stares at the floor, so Brad intervenes. "He has had some medication, but wanted to come back up to see his wife."

The doctor nods in acknowledgement. "Unfortunately, we've had to move her, it's hospital protocol, I'm afraid, but I'll make sure you get to see her if you can wait." The doctor makes a phone call and speaks to one of the nurses. He comes off the phone and turns to Dean. "They said you can come down at 4pm and if you want to bring any other family members then that would be fine too. I need you to sign some documents as well, Sir." he adds.

All Dean wants to do is to close his eyes and be on his date with Lana but realises it's not possible and knows he has the responsibility of informing the rest of their family. He looks to Brad. "I'm gonna have to go home and make some calls. I'll come back later."

Brad nods sedately. "I'll sit with Jess for a while and then I'll come straight to yours."

Dean shakes his head. "No, I need to be on my own, I've got to ring Lana's parents and..." he gulps, "just say sorry to Jess for me and I'll come and see her in a couple of days."

Brad agrees and places his hand consolingly on Dean's shoulder. "I know this is a living nightmare, but I'm here for you, you know that right?" he asks with his voice breaking. Dean nods silently. They hug then Dean drives back home.

He unlocks the door and walks in. All he can hear is silence, until he snaps out of it when Amadeus comes pounding towards him and starts running in circles around his feet. He picks up the dog and walks into the kitchen. All the breakfast items are still sitting there. The bite out of the croissant that Lana had earlier, still sits on a plate next to her half-drunk juice. He looks down at the empty gift box his watch was in and remembers the cards that they didn't give each other earlier, so goes to retrieve his from the draw. He picks it up and notes Lana's handwritten envelope and feels a lump starting to bulge in the forefront of his throat as he scans over it. He puts the dog down and sits on the sofa, then carefully pulls the card out and starts to read it.

To my darling Dean,

You make my life so perfect that every day is like Valentine's when I'm with you!

I'm so in love with you, D, you're my everything and no matter how old or bald or chunky you get, I will always feel exactly the same way about you as I do today.

Can't wait until later!

Love you always my love, Lar xxx

It all becomes too much for him, he crumbles and starts to sob uncontrollably.

Chapter 10

Aftermath...

A week and a day pass, and the day of the funeral is upon him. It's taking place at the church Dean and Lana attended regularly and were married in only a few years earlier. He is *dreading* it. Dawn is breaking and he's lying on his bed wide awake staring at the ceiling in total silence, his heart palpitating and his stomach churning.

He's been in a daze ever since the accident and awake all night anxiously worrying, wondering how the hell he's ever going to get through this day. He's blocked out all of his pain and emotion to enable him to deal with all of the heart-wrenching arrangements. Dean couldn't bear the pain of having to collect Lana from the funeral directors, so her parents have agreed to collect her body and meet him directly at the church. He wants to arrive on his own and has told Brad and his family to meet him there.

Dean pours all of his energy into just getting dressed. He fastens his cufflinks and ties his shoes, then gazes at his reflection in the mirror and straightens his tie. He feels numb. He notices how drawn he looks, his cheekbones sunken and the sudden appearance of dark circles under his eyes. Everything is silent. He's now on autopilot, and as he glances at Lana's picture on the side table, he closes his eyes and forces himself to choke back his tears. He's wearing the watch that Lana bought him and as he checks it, he lets out an extended deep breath. It's time to leave.

The church is only a short drive from his house; it only takes about ten minutes to get there. As he arrives, he parks up, turns off the engine, and sits silently trying to gather his muddled thoughts and muster his final scrap of strength. He can see all the people gathered outside the church and doesn't have the faintest idea how he's going to cope. For a split second, he even considers going home but realises he can't. He knows he has no option but to get out the car and get through it somehow.

A few moments pass, and he steadily walks down the hill to the church where he recognises the funeral car and can see the dozens of red roses he bought for Lana lining the windows and realises that the pallbearers must have already taken her into the church. His family, friends, and the priest stand outside, waiting to greet him. As he arrives, they give their condolences and best wishes. People are weeping and many shake Dean's hand and comment on what a wonderful woman Lana was.

Brad arrives shortly after with Jess who has to be helped out of the car due to her substantial injuries. Although still in severe pain, and she is meant to be at home resting, Jess has insisted that she *must* attend the funeral. She's helped into a wheelchair, her arm and leg still in plaster.

All the guests progressively start to enter the church. *'Over the Rainbow'* by Israel Kamakawiwo'ole, echoes throughout the entire room as Dean slowly walks down the aisle. It's only a ten second walk, if that, but somehow it seems to be taking an eternity to get there.

Step by step, he makes his way to the front and as the reaches the end, he's faced with something he never thought he would *ever* have to witness, a horrifying sight... Lana's coffin! He feels as though he's having an out of body experience, as if he's been catapulted into a horror movie. *'How can all this be happening?'* he contemplates.

Everyone is now seated in the church and you can hear a pin drop as Priest Hannigan appears and walks towards the podium to start his sermon. A large glossy picture of Lana stands on a wooden pedestal beside him. Although his Irish accent is strong and emphasised, he speaks clearly and concisely enough for everyone to understand him.

"I'd like to start by welcoming everybody here today and if I could ask everyone to either switch off their phones or make them silent, that would be grand. Well, what an incredibly sad day this is! Not in my wildest dreams did I ever think that I would have to stand here today and say these words. Foremost, I would like to send blessings to Lana's family and friends and everyone who is mourning Lana's passing, but especially to her husband, Dean. I know how much Lana meant to you Dean, and so may the good Lord bless you and give you the strength you need to carry you through this terrible time." Dean nods respectfully and bites the inside of his mouth trying hard to hold back his tears.

"I have known Lana and Dean for several years and I was honoured to be the one to conduct their wedding a few years ago in this very church. Lana was a *very* popular member of our community and a very special lady, a lovely woman and an extremely kind soul. She was the epitome of what a woman should be... diligent, loving, humble and obviously a very caring and devoted wife. No doubt, she will be sorely missed by her family and friends and her untimely passing will undoubtedly leave a hole in the heart of the many lives she has touched by her brief time here on earth. Now if everyone would please stand for our first hymn." Everyone stands and sings, then the service resumes.

"Speaking for us now will be Lana's good friend, Jessica. If you would like to make your way up, Jess." Brad helps her and wheels her to the front. She dabs her eyes and takes the microphone, as her voice starts to tremble. "I have no idea why *I'm* here today and Lana isn't. I've asked myself that question every minute of every day since the accident, and sometimes I wish it would've been me instead of her because she was such a beautiful person. In a way, I myself have been dealt a life sentence because I will eternally be haunted by what happened. It will stay with me for the rest of my days and I have lost one of my best friends. Lana was one of the most remarkable women I have ever met, everyone who knew her will agree. She was so kind and caring, and would immediately try and put you at ease and, although she was stunning, she really had no idea how beautiful she was," she states with a broken smile, "but that was Lana for you, such a wonderful, humble person, and an amazing friend. I will miss her every day for the rest of my life." Jess starts to break down, so Brad gently takes the microphone from her and wheels her back to her seat.

Dean rubs his head in despair, he just wants it all to be over. Another few friends and family members read poems and verses and tell stories of Lana's personality, kindness, and wit and how dearly she will be missed, then a gospel choir sings a haunting version of *Hallelujah*. There is a deathly silence in the church once more as Priest Hannigan looks to Dean. Rising unsteadily, Dean makes his way wearily to the stand, trying his utmost to stifle his emotions.

He glances at Lana's picture as he passes it, gulps, and pulls the folded paper out of his pocket, that he scribbled some notes on earlier. He irons out the creases with the palm of his hand and clears his throat. Observing all the people seated in the church, a flash of a memory of their wedding day enters his head. He swallows hard, trying to suppress his emotion, then he begins. "Thank you to everyone for coming out today, and to everyone who did a reading or said something nice, Lana would have been erm..." He clears his throat once more and continues, "Lana would have felt very loved." There's a pause and a moment of silence as Dean battles to compose himself once again. He swallows and continues.

"Lana was my wife, but more importantly than that, she was my best friend. When people use the term *my other half*, I used to think that was just something people said and I never really understood it, I mean how can you be someone's *other half*, right? That is, I didn't understand it until Lana walked into my life and *became* the other half of me. She was half of me, and I was half of her. We had an erm... We had the kind of relationship where we were so close that sometimes she would just know what I was thinking without me even having to utter a single word. Now she's gone I can never be whole again without her, but I will treasure every single second that we spent together." He glances at Lana's picture and his voice starts to break. "I know how blessed I was to have her in my life, let alone her ever agreeing to be my wife, and I will always be thankful for every moment that I had with her and..." he turns to her picture, "I will forever hold you in my heart. I love you, Lana." Everyone claps and weeps as Dean makes his way back to his seat. Brad pats his shoulder a couple of times to comfort him and rubs his arm for support.

Priest Hannigan wraps up his sermon beautifully and everyone exits the church, as Dean, Brad, and the other pallbearers are ushered towards the coffin. As Dean witnesses it again, he starts to breathe heavily and has to take several sips of water to try and calm his nerves and anxiety. Brad's watching and gives him a reassuring nod. They all move into their designated positions and carefully lift up the engraved coffin. Dean is situated at the front in prime position and leads the way. They cautiously walk down the hill to Lana's serene resting place, and after what seems like forever, gently place it onto the ground. Everyone congregates around silently, as an unusually large cluster of butterflies flutters past and the priest begins his reading.

Dean freezes and can't bear to pick it up again so stands there in stillness, staring in complete disbelief and dismay as the other pallbearers lift the coffin once more, then gradually lower it into the ground. He feels sick, like he could physically vomit at any second. Everyone rallies around trying to comfort him as the priest continues his blessing. People throw flowers sporadically onto the coffin as Brad and other family members lend a hand to fill the hole with dirt, then a temporary makeshift cross is tapped into the ground.

The priest blesses the site, then the guests sorrowfully walk back to the church in dribs and drabs. Jess starts to weep. Dean recognises her sadness and despair so bends down, puts his arm around her shoulder and kisses her cheek, trying to comfort and console her. He stands up and glances solemnly at the freshly laid grave. "Do you want me to stay, D?" Brad mutters compassionately.

He shakes his head negatively, "I just need a few minutes." Brad's inclined to stay but knows Dean need a moment to himself, so respects his wishes and carefully wheels Jess back down to the church.

Dean is now completely on his own. He bends down and places a long-stalked, plump red rose onto the soil, then takes a photo of him and Lana on their wedding day and gently tucks it into the front of the cross.

He swallows a couple of times trying to stifle his grief but as he blinks a single tear runs down his face as he silently mouths, *"I'll always love you, Lar."* Although he doesn't want to leave, he pulls himself away and sedately walks back to the church on his own. Dean is silent. His heart is broken. His soul shattered.

Nearly two weeks later...

Dean's at home. He's booked a couple of weeks off work and hasn't left his house since he came back from the funeral. He's hardly eaten but is drinking alcohol excessively, trying to blot out his thoughts and numb his pain. As he pours himself yet another triple shot, he gazes despairingly at himself in his kitchen mirror, wondering how anything's ever going to be normal again, ashamed that he's turning to a bottle and spiralling out of control, but can't find the strength to pull himself out. He throws himself back down on his sofa. Everything is still and silent. He feels like he's living life in black and white, that little by little his heartache is chipping away at his sanity, with every day drawing out like a year.

Apart from arranging the funeral, he's been silent for over two weeks now. Muted by his sorrow, stuck in oblivion, it's like he's patiently waiting to awake from his worst nightmare. He has no energy left, there's just sadness and sorrow. He can't summon the strength to even speak nor does he even want to. He's easily lost a stone in weight and although he's meant to be returning to work in the next few days, he doesn't care about it in the slightest.

The house is a catastrophe, a *complete* mess. There are empty beer cans, wine, and whisky bottles strewn across the living room floor. The trash hasn't been emptied in weeks. There's food on plates scattered around the house. The only thing Dean can bring himself to do is feed his dog. Amadeus is his only comfort; the only piece of Lana he feels he has left.

Since the funeral, Brad's been trying to contact him constantly, but to no avail. Dean's house phone and cell phone both ring out but then click to voicemail. Brad has left several messages, but Dean never returns any of his calls; he's visited his house numerous times, but the curtains are always drawn, and Dean never answers. Brad has been supporting Jess constantly and has been engrossed in her recovery, well-being, and rehabilitation, so hasn't been as focused on Dean as much as he would have liked, but due to the length of time he hasn't heard from him, he realises that he must now increase his efforts and make this his number one priority.

Brad returns to Dean's house *again*, this time *determined* to check he's alright and adamant that he won't leave until he answers. He knocks, thumps, and pounds on the door but Dean is seated on his couch gawping blankly at his television and won't answer. Brad is *very* worried and concerned by now and is becoming extremely anxious that he hasn't been able to get *any* response from Dean at all, so he shuffles past his rose bushes and peeks through his window.

Brad just manages to peer through the tiniest gap in the curtain and catches a glimpse of him sitting there, still and motionless, holding a picture in his hand. Brad can't believe his eyes, he's gobsmacked, Dean looks like death. "Dean?" he hollers as loud as he can, but he doesn't even react. Brad bangs on the window with force and shouts his name again. Dean gradually looks around. "Open the door!" he commands at the top of his voice. Dean rolls his head back and closes his eyes, then slowly gets up and stumbles to the door. He unlocks it but doesn't open it and walks straight back to his sofa. Brad lets himself in.

He enters the living room and can't believe the state it's in, he's aghast. "D? I've been trying to reach you for *days!* Why haven't you answered your phone?" Dean doesn't answer him, still vacantly staring at the television. Brad quickly opens all the drapes and windows, expelling the stale air. "You've gotta pull yourself together! You can't live like this. It's not healthy! Look at you! Look at how much weight you've lost. Look at the state of this place!"

Dean continues to stay silent. He is totally uninterested in anything Brad has to say and proceeds to gaze at his television, still tightly grasping onto a picture of Lana. Brad is now seriously concerned about his state of mind so quickly decides to change his approach. He sits down beside him and speaks in a softer, kinder manner. "D, it's gonna be alright."

Dean has absolutely no energy left. He slowly turns his head and scoffs. "Is it? Is it, B? How's it gonna be alright? Tell me? How is it *ever* gonna be alright?"

Brad feels Dean's despair and looks away for a second trying to think of some consoling, comforting words he can come back with. "It's just going to take a little time, that's all." he stutters.

Dean glares at him with his blood-shot eyes and with his voice breaking he slurs. "She's gone, man, she's not here, and no matter how long I wait she ain't comin' back. She's not going to be here tonight or tomorrow or at Christmas or for our anniversary, or *ever!* And there's not *one* thing I can do to change that, so you tell me, Brad, how is time gonna fix anything and how is anything *ever* gonna be alright?" Dean gets up, his eyes filling with tears as he staggers to the bathroom, slamming the door behind him.

Brad sits back in silence. He doesn't know what he can say to make things any better, but he's definite that he's going to do everything he can to help and that he's not going anywhere until he knows he's alright.

He pulls a trash bag from the kitchen draw and starts tidying up. He clears away all the rubbish and empty cans, places the plates in the sink, and sprays some air freshener around the room. He makes a large mug of strong coffee, leaves it on the table then gently knocks on the bathroom door. "Dean?" he calls out, but Dean doesn't answer. "I'm going to the grocery store and I'll be back in half an hour," he shouts clearly, knowing that he can hear him. Brad takes Dean's house keys and heads to the store to buy groceries.

On his return, Dean is seated in front of the television once more. Brad walks past him irrelevantly and puts all the food away in the cupboards and fridge freezer. He makes him a sandwich and gives him a bottle of water then runs up to his bedroom to get him some fresh clothes and underwear from his wardrobe. He brings them back downstairs and places them on the chair next to him. "Right, this is what's going to happen. Jess is at home now, so my mom's looking after her. I've booked a week off work and I've told Bulmer's you ain't going in for another week either, so we're gonna get through this next week *together*!"

"I wanna be on my own!" Dean mutters anxiously.

"Well, that's not an option, because you've been on your own and how's that working out for you, D?" Dean looks helpless, troubled and gaunt. Brad sighs and moves closer. "I know you're going through the worst pain of your life, but Lana wouldn't want this, you have to let me help!"

Dean turns to Brad and finally starts to crumble. "She's gone, man!" he whispers, his voice breaking, lip quivering. Brad hooks his arm around his neck as Dean weeps uncontrollably.

Chapter 11

The Waiting Room...

Situated in an expansive, serene room, seated at his desk is *The Boss*. The Boss is a very well built, extremely handsome, rugged, charismatic man. He is exceptionally kind but does not suffer fools gladly. He wears a glorious, prestigious, elaborately embroidered robe and a luminous golden bracelet. The Boss is in charge of all the incoming and outgoing souls to heaven. He has a very reliant, competent right-hand man, his assistant and confidant, Tobias.

Tobias bursts in. "Sir, I'm extremely sorry to disturb you but we have a *very* serious situation." he announces. The Boss doesn't flinch in the slightest, but instead proceeds to sip his cherry wine and writes on his translucent paper with his quilled, iridescent pen. Tobias takes a breath. "Sir, the numbers are wrong!" The Boss looks up with his eyes only. "Demetrius and Aaron, they took the wrong person!" he continues anxiously, then looks to his clipboard. "I'm not sure *how* this error occurred, there were *some* strong similarities, but one is twenty-nine years old and the other is eighty-seven!" he explains shrugging his shoulders. The Boss looks back down and flicks his left hand to the right to summon Demetrius and Aaron, they instantly appear. They turn to one another sheepishly, suddenly very aware they've been sent for, and are standing there in front of The Boss! They are both *extremely* agitated, anxious and tense.

"Tobias has just informed me that *you two* have taken the wrong person. Now tell me, how that can be?" The Boss asks calmly then sits waiting for their response.

Aaron and Demetrius are panicking. They squirm and stutter. "We're *so* sorry, Sir, we made a mistake, the names and dates, we got them mixed up!" Demetrius tries to clarify.

"How?" The Boss raises his voice sternly, "How is it possible to get two people mixed up?"

They both continue to ramble and splutter. "The names and places, they were *very* similar, *and* they have the same birthday. We just got confused, Sir." Aaron tries to explain, but The Boss is having none of it.

"*Same birthday*?! One woman is in her eighties and the other is in her twenties!" he scoffs impatiently, "But irrelevant of that, you didn't once think to inform Tobias so he might have had a chance to sort it out!" he scorns, his voice becoming even more raised. They glance at each other, outwardly on edge as The Boss composes himself. "You know, I already gave you two a second chance after you turned up late to the last meeting I called."

"Please, Boss. We're *very* sorry. We promise it won't happen again!"

"Hmm, you're right. It won't! You're both demoted!" The Boss flicks his left hand away from his body and they both disappear.

Tobias has *never* seen The Boss this angry or agitated. "So, whoever it is, just put them back on please Tobias, and I'll deal with those two later!" The Boss looks back down to his paper, breathes out heavily and continues writing.

Tobias is feeling extremely uneasy himself and clears his throat, as there's still more to tell. "I'm *very* sorry, Sir, but she's on *level three*, they've already had her funeral!" he divulges.

The Boss glares directly at him with a disconcerted gaze. "What? How is that even possible? Why wasn't I informed about this earlier?" he sneers.

"I only just found out about the numbers, Sir, and I came straight to you," splutters Tobias tensely. The Boss pauses looking very concerned. "Where is she now?"

Tobias gulps again. "She's due to arrive in The Waiting Room, Sir."

The Waiting Room is a beautiful place where souls wait to be transported to heaven. It's made of light, warmth and infinite love. Beautiful angelic voices and divine music fill the air and violins and harpsichords merge and play faintly in the distance. A calming mist floats all around.

The Boss is exasperated. He reaffirms, "So, let me get this straight, you're telling me that a person that's not even meant to be here, is on their way to The Waiting Room?" Tobias swallows hard and nods nervously in confirmation. The Boss closes his eyes, rests his hand on the bridge of his nose and sighs heavily. There's a sustained pause. "Has she got any family?"

Tobias looks down at his clipboard. "Erm... a husband, friends... a dog!"

The Boss rolls his eyes and frowns at Tobias. "Summarise!" he commands. Tobias anxiously scans his board once again and scrolls through the pages. "Lana Smith, 7887, twenty-nine years old, Pasadena. Lives with her husband, Dean. Died in a car crash due to multiple fractures and internal injuries. The woman who's meant to be here is Lana Smith, 7129, eighty-seven years old, Pennsylvania. She was resuscitated and her life expectancy could now be as much as five years."

The Boss raises his hands to his face and looks irate but concerned. After a few minutes of deep, pensive thought, he lifts his head and stands. "Alright, we have no choice." he sighs. "Level Three still isn't too late. You'll have to give her a new persona, a new identity, a house, bank account, all of it!"

Tobias blinks, appearing stunned. This is something he has only ever heard of in myth and nothing he thought *he* would ever have to be a part of. "Are you sure, Sir?"

"Just do it!" The Boss responds decisively.

Tobias nods, "Yes, Sir, right away." and hastily leaves to carry out his duties.

Meanwhile, Lana is now sitting in a chair in the corner of the hospital room gazing at herself lying on the bed. She knows she's dead, but she doesn't feel any fear. Strangely, it's as though everything is just as it is meant to be. She watches, absorbed and fascinated as Dean walks in and sits down beside her body. She sees him take her hand and kiss her face and lay his head on her chest. She hears him talking and watches as a tear falls down his face. Lana knows exactly what's happening but is still calm and unperturbed. She slowly walks over to Dean and kneels down next to him.

She gently places her hand on top of his, which he has rested on his knee. She tells him that she's alright and how much she loves him, but he can't hear her. Dean stares at Lana's injuries. He sees her necklace and starts to break down. A doctor takes Dean to be sedated. As Dean stands, a charming, adorable little boy appears in the doorway.

The second Dean moves from sight, Lana's life abruptly starts to flash before her. She glides and swerves through a passage and is pulled toward a beckoning ray of light and knowingly realises that this was the moment she was being born. She feels herself taking her first breath and hears herself cry. She gazes up at her mother as she swaddles her in a warm, cosy blanket, and notices how youthful she looks. She can feel the comfort and the immense love radiating back from her. She recollects her first day at school. How she felt when she had to leave her parent's side. Her childhood memories flash before her, one by one. Each Christmas, birthday, vacation, the good times and bad. She relives every chapter of her life through extreme speed, almost as if she were rapidly flicking through a photo album, or reliving her life as though it were a film playing on fast forward.

Suddenly, Lana sees herself running into the café and stumbling into Dean. She sees him smile at her and feels boundless love for him. She recognises how prominent this meeting was in her life.

Now she's standing in the church reciting her wedding vows. The love she has for Dean is immeasurable and she can feel his love flowing back into her. Several more chapters quickly follow and then all of a sudden she's back in her car. She's watching the accident happen like a spectator. She sees herself talking to Jess and knows exactly what's about to happen, but there's not one thing she can do to prevent or alter it.

Instantaneously, there's an almighty flash, a glimmer and sparks start to fly. Gradually an intense, luminous light forms above her and she's pulled upwards in a spiral pattern. She starts to accelerate at tremendous speed. After a few seconds Lana abruptly comes to a dramatic stop. She glances down and realises she's standing on a travelator moving through what appears to be soft dusky clouds, now travelling towards an even *stronger* beam of light. Even though this light is incredibly and profoundly bright, it does not affect her in anyway; she can stare straight into it. She is not in the least bit scared, everything feels harmonious and calm, and as she reaches the top the light disperses and vanishes. She steps off and there before her stands a monumentally large door with complex, detailed carvings. It reads *Room 8*.

Lana's not afraid in the slightest, she knows this is *exactly* where she's meant to be. Stretching out her hand, she's about to push the door open, but as soon as her fingers reach the handle, it opens of its own accord. She lowers her arm, steps forward and walks through.

Upon her arrival into *Room 8*, Lana's abundantly aware of a vast feeling of serenity and peace washing over her. The feeling of contentment is indescribable. As she stands there trying to take it all in, her attention is drawn to a woman of breathtaking, exquisite beauty, sitting at a desk in the corner of the room typing on an old-style typewriter. With vibrant red hair tousled into a bun, perfect skin and full ruby lips, this lady is a complete vision. As the woman notes Lana's presence, she stops typing and moves her cat shaped glasses onto the bridge of her nose to take a closer look. She smiles broadly, pushes her glasses back into place, yanks the paper from the typewriter and gets up from her desk.

As she walks near, Lana notices she has some intricate embroidered stitching on her lapel which reads *Laurie, CEO*. "Hi, Lana, I'm Laurie, it's lovely to meet you. I'm your Console & Enrichment Officer, please take a ticket and a manual." Laurie has piercing emerald eyes and Lana feels extremely calm, safe, and protected in her presence.

As Laurie starts organising and shuffling some papers, Lana scans the room contemplating *where* the ticket and manual might actually be. Just then, without warning, she turns her head and is greeted by a transparent, floating, rotating ball made of millions of bursts of coloured light intertwining with one another. The ball exudes endless warmth and love and knowingly Lana reaches out and places her hand inside it. She feels like she's touching the inside of a rainbow! As she removes her hand, to her surprise she finds herself holding a ticket. It has thousands of numbers printed on it, large at the top decreasing in size toward the bottom. The ticket glistens with luminosity and isn't a colour she has ever seen before.

The ball spontaneously disperses before her eyes as Laurie beckons her. "Lana, please take a seat in The Waiting Room." Laurie holds open another door which Lana did not recall seeing when she entered the room, yet feels completely compelled to walk through it. She makes her way to the door and steps through. As she does she turns around to say goodbye to Laurie, but Laurie and Room 8 are no longer there, they have completely vanished, there is only the travelator behind her once more. Lana turns back around and now faces yet another galactic, intricately engraved wooden door which reads... *The Waiting Room.*

As soon as Lana turns the doorknob and steps through, she instantly notices a small child standing beside her. The little girl is *extraordinarily* beautiful and *extremely* sweet. She has wavy, golden hair that almost seems to be shimmering with light, delicate rosy cheeks and turquoise, blue, and green eyes that gleam and shine like the sun beating down on the waves of an ocean at sunset. She's wearing the most exquisite, unique dress Lana has ever laid her eyes on. The top half is a delicate glistening material she has never witnessed before and the skirt seems to be made from embroidered white lilies.

"Hello, Lana!" greets the little girl in a welcoming soft voice and warm smile.

"How do you know my name?" Lana asks captivated and intrigued.

The little girl grasps her hand tightly. "Because I'm your guardian angel! I'm Liliana!" she explains. Everything seems *so* familiar to Lana and yet nothing does. It's almost like she has amnesia, trying hard to remember things she already knows, yet can't place them.

Liliana tugs on her hand, leading her in the direction she wants her to go. They walk a short way until they come to a fascinating, enchanting apple tree, but instead of the apples being green or red, they appear to be white and silver, and the trunk and branches sparkle and glisten with a metallic hue. Lana's mesmerized and can't take her eyes off this unparalleled sight, but as Liliana keeps walking, Lana has to pull herself away. Liliana guides her for another few steps to the front row of a large group of people who are sitting down.

"Sit here, Lana," gestures the little girl, but Lana notices that there are no chairs.

"Sit where?" she asks in a confused state.

"Just sit down and you will be seated!" the child tells her. Lana is aware of her strong connection to this little girl and feels that she can trust her, so gingerly and hesitantly lowers herself into a sitting position. To her amazement, it's as though she's sitting in the most comfortable chair she has ever sat on! Liliana sits next to her and assertively clutches her hand. The tree is situated directly in front of them now, and Lana proceeds to stare at it, totally entranced by its beauty.

She turns to Liliana. "Where am I?" she asks curiously.

"You're in The Waiting Room, and don't worry, it'll be your turn soon!" she replies excitedly.

"My turn for what?" Lana asks intrigued.

"To get on the tram, of course, silly!"

Lana shakes her head in confusion. "What tram?"

Liliana rolls her eyes with a giggle. "The tram to heaven! It arrives at 11.11, the moment in time when all the angels are present. Didn't you read the manual?"

Lana pauses for a second trying to take in the fact that Liliana's just told her that she's going to heaven! She tries hard to focus. "What manual?"

"Lana! There was a manual as you came through the first door, you were meant to have taken it and read it before you took your ticket!" she says quietly chuckling to herself.

"I didn't see any manual!" maintains Lana. "I was in that other room... Room 8? And..." Lana pauses for thought, then asks inquisitively. "Why is it Room 8? Where are all the other rooms?"

"*Everyone* has to come through Room 8! It's the room of Enlightenment, Insight, Growth, Healing and Tranquillity. Laurie's your CEO. She would have booked you in and told you to get a ticket and a manual."

"Booked me in?" Lana shakes her head hesitantly, in bewilderment. "She asked me to get a ticket and a manual, and I put my hand in this floating thing which gave me a ticket, but I didn't see a manual!" she emphasizes.

Liliana takes the ticket from Lana's hand, holds it up in front of her and lifts her eyebrows, "Well, at least you've got a ticket and that's the main thing!" Lana feels at ease and peaceful, but *still* a little perplexed. She discretely glances behind her, there are several rows of people of all different ages and cultures holding tickets. Although she's certain she hasn't met any of these people before, she seems to recognise *all* of them, and every one of them is seated next to a child. She squints. She doesn't know if she's imagining it or not, because looking past the back row everything seems considerably blurred, but it appears that there are many, many people seated on rows far, far into the distance.

Although very conscious of the fact that she is now in The Waiting Room, she's completely at ease with it, as the whole room exudes extreme, immeasurable peace and love. Everyone seems to know *everyone* in The Waiting Room, there is no sadness or sorrow. There's no anxiety or worry. There's no pain or illness and all ailments have vanished. There's just waves of harmony and tranquillity glazing over everyone's soul, the most euphoric feeling of love ever imaginable.

As Lana continues to look around, observing everybody and everything, she realises that no-one looks old, everyone seems to be in their prime. She contemplates how even the old people somehow look young! Everyone has a glow, an aura about them, like they've never been happier.

"You seem confused, Lana! You *really* should have read the manual!" Liliana notes with a raised eyebrow.

Lana smiles to herself, shaking her head slightly. "There *wasn't* a manual!" she reiterates. She feels likes she's being told off by a child, but finds it strangely amusing at the same time. It's like Liliana is a minor but with the mind and vocabulary of an adult.

Liliana turns around to talk to one of the people sitting behind her and motions to him. "Can I borrow this, please? I'll give it straight back!" The man nods and hands his manual to her. Liliana opens the book. As soon as she turns the page, an image launches out and projects about ten inches above it. She hovers her finger over it and scrolls across. She swivels it around to Lana's direction so she can see. The projections are so vividly clear that Lana feels like she's just stuck her head through a window and is watching it all in real time.

Liliana flicks each moving image one by one, whilst explaining simultaneously. "Okay! So, you go over the Bridge of Concealment, through the Tunnel of Enchanted Lilies, then up the hill to the Crescent of Colouration. As *soon* as you pass this point, make sure you get *off* the tram! Beau should call it, but just *make sure* you're ready 'cause Lunar drives *considerably* faster than she should sometimes! Then when you reach the gate, hand your ticket to Nevaeh." Liliana momentarily stops speaking and appears thoughtful and reflective. "She's *unbelievably* beautiful and has the most sublime aura... she's the *gate keeper!*" she proclaims. She looks back to the book and carries on. "Then just walk up the stairway and you're there!" She promptly claps the book closed shut and hands it back to the man behind her with a chirpy, "Thank you!"

Lana's taken aback trying to consume so much information all at once. Because Liliana spoke so exceedingly fast and Lana was so absorbed with all the beautiful visions and images, she didn't have time to take in everything she was being told. Deep in thought, and with a slight frown, Lana starts to mumble to herself. "Tunnel of Lilies? Bridge of something? Beau, Lunar, what?" But it's too late for questions now.

Lana stops in her tracks as she's distracted by beguiling, celestial, angelic music. It's a mesmerizing, divine, entrancing sound which gradually becomes increasingly clearer with every passing second. As it grows, the people behind her start to stand. *It's the tram!*

Chapter 12

Stairway to Heaven...

Lana can't quite believe her eyes. There's what appears to be a silver, scintillant mist starting to completely surround her. Suddenly, something else *very* peculiar and *exceedingly* strange happens... It starts to snow! Although it's snowing, Lana doesn't feel cold at all. In fact, with every falling snowflake she feels warmth and love swathing her, like she's wrapped in a soft, comforting blanket.

The fog is thick and dense now; it's drifting all around her so she can't fully see, but as she squints and peers into the distance, she realises there's a huge shimmering arc of light gradually starting to develop. *"What.. is.. that?"* she queries with prolonged expression, staring totally awestruck, engrossed, and fascinated.

Liliana smiles back cutely. "It's *the arc of Parhelion*."

Lana's dumbstruck at its beauty. "But... *what is it?*" she asks once again. still perplexed.

"When moonlight is bent by ice crystals it creates ice fog and diamond dust which forms a bridge and road, see... the arc of Parhelion. It's a path for the tram to travel on!" Liliana absorbs Lana's confusion. "But you can just call it a snowbow if you want!" she adds kindly.

Lana continues to stare in complete amazement, and as the mist starts to evaporate and the snowflakes become few, she can now distinctly see the clarity and wonder of the road. It's profound! It's a vast, lustrous arc, separated into seven different layers of semi-transparent silver and multicoloured light. Each layer a slightly lighter shade and more shimmering than the next. Abruptly, from the end of the arc, a road starts to perfectly form, which leads directly to the apple tree situated straight ahead of her.

As soon as they meet, the apple tree reacts and promptly starts to twist and rotate at speed, moving like a forming tornado. It shines brilliantly and sparks fly as it miraculously transforms into a glimmering, glittering tram post, dazzling with intense light and sparkle.

Lana's heart starts to palpitate in expectation. As the group of people behind her move close, she unexpectedly senses everyone connecting with her. She can feel the impatience, eagerness and intrigue radiating back from everyone else, channelling straight into her.

The crowd marvel in astonishment as the tram travels over the arc and onto the road heading directly towards them. At first the tram appears to be driving *on* the glistening moonlit road, but on closer inspection Lana realises it's actually gravitating above it. Her attention then turns to the roof and, although it's a tram, it has a large flue which is oozing out some sort of smoke. As it nears and finally arrives, it slows down and gradually pulls into the stop directly in front of her. She can now see clearly that it's not smoke at all, but billions of tiny snowflakes shooting upwards and out the top.

As soon as the tram stops, the arc promptly dispels, then the road also starts to disappear, graduating from the top to the bottom, rapidly vanishing into a wisp of glittery dust. The tram gently lowers and rests on the ground. With anticipation running high, and without warning, the door suddenly springs open and a tall slender man with an extremely positive aura jumps off. As soon as you notice this man, you have no option but to become entirely compelled and awestruck, as the unprecedented energy he exudes is contagious.

He wears an unusually shaped, hexangular bowler hat and a lustrous, glossy, shiny suit, which both seem to shimmer like they've been showered in silver stardust.

When he turns to the side, they glisten with a golden hue, then appear to alternate between the two colours. His hair is silvery blue with slight waves, and he has a ticket machine strapped horizontally across his body.

Lana's transfixed and can't stop herself from staring at him. Liliana notes her expression and appears humbled but amused. "That's Beau! He's gonna take you to the gate, but remember to get off at the stairway, okay?"

As Beau gets his machine ready, a fascinating, exotic, vibrantly coloured bird appears. Its tail is sky blue and the feathers of his outstretched wings are the most lustrous combination of oceanic colours. His crown, underbelly, and the feathers situated towards his centre have a glorious dense turquoise tone.

He flies and lands on Beau's shoulder. "G'day, mate!" he squawks in an Australian accent.

Beau turns his head. "So, you're Australian today?" he asks wryly.

"So what if I am, my old cobber?" replies the bird sarcastically.

"Can't you just talk properly?" asks Beau impatiently.

"I don't know what you're talking about, Mon!" retorts the bird in a Jamaican accent.

Beau lifts his eyebrows and Liliana laughs. "That's Taz!" she informs Lana, "Don't worry about him, he's one feather short!" she giggles. "He's a roller bird now but he used to be a parrot, I think that's why he talks so much! His *real* name's Tarrop but *don't* call him that! He doesn't like it! Everyone calls him Taz, and as you can see, he's trying out some different accents right now!" Lana chuckles under her breath, deeply intrigued and entertained.

Beau walks forward and calls out with a cheeky grin. "All Aboard! Tickets please!" People make their way around Lana towards him and stand in line. He takes a ticket and feeds it into his machine. The ticket gets rapidly sucked in and seems to shred and disappear instantaneously, then a glistening gold dust dispels into the air. A new number appears on his machine then a different ticket pops out the other side and he passes it back to them. "Thank you, you may now board!" he informs them politely with a broad grin.

As people start to board the tram, Lana notices that some of the accompanying children suddenly have a golden aura about them and are boarding the tram next to the person they're with, whilst others wave goodbye and vanish.

Lana observes that the driver of the tram is a cute little girl. Her hair is pure white with silver highlights, parted into four wavy bunches with silver and blue graduated, coloured ends. She's reading from a clipboard and has a white glowing lollipop sticking out the corner of her mouth. There's also a humongous container full of them sat next to her. Liliana beams, "that's Lunar! She's your driver for today! She loves moonstone lollipops!"

Beau continues to call out for tickets.

"Let's go, Lana!" beckons Liliana. In a hurry, still grasping Lana's hand she leads her to the tram. Lana's feels infinite love, it's like a magnet is pulling her onward.

Lana looks down at her ticket and is just about to hand it to Beau when Liliana suddenly grabs her arm and pulls her back. Looking troubled she stops her. "Wait!" she calls out abruptly. "We *have* to wait!" she commands, feeling *very* uneasy.

Lana's confused. "But I thought I needed to get on the tram!"

"No, something's wrong!" She looks up at Beau. "We'll wait for the next one, thank you!" He nods to her with a kind smile and tip of his hat, as Liliana pulls Lana away.

"We'll wait for the next one, thank you!" repeats Taz in a London accent. Liliana rolls her eyes at Taz whilst Beau continues to take more tickets.

"What's wrong?" asks Lana anxiously.

"I'm not sure, all I know is we just have to wait!"

Although bemused, Lana nods in confirmation.

"C'mon!" instructs Liliana, leading her back to the seated area. As they go and sit back down, the peaceful feeling of love and tranquillity is swept over her once more, yet concerned thoughts for Liliana creep into her mind.

Lana stares at her for a moment, then thoughtfully and inquisitively asks, "How long have you been here?"

Liliana shrugs, "It's not like earth, there's no real time here. Although the higher celestials do have their own epoch dimension system and we do work around 11.11, but that's different!" she rambles, looking toward the sky.

Lana blinks a few times, not registering anything she just said, "But... you're a child! Where's your family? Your parents?" she insists.

Liliana starts to clarify. "Well, it's when an occurrence takes place that changes the direction of the soul path. Some earth souls already arrive here before they are even born on earth, and some a short time after. Others, they might be just a few earth years old or more, then sadly some earth souls are taken abruptly before their designated time, so when we arrive here, we're given wings and become guardian angels." She smiles, "See!" She moves her hair to the side and proudly shows off her wings.

"So, you'll stay an angel forever?" enquires Lana curiously.

"No, just until our soul connection arrives."

Liliana continues to explain further. "Each guardian angel is assigned one or more earth soul to guide. Usually an earth parent or someone else they have a soul connection with, everyone has a soul connection! When a soul is experiencing a time of difficulty or emotional disturbance, you can be near to them and guide them onto the right path, or move them from harm, or just give them love, comfort and guidance. Then, when their time on earth is over and they arrive in The Waiting Room, we escort them onto the tram. If that is our designated soul connection, our angel wings will become golden and we can either go on the tram with them or fly to heaven ourselves. Then the souls who are left are designated a new angel or we carry on guiding until it's our time." she explains calmly.

"What is *our* soul connection?" she queries, but Liliana doesn't answer as she suddenly becomes distracted.

"Wait here a minute!" she advises sternly, yet anxiously.

Lana nods a couple of times in agreement as Liliana walks over to a man in the distance and starts conversing with him. Lana squints hard, she can just about make out a figure but can't tell exactly who it is. It's Tobias! He informs Liliana that Lana's not meant to be there, and that there's been a *catastrophic* mistake. Liliana motions to him, then walks back over to Lana and sits with her.

"Don't worry, Lana. Everything's going to be alright!"

Lana looks back to where she saw Tobias and now there's another man standing there with him. Although she doesn't know this man, she can't explain it but feels a huge familiarity and warmth for him... It's The Boss!

He smiles compassionately at her and she senses how enormously kind he is, but then unexpectedly, she experiences an almighty jolt which radiates throughout her entire body, and as if she's been struck by lightning, a tornado of light opens up next to her. She's forcefully sucked into it and catapulted along.

As she falls, she looks at her hand and can see her aura and soul are being pulled away. Lana is twisted around multiple times and propelled backwards then carried along until she gradually disperses, disappears, and vanishes.

Chapter 13

Angelica Karrae...

Three months later...

It's 8:12 a.m. and as another workday beckons, a beautiful woman named Angelica starts to awaken. She stirs, adjusts her pillow, and stretches. As she blinks trying to open her eyes, she yawns and squints, directing her attention towards her clock. Now fully focused, the time becomes clear and her eyes pop open. Aghast, she yells out a prolonged "noooo!" as she was meant to be in work for eight. Frustratedly throwing off her quilt cover, she leaps out of her bed in a panic, tripping and falling over herself.

Clutching some clothes from the chair next to her, she races down the stairs stumbling in her rush, but still managing to gather things as she goes. She grabs her hairbrush, toothbrush and a bottle of water from the fridge, then grapples to prize her heel into her high-heeled shoe, hopping and running alternatively to the door. In her rush, she forgets her car keys and has to double back for them, delaying her even further.

It's 8:23 now and peak time traffic, so Angelica rings her assistant to let her know she's running late but is on her way. After much discontent, and a little road rage for good measure, she finally arrives. Due to her lateness, she's a little flustered so rushes past most of her colleagues and makes a beeline for her office. Her assistant calls out to her.

"Hi, Angie. You okay?"

"Yeah, I just overslept! Can you hold all my calls for an hour please, Cass?"

"Sure, but you know you have a meeting at nine, right?"

Angelica sighs. "Ugh! I totally forgot. Alright, thanks." She shuts her office door behind her, not feeling in the greatest of moods.

A little while later, one of her colleagues peeps his head around her door. "Meeting in five minutes in Room 12 Ange!"

"Thanks, I'll be there!" she confirms.

The meeting commences and Angelica's boss takes centre stage. She leans against the front desk and claps her hands together. "Good Morning, everyone. Get your drinks and look lively 'cause I've got some *very* exciting news for you all." Everyone looks extremely intrigued. "You may or may not have heard the rumours flying about, but our sister company Bulmer's in America are expanding their advertising department and have two new openings available. As many of you know, Bulmer's is based in Pasadena, California which is only a few miles from Los Angeles, so this is an *amazing* opportunity." Everyone's excited and they all look around at each other to see who else is interested, followed by a low mumble of voices. "Bulmer's require *two* people from our office to join them in the next few weeks, as they're looking for British representatives from our branch to be part of their department. So, by a show of hands, how many of you are interested so far?" Eleven people raise their hands. "Let me also tell you, before you all get *too* excited, this is a *twelve-month contract*, meaning that whoever takes a position will have to relocate. Part of the package is that you will be provided with hotel accommodation for a month in a nearby hotel but then you will have to make your own living arrangements." There's a stifled murmur of voices. "*However*, in saying that, the salary will be *substantial* so it should be more than sufficient to cover the costs and, undoubtedly, this is a once in a lifetime career opportunity. So, based on *that* scenario, how many of you are still interested?" Only five people now raise their hands.

"Hmm! Well I don't need to give them a decision for another few days, so you all have time to go away and think about it. Go home, talk to your partners and your families, but please remember it's a *minimum* twelve-month contract, and it could lead on to an even longer period or permanent position. Bulmer's are a *massively* progressive company, it could develop into all kinds of things for you, but as already mentioned it will involve you moving to another country, which is obviously a tremendous upheaval for anyone. If you are going to apply, please make sure you are one hundred percent certain and think about all the things I've said before you make your final decision. As I've said already, there are only *two* openings available, so if everybody can check their emails, all the information should have already been sent directly to you. Go away and think about it and if you are interested, please let me know by Friday. Thanks everyone!"

There's a prolonged chatter as everyone talks about this amazing opportunity and people continue to converse as they leave the meeting.

Just as Angelica is getting up and about to leave her manager pulls her to one side. "Angelica?" Angelica looks up with a start.

"Yes?"

"I didn't see you raise your hand! Obviously, I'd be *extremely* disappointed to lose you from our office, but you are one of our best employees, and I would love it if you would consider this position. You're absolutely *ideal* for this role!"

Angelica is gobsmacked and hesitates. "Erm... thank you, but I don't really think it's for me." she stammers.

Her boss looks disappointed. "Right. Well, have a think and let me know if you change your mind."

Angelica returns to her office and immediately checks her emails and searches for the American Bulmer's branch. She knows her worth, how conscientious she is, and that she would certainly be an invaluable asset to them, but it would also be a complete lifestyle change and she's not sure if she wants that. As she makes a list of all the pros and cons, she sits quietly, contemplating all her options.

After a long day, Angelica arrives home. Sprawling out on her sofa, she stretches her tired legs, then starts to nibble at her microwave meal for one, feeling pensive and lonesome. Reminiscing about her life, her family and her career, she contemplates how exhausted she is with all the work she has, how all she seems to do is go to work, and how every day is exactly the same. She reflects on the fact she has no social life and how over time she's gradually lost contact with all her friends.

Picking up a photo album from under her coffee table she flicks through it, smiling fondly at pictures of her parents and family, but still she's alone. She places the album to one side and goes into the kitchen, heats up some blueberry pie and custard, sits back down, and turns on an old romantic film. As she watches it, she realises that she's made a great deal of money and has an amazing career yet has absolutely no-one to share it with. Everything seems pretty meaningless right now.

Angelica hears her phone ring but leaves it to click to the answering machine. It's her boss leaving her a message to say she's been awarded yet *another* bonus for all her continued hard work. It will be in her bank account in the next few days and that she'd really love her to reconsider the job opportunity. Angelica picks up her laptop and logs into her bank account, she's accumulated a vast amount of money from solidly working long hours for years on end. Sitting there lost in thought, she muses over her situation, scrutinising her options, contemplating what she should do.

She loads the American company's website once more and scours through their pages. It looks like it would be an impressive place to work and Pasadena looks like it would be a beautiful place to live. There's also a niggling thought in the back of her mind pushing her to do this.

A few hours pass and she hasn't been thinking about anything else. After much deliberation, Angelica comes to terms with the fact that there's actually nothing keeping her in England. She concludes that she has enough money to see her through should it all go wrong, so determines that she's going to take a chance and accept the position. While she's feeling so motivated and inspired, she takes her phone and rings her boss. She asks her if she's offered it to anyone else yet, which she explains she hasn't, so Angelica confirms she *will* apply for the job, much to her manager's delight.

The following day she is very upbeat and optimistic about her life-changing decision. This is the most alive she has felt in years. She speaks to her boss who happily reaffirms that she will set the wheels in motion once she receives her signed documentation, so Angelica formally makes an application for the position, completes arrangements to put her house up for sale, and starts sorting out her finances. She has only *two* weeks to sort everything out before her big move.

In a bittersweet moment, she starts to box up her belongings, checking through her things as she goes, and memories of days gone by flood her head. Although she's sad at the prospect of leaving the home she's lived in for many years, she's also eager for what lies ahead and wonders what this adventure will bring.

After two weeks of continued chaos, all of Angelica's furniture has been moved into storage and she's finally ready to set off to her new job in the U.S. She takes one last sentimental look around her empty house, and glances at a photo of her parents and grandparents she has stored on her phone. She is now finally ready to leave for the airport.

After a lengthy but smooth flight, she arrives safely and is greeted by a lovely woman from Bulmer's, named Maria. Maria has been assigned as Angelica's assistant, and they hit it off instantly. As it's early evening, Maria takes her to their local café for a chat and to discuss the formalities.

As Angelica opens the door and walks into the coffee house, she turns around and unintentionally bumps into Dean.

"Oh, I'm *very* sorry! I didn't see you there!" she apologises profusely in her distinctive English accent. As she looks at him, she feels a strange and unusual connection.

Dean is also taken aback and pauses. "It's fine. No problem." he says reservedly. He feels a curious yet strong affinity to her also, but shakes it off. Dean reasons it's because he's sadly reminiscent of how Lana had bumped into him in the exact same spot. Angelica and Maria go and sit down at an empty table and place their order.

Dean strolls back over to where he was sitting with Brad and finishes his drink. He always orders two lattes, he drinks one and leaves one for Lana, then Sam routinely and kindly clears Lana's cup away after he leaves.

Brad notices Dean's sober demeanour. "D, you alright?"

Dean looks over in Angelica's direction, tilting his head to acknowledge her. "See that woman over there?"

Brad turns to look, "Yeah,"

"She just bumped into me! She reminded me of Lana a little, something familiar about her eyes."

He continues to stare in her direction, totally transfixed on her. Brad gazes at him for a second then rubs his fingers over his forehead several times and sighs. "D, look I know it's only been three months, but you've been making some *amazing* progress, so maybe it's not a good idea that we come here anymore."

Dean glares at him, "Why not?"

"'Cause... every time we come in here it's like you take a *huge* step backwards. This place... It's all about you and Lana!" Dean lowers his eyes and looks away. "How are you ever going to get over this if you keep having constant reminders of Lana? I know how much you loved each other and how much you miss her. God, I miss her too man, but you need to try and move on."

Dean scowls and scoffs. "Move on? Lana was *everything* to me, my whole *life!* It's been twelve weeks, two days and three hours Brad, and you want me to move on!" he jeers. Shaking his head, he grabs his jacket and walks out.

"Dean?" Brad calls after him, but he ignores him and struts off anyway, leaving Brad sitting there alone. Glancing at the coffee Dean left for Lana, he feels despondent and saddened. How he wishes he could bring Lana back and make everything alright and that things could just go back to the way they were before.

After their coffee and involved conversation, Maria and Angelica begin the short journey to the hotel that Bulmer's have reserved for her. They've given Angelica the following day off to settle in, so she plans to recuperate, search for accommodation, *and* see the sites, if she can fit it all in!

The next evening, Dean is in the café as usual, drinking coffee and reading a newspaper. He goes there most lunchtimes and every evening after he finishes work as well. It's the only place he feels any real comfort or solace and he has absolutely *no* intention of giving that up for anyone.

As he starts to turn the page of his newspaper, he smells Lana's perfume waft past him. He suddenly recognises it and swiftly turns his head, stunned to see Angelica walking past. She sits on the stool Lana always sat on. He feels a shiver down his spine, and his stomach somersaults. This is the *second* time he has seen this woman now, and both times thoughts of Lana have immediately submerged his mind. Although this isn't anyone he recognises, he wonders if this could possibly be someone who may have been friends with her a while ago or a distant relative who has come to see family due to her passing, as they both seem to share a lot of the same qualities. He feels compelled to go over and ask her, so leaves his newspaper on the table and strolls over to her.

"Excuse me, Miss? I'm sorry to bother you but I come in here all the time and I've never seen you in here before, it's just that you remind me of someone. I was wondering if you know my wife, Lana Smith?"

Angelica shakes her head negatively. "Oh no, sorry I'm not from around here. I just moved here from England a couple of days ago."

"Oh! Yeah, that's a nice accent you have! Alright, well I'm sorry to have bothered you." Dean returns to his table dispirited and sits there for a moment staring at Angelica's back, reminiscing to when Lana used to sit there. He shakes it off, takes his paper and leaves.

The following morning, Dean's in his office with Brad, brooding, lost in thought. A meeting is called, and *all* advertising executives must attend. Dean and Brad sit in the boardroom discussing their notes as their boss walks in with two other people. "If I can have everybody's attention! I'd like to introduce you all to our two newest employees, who are joining us all the way from our sister company in England. Miss Angelica Karrae and Mr Ryan Bateman. I know you will all join me in making them feel very welcome. Okay guys, please take a seat." Angelica and Ryan go and sit down as their boss continues the meeting.

Dean and Brad shuffle a bit closer together. "That was the girl from the café!" Dean side whispers to Brad; he nods back in agreement.

Angelica recognises Dean and raises her hand to acknowledge him, he gestures back. After the meeting comes to an end, everyone goes about their business. The guys discuss what a weird coincidence it is, but they don't see her for the rest of the day as she has been relocated to a different floor.

Customarily, after work Dean is in the café. After about twenty minutes of him being in there, Angelica walks in. They're both highly surprised to see each other *again*, yet convey their familiarity with a courteous nod. He can see she's on her own and feels a bit sorry for her. Knowing she's in a strange country and doesn't really know anyone, he puts his drink down and walks over. "Hi, I hope you don't mind me coming over *again*! But I saw you at work today and after our conversation the other day, I know you're new in town so wondered if you wanted to come over to *my* table?"

"Erm... Okay!" she responds, thinking what a nice gesture that was. They both walk over to his booth and start to chat.

"So, you moved here *all* the way from England, for a *job*!"

"Yeah, I realised I needed a fresh start and the opportunity was there, so I decided to take it!"

"Uh huh!" nods Dean. "But what about your family? That's a pretty big upheaval to travel halfway around the world for work!"

Angelica looks dismayed. "I don't have any family," she utters quietly, appearing saddened.

Seeming dismayed, he frowns. "You don't have *any* family? No-one?"

"No, unfortunately not." Angelica explains. "My parents died when I was younger, so I moved in with my grandparents, but then just over ten years ago they both died within a few months of each other, so I had no other option but to look after myself."

"Oh, that's a real shame. I'm very sorry to hear that." he replies compassionately. She continues. "I just threw myself into my job and my career and blocked it all out to be honest. Gradually, over time I became a workaholic! But that meant I lost contact with my friends, so there was nothing keeping me there anymore."

"Well I'm sure you're going to make a lot of new friends now you're here!" he responds soothingly, trying to lift the mood.

Angelica smiles, she doesn't know what it is about Dean, but she feels safe and reassured in his presence, like she's known him all her life. "You know, you're gonna think I'm crazy but I feel like I've met you before, which I obviously couldn't have, but I genuinely get this very strange feeling every time I see you, like déjà vu or something!"

Dean appears gob-smacked. "Really? That is *so* weird that you should say that, 'cause the very first time I saw you I had that exact same feeling! That's why I came over to ask you if you knew my wife 'cause you kinda remind me of her in some way, and I was wondering if you could have been a distant relative or something, I dunno! But that's very strange you would think that!"

Angelica glances at the two cups of coffee on the table. "Oh, you're waiting for your wife, I hope I'm not intruding!"

Dean glances down woefully. "Erm... no. My wife passed away a few months back. You probably think I'm crazy, but I always buy an extra cup for her. This is where we met and used to hang out so..." He shrugs his shoulders whilst sadly gazing down at the drinks.

Angelica feels his pain. "No, not at all. I think that's lovely, and I'm so very sorry for your loss, I didn't realise." She feels genuinely concerned for Dean even though they've only just met.

He nods and throws her half a smile. They hold each other's gaze for a couple of seconds until Dean breaks away. He takes a sip of his latte and tries to change the subject. "Angelica, that's a real nice name!"

"Thanks! My dad said that when I was born, he thought I had the face of an angel, so that was the first name he could think of, but then after that he always just used to call me *Jelly*." she chuckles, shrugging her shoulders.

Dean smiles. "So how long are you over here for?" he enquires.

"I'm on a twelve-month contract at the moment, but it could be longer. I'm not sure yet, but I'm here for now!"

"Twelve months! Wow, I didn't realise it was for that long!"

"Yeah, I'm trying out the whole *lifestyle change thing!*" she jokes. "Actually, I'm going to look at a house this weekend 'cause right now they've got me holed up in a hotel, and don't get me wrong, it's very nice, but it's not home, and part of my contract is that I've only got a month to find somewhere else anyway. This house I've seen, it looks so pretty in the brochure, it's got a *massive* rose bush outside the front and I absolutely *love* roses, so fingers crossed!"

"Sounds cool!" replies Dean with a broken smile.

Just then, Brad walks into the café and notices Angelica and Dean deep in conversation. He clears his throat to interrupt.

Dean glances up. "Angelica, this is my friend and colleague..."

She cuts him off in mid-sentence. "It's Brad, right?"

"Yeah!" They both seem confused and gawp at each other somewhat surprised that she knows his name.

Brad's confused, "Er... were we introduced at work?"

Angelica looks shocked herself that she knew his name that quickly and softly stutters, "We must have, 'cause it just popped into my head!"

He nods, then sits down to join them, slightly bemused. "So, how was your first day?" he asks energetically.

"It was good, yeah! I was a bit nervous at first, but it went well. My office is *lovely* and there's a *stunning* panoramic view of the city!"

"Well, my office *isn't* lovely 'cause it's across from Dean's, so the only view I have is of him!" teases Brad pointing in Dean's direction.

"It could be worse B, you could be me, stuck in *my* office having to look at *you*!" Deans comically claps back.

Brad gives him a sarcastic grin as Angelica laughs, "You two are funny! You could be a comedy-act!"

"My wife used to say that!" utters Dean reminiscently.

Angelica and Dean stare at each other until he snaps out of it again. He stands abruptly and takes his coat from the back of his chair. "I gotta go! Angelica it was great to meet you and I'll probably see you around work sometime and B... I'll see you tomorrow," he rapidly rambles.

"You sure you don't wanna stay for a bit?" Brad calls out.

"Nah, I'm getting a headache. I'll see you at work." He rushes out as Brad is left sitting awkwardly with Angelica.

Brad manages to diffuse the situation with his playful personality, and they chat for a while about Dean and work.

Dean doesn't know how he is *ever* going to get over this. It's been nearly *four* months since Lana passed, but everything still feels just as raw as it did on the day of her funeral. Absolutely *nothing* has changed, in fact, it's all getting progressively worse. Angelica's managed to resurface yet even more thoughts and feelings of Lana, that he's been working so hard to stifle. Work is a solid distraction, so he continues to attend, but he's putting on a brave face around Brad, and everything is all just a front. As soon as he gets home, he lights a candle and tries to calm himself, but all his emotions come crashing down, he deteriorates and breaks down. Amadeus, and the fact that he knows Lana would want him to carry on, are the only two reasons he keeps going.

The next afternoon, he sees Angelica eating her lunch in the company cafeteria. He sits down to eat his sandwich and observes her seated in the corner on her own, again! He's feeling depressed and low and, although he doesn't want to talk to her or get involved in her business, she looks lonely and it's almost as if something is persuading him to go over, so he casually gets up and forces himself to speak to her.

She gazes upward to him. "Hello!"

"Hi! Mind if I sit here?"

"No, of course not, please do!"

"Thanks, it's nice to have lunch with someone other than Brad!" he comments, trying to break the ice. She smirks. Gazing over at her food, he notices that strangely they've bought the *exact* same lunch items, which he thinks is unusual but continues with his conversation. "How's your day been?" he asks kindly.

"Fine!" she responds with a sweet smile, humbled at his thoughtfulness.

He glances down at the paper she's holding. "Is that the house you were talking about?"

She nods and turns it around to Dean's angle. "What do you think?"

"Well, that looks like it would be a very nice place to live!" he comments.

"Yeah, and see the rose bush outside that I was telling you about?"

"Yeah, that *is* beautiful!"

She smiles at his positive response. "I'm going to view it on Saturday, I'm *so* excited! But I'm not entirely sure how to get there, do you know where this road is?" She points her finger to the address as he reads it.

Something is telling Dean he needs to help Angelica and, because she's on her own he feels obliged to assist her. "Yeah, that's not far from my place. I'm not busy Saturday, if you want I could take you?"

Angelica looks surprised at his kind offer, but she doesn't want him to feel obligated. "That's very kind, but I wouldn't want to put you to any trouble."

"It's no problem and you know Angelica, to be honest with you, *you'd* be doing *me* a favour 'cause weekends aren't the best for me right now with Lana not being here, I'm trying to keep as busy as I can."

She can see he's being genuine so pauses for a moment then decides to accept his kind offer of help. "Well, I was a bit apprehensive to see the realtor on my own if I'm going to be honest!"

"Great! So, what time do you need me there?"

"I need to be at the house at two."

"Alright, I'll pick you up from your hotel at quarter to, and hopefully this will be the house of your dreams!"

As she writes down the hotel address, something dramatic yet curious happens, her face abruptly changes as she has a flash of deja vu. Dean takes a bite from his sandwich but stops mid-chew as he recognises her changed expression. "What?" he queries as she shakes her head.

"I don't know, I had another one of those weird feelings of deja vu, like I've heard you say that expression to me before!"

He gulps his sandwich down in one swallow and stares at her. "Maybe I remind you of someone?" he tries to reason.

Angelica shakes it off. "Maybe! Anyway, I really appreciate you being so kind, it's a little daunting when you don't know anyone."

"Well, you know you've got two new friends in me and Brad so you're well on your way!" She smiles heartily at his kindness.

"Here, I'll give you my house number just in case, for any reason they change the time, or something else comes up and you need to cancel, you can leave a message on my machine," he tells her considerately, writing out his telephone number on the back of one of his business cards. "But if not, then I'll pick you up on Saturday!" She is overwhelmed by his kindness as they swap details.

Saturday soon comes around and it's time to view the house. Dean is right on time and Angelica is standing there outside her hotel ready and waiting. He beeps his horn, she hurries over, then clambers into his car. "Hey! You ready to see the house!"

She grins broadly. "I'm *so* excited, I can't wait! Thanks again, Dean."

"It's no problem, really." He programmes his GPS and they set off.

A little while later they turn onto the road, decreasing in speed to locate the house, then Angelica spots it. "There it is!" she points out eagerly. Dean nods in confirmation and pulls into the driveway. There sits the massive rosebush outside the front, appearing exactly as it does on the leaflet. The realtor is standing outside the front door waiting.

"I'll wait here for you, take as long as you like!" he states kindly.

"You're not coming in?" she queries.

He looks a little perplexed. "I... erm..." he stutters.

"I'd really like a second opinion!" Angelica implores.

He nods, "Alright." They both get out the car.

The realtor greets them as a couple, but both immediately and adamantly inform him of his error.

"No, you've got it wrong." declares Dean.

"No, we're not together. This is my work colleague, I just bought him along for another perspective on the house!"

"Oh, I'm sorry, I didn't mean to cause any offence," he quickly replies, thinking he may have now jeopardised the sale.

"None taken, it's fine," confirms Dean. "Shall we go in?"

The realtor nods and opens the door as Angelica walks in front of Dean and they go into the house. As Dean walks over the front doorstep, drifting along in the gentle breeze floats a white feather. He thinks nothing of it and enters the house. The realtor shows them around, room by room, with Angelica absorbing every single detail, while Dean follows behind in silence.

The realtor swings opens the impressively stunning French windows which expand out into a spectacular floral garden. As they walk through, Dean's eye takes him over to a beautifully rustic swing set. All of a sudden, he has a flash of sitting with Lana when they first dated, and begins to feel claustrophobic and panicked. He turns to Angelica. "Sorry, it's all a bit too much. I'll wait for you in the car," he announces and hurriedly retreats.

After ten minutes or so, Angelica and the realtor reappear smiling and shaking hands. She walks toward the car and climbs in. "How did you get on?" Dean enquires.

"I decided to make an offer!"

"That's great news!" he acknowledges and starts the engine.

"Can I just ask... What happened in there?"

He pauses looking agitated. "There was a swing, it reminded me of Lana. It was making me feel uncomfortable, I just had to get out of there."

Angelica feels great empathy and pity for Dean. "I know exactly what it's like you know, to lose someone you truly love. If you ever wanted to talk about it, I'm happy to listen." She places her hand on his arm and gently pats it sympathetically, but as she does something else unexpected and peculiar happens. For a split second she has a vision of

Dean smiling at her endearingly in the café. He winks at her and walks away. She seems to be standing by the door smiling back at him, but strangely she's conscious that her clothes are soaking wet.

Then abruptly, in an instant she snaps out of it. Dean's calling her name, "Angelica?"

"Hmm?" she responds in a groggy daze.

"Are you okay? You kinda zoned out there for a minute!"

She appears alarmed. "Something very weird is going on!"

He frowns. "What do you mean? If you don't like the house, don't feel pressured into getting it!"

"No, it's not the house," she shakes her head, "I'm talking about *you*!"

He looks puzzled. "What about me?" he frowns.

"Just then when I touched your arm, I had this strange thought of you and me... in that café I've been going to. You were smiling at me, but I was drenched, like I'd just been in the worst storm ever!"

Dean gulps and shakes his head a few times in disbelief, bewildered and mystified at what he's hearing. "That was how I first met Lana, in the café, she was running in from a storm!" he notes soberly. "Her clothes were soaking from the rain."

They both sit in silence trying to figure out exactly what is happening, but as nothing comes to mind and neither has a viable reason, they pass it off as they must have conversed about it at some point earlier without realising. Angelica knows in her heart this isn't the case, but she has no other answer. Dean drops her back to her hotel and they both continue to feel uneasy about the whole situation.

As the days progress and they continue to cross paths in the cafe and at work, things start to get even crazier. The more they see each other, the more thoughts and feelings Angelica receives, and the more she has no explanation for it. Although she has no previous experience or dealings with any psychic or paranormal phenomenon, she now genuinely starts to believe that Lana is using her as a channel to contact and interact with Dean. She's detailing events and conversations that only he and Lana had, and neither of them can seem to fathom how she knows any of these things. She's never had any psychic ability in her entire life and is always the ultimate professional. This is completely out of character for her, but she can't deny what is happening. As though the floodgates have been opened and information is flowing, she feels completely compelled to share it with him.

Dean's totally baffled too! But in some strange way, it seems to be comforting him. Could it really be that inconceivable that Lana could be somewhere trying to get messages through to him? Every day he becomes more intrigued and eager to get to work to see what Angelica will tell him next.

A few weeks pass and as Brad turns up for work, he notices Dean walking casually out the lift, realising that he must have been to Angelica's office. He muses over the fact that they've been around each other a lot lately, so at lunchtime decides to ask him about it.

"Hey, D. I noticed you've been spending quite a lot of time with the new lady!" Dean doesn't flinch. "I'm just helping her out 'cause she's new, that's all!"

"Yeah! But she's been here for nearly three weeks now, so you're helping her out with what exactly?"

"You know, just showing her the ropes and stuff, things on the computer! I'm going to get a sandwich, I'll talk to you later, B."

Brad recognises that Dean's trying to swerve the conversation and is acting weird and passive, so doesn't carry it on but instead decides to do some investigating of his own. Guardedly, he slowly walks a little way behind him and watches as Dean diverts straight to the cafeteria. As he continues to follow him cautiously around the corner, Brad can't believe what he's seeing. Angelica is there waiting for Dean, who casually greets her and sits down.

Brad watches them wrapped up in conversation, and as they're so preoccupied and absorbed by each other, he manages to veer around the back way and sit at a table hidden by a column, directly behind them. They don't even notice, and he can clearly hear every single word they're saying. Brad listens closely but can't quite accept what he's hearing. Angelica is talking in great detail about Lana, and Dean seems completely pulled in, hanging off her every word. Brad is beyond angry, convinced that this woman is using Dean's turmoil for her own well-being. He decides that he has to put a stop to it before things progress any further, and as they finish their lunch, he follows Dean back to his office to have it out with him.

As he is just about to close his door, Brad puts his foot in the way, pushes past him and marches in.

Dean looks confused and frowns. "What you doin'? What's up?"

"We need to talk, and I mean *now!*" Brad scowls.

Dean sits back on his chair and stares at him. "What's wrong?"

"There's nothing wrong with *me*, but there's obviously something very wrong with *you!*"

"What are you on about?"

"I saw you earlier with Angela, or whatever her name is." Dean frowns and remains silent. "I heard the whole conversation, which firstly I found *very* disturbing, but more to the point, what the hell are you thinking, D?"

Dean looks away and evades Brad's gaze, "You don't know anything about it!" he mumbles, avoiding eye contact.

Brad perches on the edge of his desk, "So tell me about it then!"

"You wouldn't understand!" he replies shaking his head.

"Try me!" he states sternly.

Dean sighs and tries to explain his point of view. "Angelica, she just knows stuff!" They stare at one another silently then Dean carries on. "She knows things about Lana that I can't explain, B. I wanted to tell you, but I didn't think you'd believe it." He gets more excited and animated as he carries on explaining. "She's got some kind of psychic thing going on and she's connecting with Lana somehow!" he grins widely, but Brad doesn't have the same enthusiasm as Dean does.

"D, this woman is *using* you, can't you see that? She's feeding off your grief and you're allowing that!"

Dean looks bemused. "Don't be silly! What are you talking about?"

"She's just moved here and told you she's got no family, and she knows your wife just died, so can't you see what's happening?"

"No... What?"

"You were *too* nice when she first arrived, then you took her to look at her house and then you helped her with her furniture, and now you're helping her at work. She's obviously got a *thing* for you and using your grief to get closer to you!"

Dean shakes his head over and over, squinting deep in thought. "No, you're wrong! She knows things."

"D, wake up! You're plainly manifesting thoughts in her head every time you talk to her!"

Dean sits there drowning in his feelings and fears. Right now, he'll take anything, even if it does sound crazy and doesn't make any sense. He's desperate for any sliver of a connection to Lana. He tries to convince Brad of her genuine gift but he's having none of it.

Brad talks over him and tries to make him realise that he's not being rational. Dean sits silent, musing over

Brad's words and can see his point of view, but he's been so involved trying to grasp any thread of evidence that Lana's been trying to contact him and finding comfort in Angelica's words, that the thought of her being a fraud never entered his head.

"Let's not go to the cafe tonight, just come to mine. I'll get us a takeaway and a few beers and we can talk about it all, alright?" Brad suggests considerately.

Dean nods, still uncommunicative, confused, and deflated, continuing to try to make sense of what Angelica's been saying, and everything that's been going on.

Chapter 14

Soul Conjunction...

As agreed, they go straight from work to Brad's house and talk for hours in great depth about recent and past events. Dean continues to try and justify his conversations with Angelica, but Brad has an answer for everything he suggests.

"What about when she was talking about my wedding or honeymoon or Lana's diary or 'Deus? She knows too much to be fake! And what about when she told me how Lana was in the storm? How could she possibly know about all that?"

"You must have been handing her information without even knowing it, and don't forget *I* had a conversation with her in the cafe that time when she first started, and she was asking me all kinds of questions about you and Lana! You *have* to listen to me on this. It's not healthy to be listening to this woman every day. I'm asking you to please stop, for your own good."

After many hours, Dean can see Brad's genuine concern, and the more they talk, the more he has his doubts about Angelica's intentions. He eventually concludes that Brad might be right and that he's just been holding on to any shred of hope that he could.

Brad goes home leaving Dean feeling saddened, used, depressed and alone. He can't believe he's let this woman pull the wool over his eyes for so long. Dean lights a candle and sits on his window sill, as the gentle night breeze brushes over him. He peers out into the clear night sky, his eyes fixed on the stars and the constellations, obsessing over his thoughts of Lana, and trying to come to some rational conclusion about the conversations he's had with Angelica over the past few weeks.

He picks up his wedding picture and moves his finger delicately over the glass, stroking Lana's face. "I wish I could speak to you, Lar," he whispers to her picture. "I *wish* you were here with me. What I'd give for just *one* more moment with you." The Boss watches through the utopian bubble. He is *extremely* affected by the situation, feeling guilt and responsibility.

Just then the candle flickers and Dean has a sudden burst of energy and inspiration. He knows he's promised Brad that he'd let it go but there's still certain things Angelica said to him that he just can't get his head around. His sadness steadily turns to frustration and anger. How could someone be so low as to reel him in, in his time of grief and sadness? He decisively blows out the candle and sets off to confront Angelica once and for all.

The Boss looks on. He notes Dean's actions, which he is stunned by, but at the same time captivated by his spirit and inwardly is spurring him on. "It can't be!" he mumbles to himself, just as Tobias is walking in.

Sitting back in his chair, The Boss is fixated on the bubble and with what's occurring.

"What is it, Sir?" Tobias asks curiously, but with a tone of elevated concern, having overheard what The Boss just said.

The Boss lifts his eyebrows optimistically, "Fate, Tobias, Fate!"

"Sir?"

The Boss swings his chair around to face him. "Remember Lana Smith?"

"Yes. Of course, Sir!"

"Well, it's what's known as a *soul conjunction*, where two souls are pulled back together. Lana and her husband Dean, they're drawing back together again!"

Tobias looks puzzled and bemused. "I'm sorry, Sir, I don't understand. How would he possibly know where she is? I moved her to the other side of the earth, into a completely different avatar, with an entirely different life *and* she's also had a total cerebral conversion!"

"It doesn't matter!" The Boss reiterates. "No matter where they are on the earth, no matter what she looks like, no matter *what you do*, when two souls are meant to be together, they *will* find each other. This is an *exceptionally* rare aspect, usually not occurring for millions of lifetimes, but it can happen. I've only ever seen this happen *once* before." The Boss reflects for a moment.

Tobias looks astounded, completely lost for words, having never heard of such a thing and can't reason how it could even be possible. "Sorry Sir, I don't mean to question you, but are you sure?" he queries once more with a squint and wrinkled frown.

"Yes Tobias!" confirms The Boss confidently. "Obviously, I'll make this my priority, but I would like you to keep an eye on the situation for me as well. Inform me *immediately* of any unusual occurrences."

"Yes, Sir." Tobias leaves the room as The Boss continues to watch over Dean concernedly.

Dean gets in his car, but he's having mixed emotions and second thoughts now. He bows his head and rests his hands on the steering wheel, then closes his eyes tightly as he tries to summon up the last bit of energy and strength he has left in his body. He lifts his head and turns the engine on. The radio clicks on and one of Lana's favourite songs is playing, I Won't Let You Go by James Morrison. Dean recalls what Lana used to say to him, no matter what is happening, music could always help you through any situation and lift your spirits, even if only temporarily. As a few raindrops haphazardly start to splatter on his windscreen, he gets another surge of motivation and determinedly makes his mind up to go, so twists the volume up full blast and starts to drive.

He makes a short cut down the next road searching for Angelica's house. The rain is beating down hard now, his windscreen wipers are on full blast and it's becoming difficult to see, but he manages to just make out the large rose bush outside the house, so pulls up in front. He gets out and storms up to the door, now completely soaked through. There's water dripping from his hair and trickling down his leather jacket, as he pounds his fist hard on the door. Angelica hears the knocking and becomes startled. She's just moved in and doesn't know anyone so who could be banging on her door at this late hour? She sneaks up to the peephole and peeks through. There stands Dean looking wet and agitated. Although she's confused as to why he's there, her stress is alleviated as it's not a stranger, so she opens the door.

"We need to talk!" he scorns, pushing past her and stomping straight into her living room.

He leaves a trail of muddy footprints and water behind him from his shoes and clothes. "You're getting my floor wet!" she snaps, maddened at his ungracious entrance.

"You think I care about your floor? We need to talk, NOW!" he yells in an exasperated, raised tone.

"You can't just come barging in..."

"Angelica!" Dean cuts her off mid-sentence. "Brad said you're a fraud, a fake, that you're using me. Please just tell me the truth, is he right?"

Angelica gulps, taken aback by his blunt and flippant accusations and drops on her sofa. "No!" she whispers, shaking her head softly. She notes the water dripping from his face so grabs him a towel and blanket, places them on the sofa next to him and sits back down. He leaves them where they are instead pours himself a shot of whiskey.

They sit on opposite seats and he stares straight at her. "All those things you said before, how did you know all that? Some of the things you said were *so* specific, things that only me and Lana knew!"

"I don't know Dean, I told you, I don't know. These thoughts and feelings, they just come to me, I can't explain it!"

He pours himself another drink and still keeping an open mind, questions her further. They both steadily calm down and start to talk sedately. Dean quizzes her over and over with question after question, but she answers *every* single one. He even adds in a couple of trick questions, but she doesn't falter. He's aggravated and baffled, but continues irrelevant. He listens to everything Angelica is saying, and can hear the words leaving her mouth but can't comprehend how she knows all the things she's speaking of. He recalls how Brad advised him that she was fishing for clues, but he's been very vigilant not to give away any information, and some of the things she's talking about only Lana would have known, as there were only the two of them there in those private moments, so how could she possibly know any of this?

He stands up abruptly and turns to her, torn between what Brad said to him, wondering if he's being taken for a fool, and trying to rationalise all the things she's told him.

"What is happening here?" he shouts.

"I have no idea, Dean, I don't know! These thoughts just come to me!" she stutters. "Nothing like this has *ever* happened to me before," she states, starting to sob. Then although she wears no ring, he notices her rubbing her wedding ring finger anxiously. This is what Lana used to do when she was nervous. Dean can't comprehend how all these things are possibly happening, and that now she's even starting to *act* like Lana.

Feeling disorientated, he doesn't know what to believe anymore. He's lost and agitated and tells her he's going home to think things through on his own, but Angelica stops him as she doesn't want him to leave. She's feeling scared and anxious herself and asks him not to go until they can figure it out together. He detects her fear, but he's still confused, cold, and exhausted so tells her to get in his car and they can continue their conversation over at his house.

He drives them back to his place, and peculiarly as soon as Angelica walks through the door Amadeus instantly recognises her, even though he's never met her before. He starts barking loudly, running around her feet, rapidly wagging his tail and licking her face. Dean just sits on his chair, bewildered, silently staring at them both. His mind is blown, but surely his eyes and ears both can't deceive him. He changes his wet clothes, then they sit together talking things through in depth.

Meanwhile, Brad's been worrying about Dean since he left, so decides to go back to his house to check if he's okay. He can't believe his eyes when Dean opens the door and he sees this woman there again. His face drops and he throws Angelica a look that could kill. "What the hell is *she* doing here D? I thought we sorted this out?"

She walks into the other room as Dean sighs and rubs his head anxiously and stammers. "Look, B, I know you think this is insane, but we've been talking, and I really feel like there's more to this than we know. Maybe Lana *is* trying to communicate with me somehow."

Brad stares blankly, pausing in disbelief. Flabbergasted, he pulls him aside and talks quietly and calmly. "Did *anything* we talked about earlier go into your head? I know you're grieving right now, but I thought we were progressing. Can you hear yourself?"

"You don't understand! Some of the things she's saying, some of those moments... there was only me and Lana there! There was only the *two* of us there, B! Don't you get that? How could she know?" Dean reiterates his frustration and confusion.

Brad listens attentively then thinks for a moment. He says it's late and that he should drop Angelica back home. To try and calm down and relax for the rest of the evening and he'll come back the next day so they can discuss it in greater depth then.

Although reluctant, Dean agrees that it's late and decides Brad's right and it would be best to drop Angelica back.

Dean believes Brad's gone home, but instead he's followed them to Angelica's house and sits in his car outside, patiently waiting for Dean to leave. Making sure Dean's out of sight, he walks up to her door and bangs forcefully.

Straight away she answers, thinking Dean has come back, but shockingly Brad marches past her instead. In an aggressive manner, he asks her who the hell she thinks she is, and orders her to stop messing with Dean's head. He explains how Dean's not in the slightest bit interested in her romantically, and how hard it's been for him over the past few months to try and get over his grief, and now that he's finally making progress, she's undoing all their good work.

"Brad, I'm sorry you feel that way. I don't want to upset *anyone*. I moved over from England looking for a new start. I don't want any problems or drama, it's affecting me as well, but I can't help what I see or feel!" Brad is *exasperated* by her continued denial and nonsense, and sternly instructs her once again to leave Dean alone then furiously slams the door behind himself and swiftly leaves.

After his strained conversation with Angelica, Brad decides he doesn't want to wait until the next day to speak to Dean so rings him whilst en route back to his house, determined to convince him once and for all that he's on the wrong path and needs to take on board his sound advice.

They sit and talk again as Brad echoes his previous advice. He reiterates how Angelica's been playing off his heartache and emotion, picking up clues along the way, and that he must have been unsuspectingly feeding her each line. How he must have continually led her in conversation and that his grief is seriously clouding his judgement, and that the time has come for him to put his foot down and tell Angelica to leave him alone once and for all.

After hours of continuous conversation, Brad finally begins to make headway and persuades Dean that Angelica isn't the person she claims to be. That since he's been speaking to this woman, he's emotionally taken a hundred steps backwards, and it's making him re-live his grief all over again. They speak incessantly for hours, until Brad finally makes Dean see sense.

Dean's starting to see things *very* differently now and makes the unwavering decision to ring Angelica and tell her that talking to her is making him feel worse, and that he can't move forward if he continues to speak to her, so she needs to leave him alone to grieve, as it's extremely unhealthy for him.

She tries to reason with him but unrelentingly, he tells her that he doesn't want her in his life and tells her not to contact him again. The more she tries to reason with him, the more he gets agitated and suspicious of her motives. He pleads with her to leave him alone and hangs up.

Chapter 15

Lost...

It's 3:12 a.m. Dean's phone starts to ring. He awakens groggily and picks up his clock, not being able to make out the time, he squints at it, it's blurry. The more he blinks, the more the time becomes clear. He drops it onto the bed and feels around for the phone. "Hello?" he answers sternly.

"Dean? It's Angelica."

Puzzled and confused, he glances at his clock again. "Do you know what time it is?" he scorns.

"I know it's late, I'm sorry, but I need to meet with you, it's *extremely* important."

Dean sighs loudly. "Look, I'm not being rude, but I've told you already, I'm not interested in *anything* you have to say and..."

She cuts him off. "It's about Lana!"

He pauses, "What about her?" he asks in a frustrated, raised voice.

"The more I'm around you, the stronger these feelings and visions become." she states pensively.

Dean sighs again, rubbing his head and face. "I was talking crazy, it's like Brad said I was just trying to hold on."

"No, Dean!" states Angelica adamantly, "You don't understand."

He stops her. "Angelica, this isn't good for me okay? Do you have any idea how hard this has been for me? I've told you already, you *have* to leave me alone."

"But, Dean" she interrupts.

"*Please* leave me alone!" he emphasizes sombrely, then ends the call abruptly, changing his ringer to silent. He pulls the covers back over his shoulder and gazes over at his wedding picture on the side table. He knows not speaking to Angelica is the best thing for him but still feels troubled and emotional. He eventually manages to doze off.

Just over an hour later, there's a knock at the door. Dean flinches, startled. He rubs his eyes and checks the time again, it's nearly 4:30 a.m. now. He picks up a large wooden baseball bat that he keeps next to the side of his bed and creeps downstairs. He guardedly bends down slightly to peek through the peephole in his door. There stands Angelica. Dean is astounded, he can't believe what he's seeing. He bows his head and groans, throws down the bat and pulls open the door. "Do you have *any* concept of time? It's *four thirty* in the morning! And what about part of 'leave me alone' don't you understand?" he questions in an agitated tone.

"I know, I'm so sorry, but I couldn't sleep. I *have* to speak with you."

He rolls his eyes at her. "Angelica, I have no interest in *anything* you have to say. Seriously this *has* to stop, I'm gonna lose my damn mind!"

She places her hands together and pleads with him. "Please, just five minutes."

He sighs deeply. He decides to agree to her request as he figures it's the only way to get her to leave. "Five minutes, then you're going!"

She nods and he reluctantly lets her in. Amadeus runs over and is highly excited to see her, he barks and jumps. "'Deus!" Dean reprimands. He picks him up, puts him in the other room then angrily closes the door.

He opens the living room door and motions Angelica to go in. He sits on a chair as she takes off her scarf and coat and sits on his sofa. She can see that Dean is starting to lose his patience so starts to talk quickly.

"I know we've had these long discussions and you're not comfortable with it anymore, and to be honest, neither am I, but I'm seeing Lana in my *dreams*, Dean, almost every night now and every time they get stronger and clearer." She carries on explaining, "I had to come and speak with you because tonight was different. All the dreams before, I've seen things, I've felt things, but tonight it was like I wasn't just dreaming about her, it was like I *was* her!" Dean stays silent. "I could see myself talking to you, and you were talking to Lana, but Lana was *me*!"

Dean sighs and cuts her off. "Angelica? This is *crazy*! I realise I've probably told you too much about myself and Lana, and I'm guessing you probably feel sorry for me or something, I don't know, but you have to just forget about all this, 'cause I'm trying to come to terms with losing my wife and you're making everything a million times harder for me, do you understand that?"

"But, Dean..."

Dean stops her, "Look, you've talked, I've listened, now you *have* to go!"

"Dean, I just..."

"*Please* just go!" he repeats resoundingly.

Angelica succumbs to the fact that Dean isn't willing to listen, and as she doesn't want to upset him any further, she nods, picks up her coat, and leaves. Dean double locks his door and goes back to bed. He's completely emotionally drained. As he pulls the covers up around him, one tear steadily trickles down his face.

The next day, Dean is in his office yawning as Brad walks in. "Hey! Tired?"

Dean scoffs. "You won't even *believe* what happened last night!"

"What?" Brad's intrigued as he perches on the corner of Dean's desk.

"Angelica turned up at my house, at *four thirty* in the morning!"

Brad's shocked and angered. "What? What did she want?"

Dean shakes his head. "She was rambling on about all these dreams she's been having about Lana."

"Is she crazy?" asks Brad dumbfounded.

"I'm starting to think a little bit!" replies Dean cynically. "I just can't believe she pulled me in like that! The more I think about it the angrier I feel, *and* embarrassed, B. I feel humiliated by the whole thing! And the fact that I told her not to contact me, but she *still* showed up at my house."

Brad shakes his head in disbelief. "I can't believe the cheek of that woman! Appearing at your door and that time, then having the gall to speak about Lana, *again*!"

"I know, man. You're right, it's nuts!" Dean quietly states and nods gently to himself in agreeance to the fact that everything Brad ever suggested was true.

"I mean if she likes you, why doesn't she just say? But using Lana, to do what? To try and make conversation? It's just sick man! The woman's off her head!"

Dean nods. "I don't know what's goin' on, I just can't worry about it any longer B. She just needs to stay away."

"You want me to speak to her for you?" Brad asks, concerned for Dean's well-being and state of mind.

"No! Just leave it, alright?"

"But at some point you're going to bump into her around work, and then what?"

"Then, I'll speak to her politely about work stuff and that's it. I don't want you getting caught up in all this, alright? Thanks for having my back, but I've already involved you enough."

"Alright!" Brad replies despondently, in the knowledge that he's *already* spoken to her, but she hasn't heed his warning.

Roughly an hour later it's break time, and as Dean's cup drops into the bottom of the vending machine, and his coffee starts to pour, Angelica spots him and hastily makes her move.

"Dean!"

Dean looks up whilst taking a sip, and a moment of awkward silence ensues.

"Hey!" he gulps, caught off guard, yet still managing to remain calm.

"I wanted to apologise for last night. I know I shouldn't have just turned up like that at such a late hour, and I can't even begin to imagine what you're going through right now. It's just I'm getting all these dreams and I feel like Lana's desperately trying to connect with me somehow."

Dean sighs. "Can we *please* not do this? I've got a lot of work to do and it's hard enough to focus as it is." Angelica's eyes lower as Dean brushes past her and walks briskly back to his office.

Brad's overheard most of their brief conversation, and although Dean told him not to interfere, he can't help himself and swiftly approaches her. "Are you *crazy* or something?" he sneers, full of contempt. Angelica appears stunned. "Do you know what Dean's going through? I've told you already, *stay away from him!*" he furiously demands, then storms off leaving Angelica standing there alone, with tears progressively forming in her eyes.

As the days pass, Angelica continues to have several more intricately detailed dreams of Lana and feelings of her presence. Although she knows she's been warned off more than once, and the situation is now bordering on disaster, she feels she has no other choice but to try once more to convince Dean she's telling the truth and to try to win him over. She tries her hardest to contact him but he's refusing to answer her calls and is now avoiding her at work, so she decides to take a different approach and starts to write a letter instead.

The next day dawns, as Dean wakes and goes downstairs to make his breakfast. He notices a letter lying there on the mat by his front door, it's from Angelica! As he starts to read it, she reveals new things that she's never spoken of before. She talks about how she saw him carve their initials into a tree and words Lana said to him on their honeymoon, things that nobody else could have ever possibly of known. He feels a shiver down his spine and is now even more baffled than before. He's actually starting to feel physically sick with all the stress of it.

The Boss looks on. "Tobias? Angelica is getting far too close to Dean. We're going to have to perform *another* full transfer *immediately*."

Dean feels that he *must* confront Angelica about this new information for his own sanity, so speedily folds the letter and pushes it into the inside breast pocket of his jacket, while simultaneously rushing to his car. He gets in, slamming the door behind him. Pulling the letter from his pocket, he places it onto the passenger seat and throws his jacket on top, but just as he's about to drive off, he remembers he's left his phone in the kitchen. He groans and rushes back into the house.

Strangely and co-incidentally, at that precise moment Tobias performs the transfer and in an instant, Angelica, and any trace of an existence of her, is no more.

Dean rushes into work and heads straight for Angelica's office to question her. As he walks up to her door, he notices the office walls and décor look somewhat different. He knocks on her door, but a man's voice answers, "Yep?" the strange voice calls out assertively. Dean frown suspiciously, unable to recognise the voice and pushes the door open. Everything has changed and all signs of Angelica are no longer. There's a random man sitting behind her desk, leaning back in her chair.

Dean squints curiously. "Hi, erm… I was looking for Angelica?"

"Angelica who?" queries the man, shaking his head looking bemused.

"You know the new lady who was transferred here, from our England branch? This is *her* office!"

"No, there's no Angelica here."

Dean looks totally bemused. "Whattt?" he stammers. "She was in here *yesterday*!" he states adamantly.

"No! *I* was in here yesterday! This is *my* office and has been for the last *five* years! You must be on the wrong floor or something, I can't help you. Now if you don't mind I've got work to do! Shut the door on your way out?" he instructs harshly, motioning Dean to leave his office.

Dean's completely lost as to what's going on. He walks out the room, slowly closing the door behind him and stands there for a moment, composing his thoughts. He decides to go and speak to Angelica's assistant Maria, who's situated just a few offices down. "Hey Maria! Is Angelica around? Has she moved rooms or something? 'Cause I just went into her office and there's some other guy sitting at her desk!" he tells her, pointing in the direction of the room.

Maria frowns. "Who's Angelica?"

Dean scoffs. "Okay, is there some kind of weird joke going on here? 'Cause I really just need to speak to her for a couple of minutes."

Maria shakes her head. "Sorry Dean, I honestly don't know who you're talking about, I don't know an Angelica!"

He stands there for a minute completely dumbfounded. Bewildered, he tries to gather his thoughts, dazed as to what is happening. He realises his only sanctuary will be discussing it with Brad. Brad's sat at his desk checking his computer for clubs that he can go to at the weekend, as Dean runs in. "Brad!" he gasps.

Brad jumps up, startled, quickly closing his laptop. "Shit, D! I thought it was the boss man!" He opens it back up and is excitedly about to discuss his nightclub findings, but hesitates as he detects Dean's distress. "You alright? What's wrong?"

"I can't find Angelica, there's some guy sitting in her office and everyone's pretending like they've never even heard of her. I know you said not to speak to her, and I wasn't going to, but she left me a letter this morning and I have to talk to her about it!" he pants.

"Alright, just calm down." Reassuringly, Brad tries to calm his nerves and passes him some water. Dean takes a sip. "Okay, now you mentioned *Angelica*. So, who's that?"

Dean gulps his water, spits in out and nearly chokes on it. "Are you serious? Do you think that's funny? This is not the time for jokes B!"

Brad looks around to see if anyone's listening as Dean's getting loud and agitated, so he gets up and gently shuts his door. "Dean, I swear to God, I don't know any *Angelica*," he reiterates in a whisper.

Dean can tell from Brad's facial expression that he's being deadly serious and starts to get alarmed. "What are you talking about? We saw her *yesterday*, you were at my house with her *yesterday*, we were upstairs in her office last week! Now there's some rude guy in there who I've never seen in my life!"

"Rude guy? Upstairs? Who Craig?" Dean looks serious. "D, What are you talking about? He's worked here for like four, five years! And I wasn't at your house yesterday!"

Dean shakes his head in disbelief, and in an anxious and bewildered state storms back to his office. Brad calls after him but he carries on walking.

Dean quickly loads up his computer and searches the website for their sister company in England, but there's no record of Angelica ever working there. He scans through his phone contacts on his desk, but she's not in there either. He gulps in despair. He is one *million* percent sure that he wrote her extension number on his phone list, but it's like it's vanished into thin air. Dean's starting to get extremely anxious now. Brad phones his office and Dean sees him calling, but ends the call and continues to investigate. He loads the company website and searches for her job description, but to his horror and dismay a picture of *Craig* appears on the page, indicating that he *has* worked there for the last five years. Dean takes a deep breath as his heart palpitates at double speed. He leans back in his chair. "This can't be! I'm losing my damn mind!"

Brad walks into his office and notices the picture of Craig on his computer. He sits down. "Dean, I'm seriously worried about you, you know," but Dean doesn't even acknowledge him.

"Wait! That letter she wrote!" Dean frantically rummages through his jacket, almost ripping the pockets off in his hurry. "Where is it?" he stammers, desperately trying to find the slightest remnant of Angelica's existence. "I'm definite I put it in my pocket before I left." he mutters to himself. Brad's starting to feel frustrated, he wants to help Dean, but he's not even listening.

"It's in the car!" he realises.

He takes his car keys and rushes to the door. "Dean! You've got to stop this, you're acting crazy. Your behaviour's erratic, you're scaring me D!" Brad shouts as he races after him.

They get to his car, Dean jumps in and starts frantically to search everywhere for it, but he can't find it anywhere. Brad recognises Dean's frustration and sheer panic so pulls a card out of his wallet, and starts to talk in a calm manner. "Jess has got this friend, she's amazing!" He places it in front of Dean's face. "I've seen her a few times myself, but don't tell anyone that!" he jokes, trying to lighten the mood.

Dean glances up at the card, "A shrink?"

"Well... yeah!... *but* she's a fully qualified doctor, a specialist in situations like this, she has *years* of experience."

Raising his voice, Dean states adamantly, "I *don't* need a shrink B!" and carries on with his desperate search.

"*Please*, just see her for an hour. I can make a phone call *right now* and you'll be able to see her straight away." Dean shakes his head negatively, so Brad pushes forward. "Dean, there's *no* Angelica. You said yourself, no-one's ever heard of her, you're pulling your car to shreds. Lana wouldn't want this D!"

Dean stops and sits back in his seat, drained and empty. Sullen, he tells Brad to leave him be and go back to work.

"I'm not going *anywhere!*" Brad retorts.

"She came to my house, we had coffee with her!" Dean squints, muttering quietly under his breath.

"*No, we didn't D!*"

"She wrote me a letter, *this morning!*"

"Then where is it?" Dean feels tormented. "*Please* Dean, even half an hour at lunchtime, just talk to her, that's all I'm asking."

Dean sits in silence, pondering what to do. How can all this be possible? How could he have imagined the whole last couple of weeks? How could he have imagined a whole human being? Dean imagines what Lana might say to him and pauses. The last thing he wants is to sit in some doctor's office, getting even more depressed, but as he notes the genuinely worried expression on Brad's face, and realising he can't find any morsel of evidence to prove his claims that this woman ever walked the earth, he has to conclude that maybe something is actually wrong with him.

They gingerly walk back to Dean's office, and after nearly an hour of mulling over what to do, he loathingly admits defeat and agrees to see the doctor. "Half an hour, no more!" he states defiantly. Brad happily agrees and pats Dean gently on his shoulder a couple of times for reassurance. He makes the call and manages to secure a midday appointment.

Lunchtime arrives and they drive to the doctor's office. Brad waits outside in the car as Dean walks into the reception downheartedly, books himself in and waits. A couple of minutes pass and she calls him through. "Hello Dean, I'm Doctor Esmé Reynolds, please come in." He sighs deeply to himself and reluctantly walks into her room. They both sit down adjacent to one another. "Okay so we'll start with what I know already, and you can fill in the gaps. Brad told me briefly what happened and said that you'd lost your wife recently in a car accident. Let me start by saying how deeply sorry I am for your loss."

"Thank you!" he replies softly and solemnly.

"I understand you've been having a very hard time recently trying to deal with everything, which is completely understandable, so if it's alright with you Dean, I'd like you to tell me in just a few words how you're feeling at this moment in time, and how you're managing to cope with everything."

There's a brief silence. Dean *really* doesn't want to be there or speak to anyone about anything, especially not a complete stranger, but now he is, he forces himself and starts to mutter quietly. "Well, I thought I *was* dealing with things. At first, I.... I nearly lost my mind. The whole void of her not being around... that alone..." He stops as emotion starts to take over, but manages to get himself together. "But the thought of her stuck in that car and I wasn't there to help her, I wasn't there to save her, I just..." He shakes his head and frowns, looking away, trying to control his emotion. The doctor can see he's struggling so passes him a large glass of mineral water and takes charge of the conversation.

"Some situations are completely out of our hands. Sometimes we blame ourselves for things that we have absolutely no control over. You obviously loved your wife *very* much, but you have to realise there was *nothing* you could have done to change what happened."

Dean glances up feeling bitter and angered. "*I was her husband*! *I* was meant to be the one who could protect her, to be around to make sure she was safe!"

"Yes, but no two people can be together every minute of every day, and even if you were there, there was nothing you could have done. You can't think like that, or allow yourself to have those kinds of thoughts. You have to let it go, because if you don't, it's only going to prolong your grief and have a seriously detrimental effect on your health!"

He closes his eyes, feeling nauseous. "It's not just that!" There's silence for a second as he knows he has to tell her the rest. He sighs heavily, then proceeds. "There's this woman at work." Doctor Reynolds looks on intently and nods. "I've seen her after work with Brad for coffee. I've been to her house. She was even at my house *yesterday*! We've had *long* discussions. I've had in-depth conversations with her about Lana. Now there's nothing strange about that right? But what's weird is that she was describing things that only Lana and I knew. So today I went into work to talk to her, but she's wasn't there, and when I say she wasn't there, she hasn't moved or left or been fired, she's *vanished!* Vanished off the face of the earth apparently!" The doctor appears puzzled but intrigued as she writes several notes on her clipboard.

Dean continues, "I'm walking around asking people who've spoken to her *several times* if they've seen her or know her whereabouts, and no-one's even heard of her!" he scoffs. "And if you think that's strange, even her *office* has changed! There's another guy in there, who says he's worked there for FIVE years! Who I've *never* seen before in my *entire* life! Even her assistant doesn't know what I'm talking about!" He laughs nervously to himself under his breath. "I feel like I'm literally going insane. I mean how the hell could I have imagined a whole human being and had conversations and meetings with them and..." Dean hears himself and stops talking, shaking his head. "How could that be possible? None of it makes any sense!"

The doctor looks perplexed and concerned, she puts down her notes. "Dean, your wife's passing came as a massive shock, it's a life-changing event. Sometimes stress can have a harrowing effect on the mind. Wishing so desperately for her to be here, could have resulted in you suffering from some temporary delusions due to the *immense* grief you've had to endure."

Seeming confused, he squints. "So, just to confirm, you're saying that for the last *two* weeks, I've imagined the whole thing? All the conversations, her being at work and in my house!" he mocks sarcastically.

She scribbles some more notes down, then glances back up and starts to speak in a very slow and composed manner. "I realise this is a big ask, but I want you to try for just *one* minute, to imagine that you're not emotionally attached to this situation. Try and think about this in a calm and logical manner. If no-one else knows what you're talking about, and there's no evidence of this woman's existence, then that can be the only reasonable conclusion! Sometimes people can also have *very* vivid dreams that seem so realistic that you actually think these things have happened!"

"I didn't dream *anything*! She came to my house! I was in her office *yesterday*!" he retorts loudly.

"You're not thinking about this rationally! If you're telling me that her office has somehow changed and another employee that you've never seen has been working there for *years*, then what your saying is not plausible, it's just not possible!"

Shaking his head over and over uneasily, he bites his fingernails anxiously. "I have no explanation for that, but I know I couldn't have imagined it all."

The doctor squints slightly then picks up her prescription pad from the table and continues. "Alright, let me start you on some mild medication. Take one at night before bed and they'll help you sleep." She starts to write as he looks on. "And if I were you, I'd seriously think about taking some time off work." Dean sits there in silence and uncertainty as the doctor hands him the prescription. She smiles reassuringly. "Take a vacation and come back and see me in a month. If you're still having these thoughts or visions, then I'll make an additional appointment with myself and another one of my colleagues, where we can do some more tests and diagnose you in greater detail. Make sure you take the tablets an hour before you sleep and try to get some time away, and more importantly give yourself time to grieve and come to terms with everything. It's a major life changing event Dean, and not something that's going to alter overnight." Nodding passively, he takes the prescription and promptly leaves.

He walks back to the car earnestly as Brad anxiously watches him approach. "How did it go?" he asks optimistically, but still a little concerned at Dean's downcast composure.

"Great! She said take a vacation! Oh! *And* also, she thinks I'm crazy *and* delusional *and* she's given me a bucket load of pills to take!" he replies dismissively, raising his eyebrows.

Brad pauses, then reacts sedately, trying to take the seriousness out of the situation. "Well, a vacation sounds like a *very* good idea!"

Dean shakes his head, "I don't want any more time off work!"

"I'm sure they'd be fine with it!"

"It's not that, *I don't want to*!" Dean repeats sternly.

"Well maybe the tablets will help you get some sleep, at least!"

"I'm not takin' any pills!"

"D, she obviously gave you them for a reason!"

"I *said* I'm not taking them! Let's just go back to work, we're gonna be late." he retorts sharply. Brad drives them back to work, dismayed at his obstinate attitude.

As soon as they arrive, Dean swiftly returns to his office. He sits there still dazed at events, now even more confused and fragile than ever before. Brad is still *extremely* worried about his mental health so irrelevant of what Dean said to him, he takes it upon himself to speak to their boss on his behalf anyway. A few minutes later, Brad enthusiastically rushes back to Dean's office and proclaims proudly, "I've spoken to the manager and he says he's happy for you to take as much time off as you need, D." But Dean's response isn't exactly the one that Brad was expecting. He interprets Brad's actions as a betrayal of his trust. He's irate that Brad felt he needed to take matters into his own hands, especially when he told him not to.

"I don't need you speaking on my behalf, I'm quite capable of doing that for myself, and I already told you, I'm *not* taking a vacation. I'd rather be at work so I can stay busy and keep my mind off things. The last thing I want to do right now is stay at home on my own or go somewhere where I'm going to feel even more isolated than I do already! I almost had a breakdown last time, so just try and understand that." Brad nods despondently and leaves, frustrated by Dean's stubbornness.

Meanwhile, Tobias heads in to see The Boss. "Sir, something's happened and I have absolutely *no* explanation for you."

The Boss turns his head. "What is it?"

"In the matter of Lana Smith, I followed your instructions to the letter, I deleted all memories, records and traces of Angelica Karrae and moved Lana to an alternative entity."

"Yes,"

"But somehow Dean still remembers Angelica."

The Boss looks baffled. He frowns and blinks several times. "So, the cerebral transition wasn't completed correctly?" he enquires.

"Yes, Sir, it was, I've triple checked! I have no idea how he still remembers!"

The Boss scoffs. "So not only has Dean lost his wife, but now he must think he's losing his mind as well!" Tobias gulps nervously. "Where is Lana now?" The Boss continues, his patience quickly dwindling.

Tobias looks to his clipboard. "She's a waitress in New Orleans."

"Location?"

"7D4628ZZ3X."

The Boss opens the visionary bubble. "What's her name?"

"Seraphina."

The Boss locates her and zooms in several times. Squinting, he appears stunned and flabbergasted at what he's seeing. "*Why* does she look *exactly* like Angelica?"

Tobias swallows hard again and quickly rambles. "Unfortunately, Sir, due to the serious nature and urgency of the situation, we had to move her so quickly that we had no time to replace her with a new interface, so we were forced to use Angelica's avatar again."

The Boss is incensed. "*Why* was that decision made without *my* authority? Do you realise how dangerous this is Tobias? Have you any clue?" Tobias looks seriously alarmed and with a bowed head stands in silence as The Boss scans back through the bubble and concentrates his attention back to Dean.

The workday ends and Dean finally arrives home. By now his head is pounding and throbbing. He sinks into his chair clasping his head in his hands feeling heartbroken, lost and depressed. Still so overwhelmed with the whole 'Angelica' situation, he has no clue where to turn anymore. He thought he'd made so much progress in trying to come to terms with everything, but now feels completely overwhelmed, like he's taken one step forward and a thousand steps backwards.

He can't fathom how he will *ever* get over losing Lana. He's so drained and tired of putting on a front for everyone and suppressing his emotions. In his despair, he holds Lana's sweater and breaths in deeply, catching the last subtle remnants of the perfume that still linger there.

Grabbing a bottle of bourbon from his kitchen, he launches himself onto his sofa, then pulls the bottle of pills from his coat pocket that the doctor gave him earlier, staring glumly at the label. NOT TO BE TAKEN WITH ALCOHOL it clearly states. He glances at the bottle for a few seconds, then unscrews the top. Dean has reached his lowest ebb and for a split second considers downing the whole bottle of pills with his freshly opened bottle of liquor.

The Boss is still guardedly overlooking the situation, he feels so much empathy for Dean and knows he can't let him completely deteriorate. As he flicks his finger towards the bubble, Amadeus suddenly runs and jumps up onto Dean's lap. Amadeus gets a bit too exuberant and knocks the pill bottle out of his hand. Dean abruptly snaps out of it, as the bottle rolls underneath the sofa and the pills scatter all over the floor. "'Deus!" he scorns. He gently pushes the dog away, placing the bourbon on the floor, then gets down on his hands and knees picking up the pills one by one, while frustratedly searching for the empty pill bottle.

He peers underneath the sofa and can see it lying there, but it's just half a finger length out of reach. He tuts as he extends his arm. He stretches but as he does he notices something else out the corner of his eye. He squints as he focuses. "No way!" he gasps. He speedily springs up and pulls the sofa away from the wall. Dean feels a shiver down his spine and reels in total shock... it's Angelica's scarf! He yanks it out then drops back down on the floor, as his heart starts to pound at phenomenal speed. He breathes heavily, almost hyperventilating. "How can this be?" he mutters. Turning the scarf around and around, he feels the fabric and starts to study it. "It was real? It was *all* real! Angelica *does* exist!" he mumbles, dazed and dismayed, but then how could her office have changed, and no-one's ever heard of her? It's like she's been erased from existence!

Slouched on the floor in disbelief, examining the scarf over and over, he tries to catch his breath and comprehend the impossible.

Chapter 16

Visions...

The depth of what's occurring suddenly hits him and he starts to become terrified and isolated, so decides to go to the only place left he can think of to get any peace of mind, near to Lana at the cemetery. He speeds there as fast as he can, then alternately, he sprints and staggers down the hill to her resting place. He is desperate now. As he arrives at her spot, he falls hopelessly to his knees, staring solemnly at her stone. He reaches out tenderly, "Lana, help me. Please help me. I'm losing my mind; I can't go on. I don't even know what's real and what isn't anymore. I don't want to go on without you, please help me!" he begs out of desperation and despair.

Consumed by his grief, he closes his eyes and bows his head. He places his hand on her headstone to steady himself, whilst still grasping Angelica's scarf in his other hand.

All of a sudden, something exceptionally strange but miraculous happens. Because Dean has one hand on the stone *and* he's holding the scarf in his other hand in unison, it starts to stimulate a galvanic reaction. A sudden jolt infiltrates his body, and for a split second, he powerfully senses Lana's presence. She appears to him in his mind's eye, so vividly it's as though she's standing right there in front of him. She's smiling. She's laughing. It's like she's glowing. Dean is overcome with an emphatic feeling of love and emotion washing over him like a tidal wave, but then abruptly, as quickly as she came, she's gone.

More peculiarly still, he now envisions a random, yet completely distinct image of a restaurant, a place he's never been to and never seen before. This image is as crystal clear as the one he just saw of Lana, *so* clear in fact that it's like he's actually standing outside on the street gazing up at the building. The surroundings are graphic and intense. In his mind's eye, he glances upward and notes a sign which reads, *The Jambalaya Hut*. He can feel himself walking through the entrance into a very busy, lively environment. People are eating, talking, and laughing. Although it's crowded and brimming full of people, he feels a serene and peaceful energy radiating through him as he stands watching.

The realisation unexpectedly sets in as to what is happening. Horrified, he wrenches his hand from the stone and continuously blinks his eyes in shock, as an unexplained energy catapults him backwards and he falls to the ground. "Lana!" he whispers, as he recollects feeling her presence and recalls the image of the restaurant.

As he rethinks and relives his vision, he becomes shocked and scared and starts to fight for air. Battling to compose himself, he attempts to remember. "Jamba or something?" he mumbles, desperately trying to pinpoint the name. Suddenly, it comes to him, "Jambalaya Hut!" he shouts out loud. But what could it mean?

He sprints back to his car in a daze, feeling agitated, petrified and bewildered. He slams the door shut and locks it, sitting there gasping for breath, frightened and out his depth, trying to comprehend the chain of events that have just occurred.

He drives as fast as he can, then slams on his break and parks up at the side of the road. He rummages through his pocket for his cell phone and loads the search engine. With trembling fingers and shaking hands, he types the name of the restaurant. His heart is palpitating. He can no longer distinguish between reality and his own imagination anymore. He clicks onto the images tab and anxiously scans through the pictures.

After a couple of minutes of frantic searching, he notices a photo of the restaurant, but in his hurry he's scrolls past it. He drags his thumb across his screen and the picture re-emerges. The *exact* same picture he's just seen sits there before him on his cell phone screen. The *exact* image he just envisioned in his mind's eye. His heart start to miss a beat as he moves his face closer to his phone, and does a double take. His pupils dilate. "It exists!" he whispers to himself in total uncertainty and confusion. "It can't be real! This *can't* be happening!" He shakes his head in hesitation. "It's an actual place!" he scoffs. He investigates further by trying to find an exact location. It's nearly *two thousand* miles away. "New Orleans!" he gasps to himself. Dean doesn't understand why he's been shown this place or how it's relevant to anything, but he realises that it must be significant to Lana in some way, and that he must have observed it for a reason.

Shaken, weary and confused, he makes the resounding decision to go back to the church. As he drives, his mind's in a whirr, on overdrive. He arrives and shuts off the engine, then sits there in complete silence for a moment, contemplating whether he should go back to Lana's grave or not. He's so lost, scared and bemused.

He vacantly saunters down the hill, but instead stops and decides to make a diversion into the direction of the church. He shuffles into one of the pews despondently, totally perplexed and withdrawn.

After a few minutes, Priest Hannigan notices him. He walks over and casually sits down beside him. "I haven't seen you in here for a while, Dean. You alright?" he asks attentively, in his strong Irish accent.

Dean forces himself to look up. He closes his eyes and replies in a solemn whisper. "No, not really."

A moment of silence follows as the priest looks on, recognising how disturbed and troubled Dean is. "You know, Lana was a beautiful woman, a beautiful soul, a one-off. It'll take a long time, Dean, but I can assure you that the Lord will have a special place for her with his angels."

Dean nods, his head slightly bowed. "The church is a wonderful place to come for some solace when you need a few moments to yourself, but you have to allow yourself time to grieve."

He nods once more. "I know, but it's more than that, some things happened and I...." He stops himself, sighs and rolls his eyes.

"You wanna tell me about it, lad?" the priest enquires considerately.

Dean scoffs. "You wouldn't believe me even if I *did*!"

The priest smirks. "You know, I have been around a bit, I may be a man of the church but I'm also Irish. I think you might be embarrassed to know some of the things I know!" he quips.

The corner of Dean's mouth upturns a little, but he still looks disheartened and in turmoil. He hesitates for a moment but then realises he has nothing to lose by confiding in the priest. "Alright!" he takes a deep breath and starts to explain. "Since Lana..." he stops himself. "Since the accident... I... I've struggled with just the normal day to day things. Getting out of bed in the morning in itself is an accomplishment, but I've tried to keep it together... for Lana." The priest nods and conscientiously continues to listen. "But lately I've been experiencing some... *odd* situations, and I don't know what's happening anymore!" Dean starts to bite his nail nervously as he continues. "I met this woman at work, there was nothing in it, I just really seemed to gel with her, but as we got to know each other more she started talking about Lana. She said she was having thoughts and dreams of her. She told me things that only Lana and I knew! So, a few days ago, I was pretty mean to her, I said some things I shouldn't have. Then I found a note she'd pushed through my door describing situations that no-one knows but me, so I went into the work to speak to her. I went to look for her, but she'd disappeared. Everything was gone. Her office had changed, no-one had even heard of her. I nearly had a panic attack, so I went back home, and then there in my house, I find her scarf! So now apparently I have a scarf belonging to a woman who doesn't even exist!" He says sarcastically holding up the scarf to show him. The priest nods deep in thought. "That's not all of it!" Dean continues.

"I went to Lana's grave earlier and I had some weird premonition or something! I had my hand on her stone and I suddenly had this crazy feeling that she was there, I had this *vividly* clear image of her. It was like I could see her, like she was standing right in front of me, and she was alright. She was happy! She wasn't hurt or anything. She was looking straight at me, smiling!" he gulps. "Then the next thing I know I'm looking at a restaurant, some place I've never seen before. The image was so lifelike, it was as though I was *in* the restaurant. I can't even explain it." Dean shakes his head as he continues, "I know what I saw, but here's the thing... something was telling me to look it up, so I searched for it on the internet and guess what? It's an actual place! It *actually* exists! A restaurant in New Orleans, a place I've *never* been to in my whole entire life, exists!" Dean sighs heavily and bows his head, rubbing his forehead in his distress.

After a few seconds of silence, the priest lifts his eyebrows. "Right! Well, that's a lot of information to be taking in, but the way I see it, lad, there can really only be *two* possible explanations. Either one is that you're a complete raving lunatic," Dean glances at him with a double-take, "or two, is that Lana's trying to convey some sort of message, so if I was you, I would definitely be looking to the second!"

Dean frowns slightly. "You believe in all that... afterlife stuff? Messages? Ghosts?" he stutters.

"I'm open to a lot of things, the good Lord works in mysterious ways, so he does! I think you're maybe looking at this in the wrong way Dean. You see, sometimes what the Lord sends you isn't a curse at all, but a blessing in disguise. I know if someone I loved had just passed and I had been lucky enough to receive any kind of message, then I would definitely have to think seriously on that, and New Orleans, what a beautiful place that is! Would be a shame not to go, don't you think?"

Dean frowns again, confused, scrunching his eyebrows. "Wait, so you're saying... I should actually *go* to New Orleans?"

"And why not? Where's the harm in it, lad? And by the looks and sounds of things you could do with a change of scenery anyway!"

Another Pastor approaches. "Sorry to disturb you Priest Hannigan, but the congregation is waiting."

"I'll be right with you." He stands, but turns back to Dean and speaks in a composed, compassionate fashion. "We're only here for a short time, each day given only by God's good grace. Sometimes opportunities present themselves, but people are too blind to see them, they choose to close their minds and squander them. You think on it, and you know where to find me if you need me, alright?" Dean reciprocates with a gentle, repetitive nod.

Sitting there silently on his own, dumbstruck at events and the conversation he's just had with the priest, he takes in his surroundings. The feeling of peace exuded from the candles, the familiar smell of incense burning, the image he relives of Lana standing at the alter in her wedding dress, her funeral. He recollects everything that has just happened and the advice the priest has given him. He stares at the scarf and then back up to the alter, wondering what he should do and what all of it means.

Tobias has seen everything, but he doesn't understand any of it either. "Sir, I have absolutely *no* clue as to what is happening right now! How can Lana contact Dean if she's with us? And how does he still have the scarf and remember Angelica?" The Boss rapidly clarifies as he continues to watch over Dean. "Lana's subconscious is trying to come through, her soul's trying to reunite with Dean's and the scarf was in their house. It was protected by Lana's spirit, so when you did the transfer it didn't disappear."

Tobias frowns, even more confused. "Sorry, Sir, but I *still* don't get it!

The Boss turns around to face him and reiterates slower. "The spirit protects what it loved the most or where it was the happiest, so for Lana, obviously that was Dean, *but* it was also their home, the place where she felt the most love and peace. When Angelica was dissipated, all memories and belongings connected to her were depleted *apart* from the scarf, because she'd dropped it in their house, and because Dean was also in the house at the *exact* moment Lana was reassigned, *he* was protected too. So, he's the only one who remembers Angelica, and the scarf still remains."

Finally enlightened, Tobias nods a few times, replying with a prolonged "righhhhht!" They both continue to protectively watch Dean through the visionary bubble, but Tobias seems pensive. "Sir, isn't it a bit strange how Dean was in the house *with* the scarf at that *exact* moment that the transfer took place?"

"Hmm, isn't it!" The Boss replies, insinuating the fact that fate might have lent yet another helping hand.

Dean leaves the church still in a daze and makes his way back to his car. He gets in, pulls his door shut and sits there silently, his hands encasing his face. Conflicting thoughts race through his mind as he contemplates and tries to reason through everything.

As he bows his head, his concentration moves to the glove compartment. He flicks the catch and it falls open. As he stares at the belongings, a million memories fill his thoughts. He pulls out some papers and starts to rummage through the rest of the things inside. An unopened fortune cookie falls to the floor, one that Lana had left for him when they had a Chinese takeaway some months before. A lump starts to develop in his throat as his breaks the seal and tears it open. He gently pulls out the proverb. It reads... *The man on top of the mountain did not just fall there*. Dean gazes at it, reading it over and over. Brushing away a tear with the back of his knuckle, he knows he can't go on this for much longer.

He sits there questioning himself. Is this a sign that he should go? He's torn, scrutinising his own sanity, musing everything over. Would it really be that insane to go to New Orleans? The priest certainly didn't think so, but what would he do when he got there? What does it all mean? He's never been that far away from home without Lana but if nothing else, maybe a vacation is *exactly* what he needs.

He realises that the only thing stopping him from going is work. As he recalls what the priest said to him about keeping an open mind, he gazes down and reads over the fortune cookie message once more. Suddenly, he has a surge of energy and determinedly makes the positive, definitive decision to follow his instincts, no matter how ludicrous it sounds. Somehow, he's holding the scarf, that's real! He can't be that crazy, can he? If Lana is trying to send him some kind of message then surely this restaurant must hold the answer.

On returning home, he prints out a picture of the restaurant with the address, then folds it up and tucks it securely into his jacket pocket. After searching for the travel details online, he finds that it will take him over three hours on a plane to get there. He rings work and tells his boss that he's had a change of heart and would like to take some time off after all and asks to take a couple of weeks off. His boss kindly agrees, so he books it then phones Brad.

Dean explains that he's changed his mind and reluctantly agrees with what Brad said earlier about taking some time off, conceding that he must be stressed and grieving, and that he probably returned to work too soon. He informs him that he's going to go to the beach for a while to try and relax and get his head together. Brad responds with kind words, positive energy and is in complete agreement, and he couldn't be happier with his decision. He urges Brad not to contact him for a couple of weeks as he wants complete rest, and after ending the conversation, starts to search for direct flights to New Orleans.

He manages to track down a flight leaving in the next few hours, so quickly purchases the ticket online then realising he has no time to waste, hurriedly packs a bag, grabs his credit cards and starts a frantic search to try and locate his passport.

He can't miss this flight so scours through his draws in a mad panic. He opens Lana's closet and rifles through her things. To his relief, he discovers it sitting there in between some of her papers. As he stands, Lana's passport drops to the floor. Stopping dead in his tracks, he turns, picks it up and gazes sentimentally at her photograph. She was so beautiful, he ponders, smiling lovingly at it. Flicking through the pages, he reminisces of all the places they travelled together and all the amazing vacations they went on, memories that will stay with him forever.

He gathers his thoughts and manages to pull himself together, throws her passport on his bed then walks over to his closet, pulls a random bunch of clothes from the hangers and hurriedly shoves them in his case. Momentarily, he pauses, perching on the edge of his bed, holding his face in his hands. Has the grief of losing Lana ultimately taken its toll? "This is crazy. What am I doing?" he mumbles, trying to reason with himself. Retrieving the picture of the restaurant from his pocket, bit-by-bit, he unfolds it. He re-reads it and starts to rethink events, as he tries to rationalise everything once more.

Glancing up at a picture of Lana sitting on his bedside table, he holds it up and starts to talk to her. "I felt you Lana, I know I'm not imagining all this. How could I have even known about this restaurant? And Angelica just disappearing like that! I didn't imagine all that 'cause I have her scarf!" he rambles, shaking his head, still striving to make sense of it all. "I don't know what's happening, but I do know that I'm certain I've seen this restaurant and, even though I don't have any clue as to why, I'm going to go. If it does turn out that I am really losing it, well, at least I'll have been to New Orleans!" he jokes half-heartedly with a broken smile.

Suddenly, the dog runs in and jumps up at him, licking his face. "Deus! Oh! I forgot about you!" he gasps, gently stroking his head and scrunching his soft fur.

Dean rings Lana's dad, Joe.

"Hello?"

"Hi, Joe. It's Dean."

"Hi, Dean. I haven't heard off you in a few weeks, we were getting worried. How are you holding up, son?"

"I'm sorry, I know I should have called, it's just been erm... well you know," he replies seriously, not really knowing what to say. "How are *you* coping Joe?"

"Just taking one day at a time, that's all I can do right now."

"Yeah... and how's Margot?" Dean asks despondently.

"I'm not gonna lie, she's not so good. I'm not sure how to help her with the grief, Dean, I'm not even sure how to help myself!" he sighs. "But I know Lana wouldn't want any of us to be going through this pain, so we're just taking it a day by day."

In agreement he sighs. "Joe, I know everyone's having a really hard time right now, but I need to ask you a favour. I would've asked Jess, but obviously she's still recovering."

"What is it, Son?"

"I need to get away for a few weeks to be by myself and I've seen a cheap flight leaving out today. I know it's really short notice, but I need someone to look after the dog, and I was wondering if you'd be able to have him? I'll bring all his food and things round to you; I just need a couple of weeks."

Without hesitation Joe replies, "Yeah of course, Dean! I've told you before, we'll have him whenever you need us to, we love that little dog! Lana loved him like he was her child! It's no problem, and to be honest with you, son, it might do Marg the world of good!" Dean smiles to himself sentimentally. "Just bring him over whenever you're ready!"

"Thanks Joe. You don't know how much I appreciate it. I'll be there in about twenty minutes."

"No problem."

Dean rings off and finishes packing his things. He gathers all the dog's belongings together, then calls a cab. He drops Amadeus off to Joe, has a quick chat with Margot, then heads directly to the airport.

Chapter 17

New Orleans...

Dean arrives at the airport with mixed emotions, feeling severely apprehensive, torn and anxious. As he stands in the queue, holding tightly onto his luggage, he begins to wonder what he's even doing there. As he looks around, he observes people rushing past him, families happily chatting to one another and others who are extremely excited for their forthcoming vacations. There are several couples who appear to be hopelessly in love, and groups of teenagers enthused and energetic. He's never felt more alone in his life but as he peers down to his hand luggage, he notices the corner of the scarf poking out from behind the zip which instantly dispels any further doubt. He becomes focused once again and a burst of energy and optimism flows over him as he moves forward in the queue.

After checks and more checks, Dean finally boards the flight. He locates his seat number, shuffles along the plane and sits down. He's happy to have a window seat and promptly orders a drink from the stewardess. The flight is nearly four hours long, so he reclines his seat back a little to try and get comfortable and watch a film. Dirty Dancing is playing, which was one of Lana's favourites. He leans back and sips his drink while intermittently reminiscing over the film and gazing out the window.

After a smooth flight, the plane lands without a glitch and everyone sequentially make their way off. Dean heads to the baggage carousel to collect his luggage, then moves through the departure terminal and out of the airport towards several cabs lined up outside. He's managed to book a hotel just a few miles from the airport so gets in the taxi and gives the address to the driver to locate.

As he stares out the window, he can already sense the electric atmosphere, and he's not even anywhere near the town centre yet. As he nears his hotel, there are people as far as the eye can see, lining the streets. It's Mardi Gras week in New Orleans and this wasn't something Dean was expecting or prepared for.

Upon arrival to his hotel, he gazes upward, the height and stature are profound. He pays the cab driver, takes his luggage, walks inside, then books in. He picks up his door key and takes the elevator up to his room, and as he swipes his key card, the door clicks open. He can't believe how glorious it is inside with gold and cream lavish furnishings. Dean hangs his clothes and takes a shower, then knocks back a small bottle of liquor from the mini-bar fridge to calm his nerves. He's as ready as he'll ever be, so he picks up his jacket and wallet, locks his door, and makes his way back downstairs.

There's a parade on every day for the next few days so cabs are in high demand. Dean tries to flag one down, but several go by before he finally manages to stop one and jumps in. He shows the picture of the restaurant to the cab driver, which is situated on a road aptly named *Hope Street*. "Do you know where this place is?" he asks hopefully, in anticipation.

"Yeah, I've been there a few times, they do some *good* Jambalaya in there!"

Dean still feels anxious, yet relieved and elated. "It exists!" he mutters to himself under his breath. "Can you take me there?" he asks.

"Sorry, I can take you *some* of the way, but the Parade's going through so no cars can get down there."

"What about them tram things?" Dean enquires.

"Streetcars? They don't run two hours before or after the parade. You could try a bus, or you'll have to walk the rest."

Dean feels slightly discouraged, but still enlightened to think it actually exists and he's not that far away.

The whole place is amazing, dripping in jazz heritage. The uniqueness of the culture, tradition, music and fashion is like no other. Dean can't help but feel moved and inspired. *Lana, you'd love it here*, he thinks to himself as he passes some talented street musicians. How he wishes they had come here together, and shared this experience.

The cab driver takes him as far as he can, Dean thanks him, pays and gets out. The Parade is in full swing now and the atmosphere is exhilarating. There are vibrant, colourful floats travelling along the street, back to back, filled with vivacious people wearing intricately decorated and flamboyant costumes and extravagant masquerade masks.

There's addictive, exuberant jazz music radiating from absolutely everywhere. Musicians playing trumpets, trombones and numerous other instruments and many singing in high spirits. Most people are wearing bowers, hats and beaded necklaces. The necklaces are thrown from the floats as they pass by, and some people are wearing several of them all at once.

Dean decides against getting a bus as he can see how rammed full of people they are, and as he doesn't even know where he's meant to be going, he's not convinced it would be a good idea. He determinedly starts walking in the direction that the cab driver indicated, but with so much going on, and with the streets becoming completely lined, it gradually becomes progressively more difficult to get through the crowds.

He continues to shuffle through the masses of people, but as his main focus remains the restaurant, the noise and sound of talking, laughing and shouting starts to become disconcerting. The noise that was once energetic and positive is now starting to become distracting and deafening.

Dean manages to stop random people to ask if they know where the restaurant is located. Many blatantly or dismissively answer '*no*' or brush him off with a submissive '*sorry*' and some just push past him and totally ignore him completely. Starting to feel frustrated and decidedly anxious, he sighs. He pulls himself together, takes a breath and starts again.

He stops a passer-by and holds up the picture. "Excuse me? Do you know where this restaurant is?" he shouts above the noise. In a Liverpudlian accent the man replies, "Ah, sorry, mate I can't help ya, I don't live round 'ere, I'm just on holiday with me girl, like."

Dean half smiles, puts his hand up and nods, "Not to worry, thanks anyway." He carries on and tries to surge through the masses of people as quickly as he can, but before long realises that because of all the bustle and chaos, he must have gone too far and wandered way off track. He's lost now, getting weary and feeling uneasy and stressed. He asks more and more people, some even seem to optimistically point him in the right direction, but as so many of the roads are blocked off, he ends up roaming down the wrong street *again*.

Dean's drained, feeling claustrophobic, tired and deflated. He thinks he's travelled down the same road at least three times and back again. He double checks his watch and realises he's been searching for nearly an hour now and has gained absolutely nothing as he's almost back to square one. Feeling as though he's about to become unhinged, he decides to take a break and strolls into a nearby shop for a refreshment.

As he takes his drink and walks back outside, he notices a bike shop opposite on the corner. They hire bicycles, mopeds and motorcycles; Dean realises that this could be the quickest way to get round the town. "Sorry, Lar, I know I promised you, but I need a bike!" he softly whispers under his breath.

Dean necks his drink, bins his plastic cup, walks over and goes in. "Hi, have you got any motorcycle's for hire for this evening?" he enquires.

"We're all out I'm afraid, Sir, what with the procession being on, but we've still got bicycles if that's any good to you?"

Dean sighs. "Is this your idea of a joke, Lar?" he mutters to himself.

"Sorry, Sir?" the shop owner queries.

"Erm, nothing. Yeah, I'll take a bike please, whatever you've got." Dean fills out the required documentation, pays the hire cost and takes the bike.

Since he's been inside the shop, somehow it seems the parade has become even more extravagant and lavish, and now there's even more elaborate floats taking part in the parade. Dean peers down to the floor. There's beads, wooden coins and decorated cups strewn everywhere. He knows he has to stay focused so summons all of his energy and strength and continues his search.

After nearly half an hour passes, still without any progress, and just as he's about to give up for the evening and head back to his hotel, miraculously, by chance he spots the restaurant out the corner of his eye. He abruptly halts the bike and stops with such a jolt he nearly topples over the front of the handlebars. Standing there staring in disbelief, he pulls the printed picture out of his breast pocket and holds it up next to the building. "It can't be!" he mumbles, dumbfounded. "That's it!" he exclaims jubilantly, still in shock, yet in complete and utter relief. Although there's tremendous noise and chaos, with overly loud music and rowdy people everywhere, everything now suddenly falls silent as Dean's focus is completely on the building standing before him.

Quickly tucking the picture back into his breast pocket, he jumps back on his bike and speeds towards the restaurant narrowly missing people in his rush. He locks the bike up around the side of the restaurant, then sprints to the entrance and unreservedly bursts through the doors. He slows and steadies himself then stands there making as many mental notes as he possibly can. He looks to the side and can see an employee rota board with all staff names written on in chalk. The whole restaurant is covered in pictures of Louis Armstrong, Fats Domino, and an array of legendary jazz musicians and memorabilia. It is *exactly* how he envisaged it when he was at the cemetery.

Although the restaurant is brimming with people, he waits patiently until he's ushered to a table by the waiter. "Please take a seat, Sir, and I'll be back with you shortly." Dean sits down and tries to catch his breath, not quite believing he's actually sitting *in* the restaurant. Everything feels surreal. He's starting to feel queasy and panicked, but knows he has to remain calm else it's all been for nothing. Shuffling to the back of his seat he looks around and scans every corner of the room for answers, desperately trying to see if he can find anything vaguely familiar in his surroundings, or to understand the purpose of him even being there, but nothing immediately springs to mind. He picks up the menu and studies it scrupulously cover to cover, back to back.

A few moments pass and the waiter returns. "Sorry about that, Sir. What can I get for you?" he asks politely.

Dean glances back down at the menu. "Erm..." he clears his throat. He wants to stay there for as long as possible to try and work things out and make sense of everything, so he decides to make a massive order. "I'll have the Cajun Chicken Flamer, with a *large* bowl of the house Jambalaya and a portion of chorizo cheesy garlic bread with an XXL coke and erm... *all* of the sides please."

The waiter looks stunned. "*All* the sides Sir? Are you expecting other guests?" he asks looking around.

"No, it's just for me!" confirms Dean. He looks at the waiter's surprised expression. "I've... been... unwell!" he stammers. "I haven't eaten in a few days, I'm *very* hungry! Also, for dessert, I'd like a large slice of pecan pie, with hot custard, please."

The waiter lifts his eyebrows, "Okay! This may take a few minutes and unfortunately I'm finishing my shift now, but I'll pass your order over and someone will tend to you straight away. Don't worry, it won't be too long."

"No problem," nods Dean. He's happy to wait around, so any delay in his food order is *exactly* what he wants.

A couple of minutes later, a waitress approaches his table balancing plates on both her arms, containing a seriously *galactic* amount of food. Dean is distracted, hurriedly glancing back and forth over the menu, looking for anything that could possibly give him some clue as to why he's there or how any of this is linked to Lana.

The waitress places some of the plates on the table and as Dean snaps out of it and peers up from behind his menu, he can't believe his eyes, he's in shock, and it's not because of all the food... it's Angelica! Dean throws down the menu and stands up abruptly. "Angelica!" he gasps, completely stunned.

The woman places the rest of the food calmly on the table and stares at him in a bemused, confused state. She glances behind her and around the room, "Erm... I think you must have me confused with someone else, my name's Seraphina!" She corrects him, pointing to her name badge.

Dean frowns and squints his eyes in bewilderment. "Seraphina? What? But..." He notes *her* confused state. "Don't you know me?" he queries.

She seems thoughtful and tilts her head a little. "I don't think so. Have we met somewhere before?" she asks curiously.

He gulps, trying once more to catch his breath. He's not even sure himself anymore. Is he seeing things? "Have you ever been to Pasadena?" he asks.

"No! Unfortunately not. I've never even been out of Orleans, not on my salary!"

Dean nods baffled as to what to do next. He can see she genuinely believes she's the person she's saying she is. Sporadic, even wild theories flitter through his mind. Is there any way this could be her doppelgänger? Is she in some kind of trouble? Could she have been in an accident and now have amnesia? But then that wouldn't explain her whole office changing and her existence being erased! He decides to back off as he doesn't want to cause her any stress and needs to give himself some time to process the situation and work out his next move. "I'm sorry, I must've got you mixed up with someone else." he stutters.

"It's fine," she smiles, "I'll just get the rest of your order."

Dean is ninety nine percent sure that this is Angelica, but he doesn't know why she's now calling herself Seraphina. Why is she in New Orleans? Why doesn't she remember him? He's totally confused and fatigued as a result of all the events taking place and fretfully deliberates what to do next.

The waitress brings the remainder of his food over and tells him if there's anything else, he needs to call her over. He has a *whole* table full of food in front of him now, but eating is the last thing on his mind.

He notices a manager walking by and flags him down to see if he can find out any information on Angelica. "Excuse me?" he beckons.

"Yes, Sir, can I help you?"

"Erm... that waitress over there, Angelica," he indicates by pointing her out.

The manager turns his head to look. "We don't have an Angelica working here I'm afraid, do you mean Seraphina?"

"Yeah... erm... Seraphina, how long has she worked here?"

"Oh, it must be nearly three years now, I think." he recalls.

"Three *years!* Are you sure?" Dean can't believe what he's hearing.

"Yes, I think so. Why? Is there a problem, Sir?" Dean doesn't want to get her into any trouble or bring attention to himself, so backtracks.

"No, not at all, she was waiting my table and I haven't seen her before and... well... she's doing a great job!"

"Oh, well, thank you for letting me know Sir. We always strive to ensure our customers are satisfied, and if there is anything else you need, please let us know. Enjoy your meal, Sir."

"Thank you!" he nods.

Dean's lost for words. His thoughts are racing around his mind at a hundred miles per hour. This is *definitely* Angelica, but then how can it be if she's worked here for three years? And now she's called Seraphina? Nothing makes any sense. His mind's foggy as he continues to stare at her every time she walks past him. He feels distressed and dazed, trying to comprehend the significance of it all. He orders a double bourbon and sips it as he contemplates his next move. As he continues to watch her walk by and wait tables, he sits there drowning in his alcohol and his own befuddled thoughts.

Chapter 18

Revelations...

The Boss is still fervently following Dean's every move through the summary bubble. He is now vastly concerned that he's channelling into Lana's soul once *again* and that his behaviour is becoming too erratic. He doesn't take his eyes off the bubble for a second.

Just then, Tobias rushes in, gasping, trying to catch his breath. "Sir?"

Without taking his focus from the bubble, The Boss stops him with a raised hand, "I know Tobias, I know."

Tobias gulps. "Sir, it's moving to Stage *Four*. It's causing a kinetic reaction with the ambrosial link patterns."

"I'm well aware of that, *thank you* Tobias!"

Tobias knows that he's already treading on thin ice but continues irrelevant. "Sir, if it reaches Stage Five, The Board *will* want to see you. I've already had word that they're considering dispersing Lana's soul."

The Boss turns his head and stares Tobias dead in the eyes. Although extremely concerned he remains calm and focused. "*I* have the final say on that decision, and I'm saying we wait! I just need a little more time to see what Dean intends to do and how he's going to react."

Tobias proceeds with caution, "Sir, can't we just move her again?"

"No! I told you before, it doesn't matter where we put her, it *won't* work. Their souls are drawn to each other, they are *bound* together. The only option we have is to wait!" he clarifies clearly.

"Sir?" Tobias is extremely concerned.

The Boss can see he's becoming fearful and troubled so takes a breath, sighs, and tells him to take a seat. "Tobias, sit down." he directs. The Boss leans back in his chair seemingly pensive and reminiscent. He turns to Tobias and sighs, then begins to speak in a quiet, sullen voice. "Do you remember when I told you that I've only ever seen *one* soul conjunction before?"

"Yeah," replies Tobias fascinated as to what The Boss is about to tell him.

"Well..." The Boss hesitates and looks downcast, "the only other person to have a soul conjunction... was me!" Tobias gulps as his face drops. "It happened with my wife, Draya."

"Your wife?" he gasps in total shock. "I didn't know you had a wife Sir!"

The Boss slowly nods. He takes a picture of her from a secret compartment in his draw and places it on his desk. "She was the most beautiful woman I'd ever seen in my life. From the moment I met her, I just couldn't take my eyes off her. We fell in love instantly, but I could never understand how she felt the same way about me as I did about her! Every day was a blessing. We spent as much time together as we could, and the few moments we were apart, we'd call. We were inseparable. Getting married to her was the happiest day of my life."

The Boss pauses momentarily, smiling nostalgically at her picture, but then sadly his demeanour changes as he continues. "Then one day I was finishing work when I got a phone call from one of our friends telling me to go to the hospital urgently. Draya had suffered a major heart attack while out shopping and it turned out to be fatal." He pauses again, looking solemn. "I remember the feeling like it was yesterday. My stomach sank and my heart was beating so fast. I had this weird eerie feeling. I was *praying* someone had made a mistake. I mean how could that be? She was young, fit and healthy, she'd never complained of *any* heart problems, the doctors seemed baffled and couldn't understand either. They tried to revive her but couldn't, and the tests came back inconclusive, so I never got to the bottom of it, I never did find out what happened. All I knew was, we'd spent nearly every living moment together for thirteen years, and then she was gone. I can't explain the *piercing* pain, the extent of the feeling of loss was unfathomable. I can't begin to tell you how heartbroken I was, Tobias. There are no words that could even come close to that feeling of emptiness."

"I went to her grave every day just to be near her. I didn't want to live without her. Every day was a nightmare, a constant struggle. It was like I had this huge black cloud continuously hanging over my head, following me around everywhere. It took everything I had just to get through a single day, I was a broken man." Tobias looks sad and tearful. "Then about six months passed, and I met this woman at the food market. I was instantly drawn to her for absolutely no apparent reason, her name was Catherine. We started talking and, although we'd never met before, she had this strange sense of familiarity about her. The more we talked, the more she reminded me of Draya, and before long she was telling me things that only me and Draya knew, only things we'd been through together. She didn't know how she knew all of these things and neither did I, but the longer it went on, the more she could recite the most intricate of details. Neither of us could explain any of it, and you might think bad of me, Tobias, but I persisted to see her because it helped me through the grief."

"I saw her continuously for nearly a month and then one day, out the blue, she just disappeared. As though she'd vanished off the face of the earth. I searched for weeks, I looked everywhere, but there was no sign of her, she was just gone. I went to the food market every day trying to trace her, but no-one had ever heard of her. People, who I *knew* had spoken to her, told me they'd never heard of her.

I didn't have an address for her so there were no other options. I nearly went mad and had to live the rest of my life longing for Draya and wondering what happened to Catherine."

"When I got up here I was hoping that I would see Draya and that we'd be united again, but I was told that someone in the lower ranks had made a catastrophic error." He bows his head, shaking it slightly. "They'd put Draya's soul into Catherine's body and because our souls were drawing together again, it was causing complications that were becoming too dangerous, so they decided to disperse her soul to rectify it. It wasn't Draya's time either. I don't know how or with who they filled the void, they never told me. All I know is that none of it was our fault, but Draya still paid the price. We both did."

"They gave me this job as compensation. They granted me supreme, superior authority and great power. I was bestowed with a *monumental* amount of love. Every time a soul passes through, the feeling is *overwhelming*, it's incredible, but it still won't ever change the fact that Draya's gone *forever,* and, even though, I have this almighty power, there's not a single thing I can do to change things." The Boss stands up and composes himself. "And, that's why, Tobias, I *can't* take Lana from Dean, *I won't!*" he states defiantly. Tobias appears profoundly upset at what he's hearing. He feels deeply sympathetic towards The Boss, knowing that he's lost the love of his life and that he's suffered all these years in silence.

"Remember Tobias it's a soul for a soul, that's the only way to fill the void, so we correct Lana's path and stabilise the link patterns. We wait as long as we can and do whatever we have to, to make it possible. If it becomes too dangerous, I will take *full* responsibility."

Tobias jumps into action, nodding confidently in agreement. "Yes, Sir!" he replies assertively, his eyes overflowing with tears. The Boss smiles compassionately and Tobias leaves. The Boss directs his focus back to the bubble, feeling the intensity of the dilemma, but still determined to save Lana and Dean, knowing that time is now against them all.

Dean's heart rate accelerates and palpitates irregularly. He feels as though his head is only moments away from exploding. "What do I do?" he whispers to himself over and over. He thinks about everything that happened with Angelica and realises that he didn't ask the right questions quickly enough. This is his *only* chance, he hasn't come all this way for nothing and can't squander this opportunity, so decides to blow caution to the wind, and not make the same mistake again.

This time he's going to ask Seraphina directly and concisely. He leaves all his food at his table, gets up and approaches her. "Seraphina?" he calls out to her; she turns around.

"Hi, can I help you? Is everything alright with your food?"

Dean ignores her questions and starts to bombard her with questions of his own. "Look, I don't know what you're doing here and how it is that *I* even came to be here, but I do know that you're not who you say you are, and there's definitely something going on that I need to get to the bottom of!"

Seraphina seems lost and squints. "Sorry, what are you talking about?"

Dean rolls his eyes. "C'mon, we both know you're Angelica!" he sneers.

Seraphina frowns, "Why are you calling me that again? I thought you said you'd me mixed up with someone else?"

The manager hears the commotion and rushes over. "Is everything alright?"

"Not really, no!" she replies nervously. "I think this gentleman has me confused with someone other person."

The manager recognises Dean. "Sir, didn't we speak about this earlier?"

Dean feels embarrassed and is starting to become increasingly frustrated. He's aware he starting to make a scene, but he doesn't want to let it go. "Look, I have no problem with you, I just need to talk to Angelica."

The manager looks perplexed, "I'm sorry, Sir but you're mistaken. As I told you earlier, there's not a person of that name working here."

Dean interrupts. "*This* is Angelica!" he reiterates, starting to get loud as he clearly points to Seraphina.

Seraphina looks at her manager with a worrying side glance. He can see she's starting to feel uneasy and intimidated, so steps in to take control of the situation.

"Sir, it's obvious that you have our waitress mixed up with someone else."

"No.. I.. don't!" Dean scorns in an aggressive, heightened, agitated tone. He's starting to feel seriously unhinged now as other customers turn to see what all the commotion's about.

The manager intervenes once more. "It's obvious to me that this conversation doesn't seem to be going anywhere, so, unfortunately, I'm going to have to ask you to leave!"

Dean grits his teeth and flares his nostrils in anger. "I've come a very, *very* long way and I'm not going *anywhere* until I've spoken to Angelica." Seraphina glares worryingly at her manager, who calmly tells her to take her break while he deals with it. She nods and hurriedly scurries off. "Angelica!" Dean shouts out after her.

"Sir! Please!" The manager interrupts boldly, but Dean continues to call out...

"Angelica, I just need to talk to you for *one* minute!"

The manager stands in Dean's path to prevent him from pursuing her. "It's clear that you are in some sort of confused state and it's apparent that we're unable to resolve this matter satisfactorily, so I think it's in everyone's best interest that you leave *now*, before I am forced to call the police."

Dean's emotional, angry and overly frustrated, not knowing what to do next. How can he just leave when Angelica's so close? How can he go when he's come all this way and the restaurant actually turned out to be real?

He reflects on everything for a second, but noting the manager's earnest expression, concludes that if he doesn't go now he'll be in even more trouble. Unwillingly and defeated, he decides his only option is to leave.

Loathed, he storms out the restaurant. Breathing hard, he stands outside the front, deliberating what his next move should be. He walks around the side of the building to retrieve his bike but then remarkably, by chance, he notices Seraphina out the corner of his eye smoking a cigarette around the back.

Realising this could be his very last chance to speak to her, he glances all around, then quickly scales a large trellis fence to get to her. Alarmed to see him *yet again*, she drops her cigarette to the ground and starts to cower in fear. Dean sees her distress and puts his hands up to calm her.

"Angelica, I'm not gonna hurt you, I just want to talk!"

"I'm *not* Angelica, how many times have I told you?" she trembles anxiously.

Dean looks to the side. He can see the manager approaching. In the knowledge that he has no time to jump back over the fence and that the police will *definitely* be called this time, he starts to panic, as Seraphina quickly scuttles back inside.

The Boss bows his head ruefully and sighs, "I'm sorry, Dean." Murmuring dolefully, he flicks his finger towards the bubble.

Dean suddenly feels a shudder throughout his entire body as the manager approaches, but to his astonishment he greets him pleasantly. "I'm sorry, Sir, but no customers are allowed back here. This is for staff only. If you would like to make your way back inside." Dean's baffled, he doesn't understand why he's being so polite when they just argued so aggressively.

They slowly walk inside together whilst still conversing. "I was just talking to Angelica, I mean Seraphina," Dean explains in a stutter.

"Seraphina?"

"One of your waitresses!"

"We don't have any one of that name working here I'm afraid, Sir!"

The Boss looks on, severely downhearted at Dean's distress, but knows he had no other option but to move Lana for their own good. Lana has now been transferred to yet another avatar to give The Boss more time to work things out and Seraphina is no more. Dean breathes heavily, his mind blown at what he's hearing. How can this be happening for a second time? He stands in silence for a moment, then deciding he can't take any more, calmly walks out the restaurant. As he passes the staff rota board he recognises that Seraphina's name is no longer there. It's disappeared, like she's been erased from existence, just like Angelica.

Dean unlocks his bike and rides back to his hotel, muted by shock and in complete disarray. Feeling scared, nervous and unsettled, he decides to urgently check out of his hotel and manages to get an earlier flight back home. He sits in silence and stillness throughout the whole journey, bewildered, lethargic and dispirited.

This trip has made him feel even more unstable and confused than ever before, how he wishes he had never even gone. As soon as he lands at the airport, he waves down a cab, drops his bags off home then drives directly to the cemetery.

Chapter 19

Thank You, My Dear!

Dean slumps to the ground next to Lana's grave, curled up in silence and despair, clinging onto his last thread of sanity, wondering if he will ever truly be at peace again or whether he must live in this nightmare eternally.

After an hour or so he gets up and sluggishly wanders to a nearby bench, situated under a beautiful pink blossom tree and takes a sip of his bottled spring water. He stares out into the clear blue sky, as a thousand scenarios enter his head.

He contemplates where Lana could be. Is she alright? Could she have been reincarnated? Could she be in heaven or somewhere else? Or is she just no more? Does she know she's dead or completely oblivious to what's been going on and everything he's been going through? He speculates what could have happened to Angelica and Seraphina, or if all the grief has finally become too much and he's just imagined the whole thing.

After a short while, an elderly woman approaches the bench. Dean fleetingly glances in her direction as she slowly lowers herself and sits down beside him. The only sound radiates from the continuous chirping of the singing birds. "It's a lovely day, isn't it, dear?" she notes. Dean stares directly at her but doesn't respond, instead he quickly looks away. He's lost in his thoughts and not in any kind of state to be conversing with someone, let alone a stranger. The woman notices him twisting his wedding ring around his finger. "My husband will have been gone twenty-one years next month and it seems like only yesterday he was waiting for me at the alter! I wish I could tell you it gets easier, my dear, but unfortunately it doesn't; you just learn to deal with it in a different way in the hope that you'll meet them again one day. You can't wallow in it and let the grief overtake you, unless of course you're looking to lose your marbles! You just have to remember the good times!" Dean listens but still does not respond. "I've come to see my daughter. Unfortunately, I don't live around here now, but I've managed to come back every year on her birthday, for nearly sixty-five years now! Would you mind helping me up dear, my legs aren't what they used to be!"

Dean sighs. He doesn't want to speak to *anyone*, but he can't let the old woman struggle on her own. She pulls herself up with the help of her sturdy wooden cane as Dean steadies her by clutching onto her arm. As soon as her arm touches his, he's aware of a calmness and familiar feeling emanating from her. "It's just over there!" She points out with her cane in the direction of the grave, and they very slowly walk towards it.

The grave is dirty and unkempt. "Oh dear, Oh dear!" she sighs, shaking her head in exasperation. "Unfortunately, I can't get here as often as I'd like, so it's not as well looked after as it should be!" She tries to reach down to place some flowers on the grave, but has trouble bending and starts to cough, so Dean quickly grabs them from her.

"It's okay, I'll do it!"

"Thank you, my dear, that's very kind," she responds gratefully.

As the old women steadies herself, he brushes the dirt away and yanks out some weeds that have grown around the stone. "You don't have to worry, I'll make sure I tend to it whenever I come down," he reassures her.

"Would you, dear? That's wonderful. Thank you so much!" she replies appreciatively.

Dean takes his water and pulls a crumpled tissue from his pocket. He washes the inscription as best as he can then dabs and dries it with the tissue. The old woman smiles brightly. The lettering reads, *Liliana Rose Smith. Our beautiful daughter, taken by the angels too soon, but alive forever in our hearts*. Dean places the bunch of white lilies on the cleaned area next to the stone and stands up. The old woman stares at the words.

"I was married at eighteen and by nineteen was pregnant with our first child." she reminisces. "When she was born she had breathing difficulties and a lot of other problems that technology just wasn't ready for. We were very lucky to have had her in our lives for the few short years we did, but when she died a piece of us died along with her. She was *so* beautiful. It's not something you can ever prepare yourself for, losing a child. My husband couldn't stay, the grief was too much for him, so I agreed to move half away across the country to Pennsylvania. He never really recovered from it, dare say did I, but how do you, dear?"

Dean shakes his head, feeling her pain. "I'm so sorry for your loss, I can't even begin to imagine what you went through, it must have been unbearable."

She nods in agreement, but appears frail. "Could you help me back to the bench, dear? I'd like to stay here a little while longer."

Dean nods and walks her very slowly back to the bench, acknowledging her weak state. She starts to cough. "Are you alright?" he asks, alarmed for her wellbeing.

"Oh yes, dear, don't you worry about me."

Dean looks around but doesn't see anyone. "Can I give you a lift somewhere?" he asks graciously.

"Oh, thank you, that's very kind, but my son will be here shortly to take me back home." She looks across the cemetery and sees his car. "Oh, yes, here he is now!" She thanks Dean again and he walks back to his car, only turning momentarily as he hears her cough again.

The Boss is overlooking this whole situation and sits back in his chair in disbelief at the realisation that Dean has actually been talking to *old* Lana and that she is also Liliana's earth mother. He can see how much she weakens when Dean is close to her and that this is accelerating the chain of events. He knows how dangerous it is and urgently summons Liliana to his office to inform her of the situation and the events that are now taking place. He knows it is only a matter of time now.

Chapter 20

The Reversal...

Just as things are about to reach a critical climax and a point of no return, and the board are about to summon The Boss, Tobias bursts through the door. "Sir? Lana Smith 7129. She's in limbo, she has twelve minutes." he pants.

The Boss nods with a glint in his eye, "thank you, Tobias." Tobias leaves as The Boss stretches out his hands to make a larger visionary utopian bubble, then sends Liliana to collect her. He watches as it all unfolds.

As Dean drives off out of site, *old* Lana has a heart attack and dies peacefully seated on the bench in the sunshine under the blossom tree. Her son tries desperately to resuscitate her, but nothing works. He calls an ambulance, but it's too late. Her soul projects out of her body as Liliana walks into cemetery to collect her. She reaches out her hand and with the old woman appearing much younger now, they happily embrace, content and overjoyed to be reunited. The Boss then watches and waits patiently for old Lana to arrive in Room 8.

Peering down to his desk, The Boss squints and frowns. A feeling of uneasiness suddenly washes over him as there's something off with the pattern alignment. He realises the urgency that this is his only chance to rectify the error and make things right, and although Lana's formation isn't one hundred percent complete, it's still enough to continue. He holds on for as long as he can but knows he must reverse them *now* or the souls won't change places.

To ensure minimum risk, he waits until the very last second for them to align, but as there's no more time, he presumes they will automatically re-align themselves or he'll have to figure it out later.

As old Lana makes her way to The Waiting Room, The Boss places both his hands firmly on the sides of the bubble, clamps them together, squeezing gently and commands... "*stop!*" Everything is silent. Everything is still. The bubble decreases in size slightly as everything comes to a sudden, dramatic halt. For a split second every single atom is frozen in time.

As he delicately let's go, and releases it, the bubble bounces back with a gentle quiver and sway and expands once more. He starts to spin it in an anti-clockwise direction, powerfully commanding, *reverse*. Young Lana's life starts to rewind at a remarkable speed. Although the images are all moving at a tremendously fast pace, The Boss can still see each one perfectly clearly. He watches diligently as everything in Lana's life is reversed and rewound and each chapter is played out one by one. After a few moments, he spins it even faster and repeats the word *reverse* again, but this time more powerfully and with greater strength and exuberance, watching as each chapter unfolds. He periodically glances down to Draya's picture sitting on his desk as he thinks of her.

After several minutes have passed and it's nearing the exact point in time, The Boss abruptly stops the bubble from spinning by pushing the edges together and once again clearly commands, "*stop!*" All things in life are frozen once more. He lets go and clasps his hands together on his lap, his fingers entwined, thumbs together, then calmly states with a slight nod... "begin!" Lana is thrust onto her bed as her avatar's body dissipates and vanishes. The Boss watches on optimistically, yet with caution.

It's a beautiful, glorious day. Rays of sunshine stream through the crack of the slightly open curtain and the alarm starts to beep. Lana hits the top of the clock to turn it off whilst her eyes remain tightly shut.

Dean grabs her and pulls her toward him, placing a gentle kiss on her forehead. "Hey baby, you know what day it is?"

"Sunday?" murmurs Lana, slumberous with her eyes still closed.

"Yeah, but also, it's the day of *love!*" The corners of her mouth start to upturn slightly. He kisses her again on the curve where her lips align and implores, "Don't go out today, let's just stay in bed."

She yawns and opens her eyes. "I can't, D, Jess is coming over. I've promised I'd take her to the office and go through all that stuff with her today. I'll only be a few hours, I promise!" Dean half smiles but looks rejected and dejected. Lana feels bad, she doesn't even really want to go, but she's already promised Jess and she only intends to go for a little while anyway. She sits up, takes Dean's face in her hands and continues, "So, *you* need to get up and make me some breakfast!"

His magnetic smile emerges once more as his good mood returns, and he nests his face into her neck. Lana laughs uncontrollably as his nose touches the funny bone on her jawline and goose bumps travel down her arm. They play fight then she hesitates and gazes up at him seductively, his alluring charm luring her in once more. With desire taking over and unable to resist the magnitude of his charisma, once more she falls under the spell he has cast and zealously they make love.

He jumps off the bed as she smiles back at him. "And that's why *I* am the King!" he wisecracks, with a cheeky wink.

Lana laughs, shaking her head. "I don't believe you just said that!"

"Oh yeah!" he replies with a brash grin and knowing nod. He starts to run a shower, as Lana is left there giggling to herself. He scrolls through his phone and loads his song list. As reggae music starts to play, he jumps in the shower and starts singing along to the songs. He calls out over the noise of the streaming water, "So angel, that reminds me, do you fancy going to that Caribbean place that opened in town? The food and cocktails are meant to be *amazing*, and I heard they play R&B and reggae music... *all* night!"

"Yeah! That sounds great!" she calls back enthusiastically.

"Alright, I hope they're not fully booked! I'll try and book it for around seven okay?"

But this time she doesn't respond, instead she abruptly pulls open the shower door and looks Dean up and down flirtatiously.

"Wit Woo!" she whistles. Dean grins, wittily nodding in recognition of himself, takes her hand and pulls her in. They laugh, kiss and embrace.

As they emerge from the shower, Dean dries off and Lana starts to diffuse her damp hair.

"I'm gonna make some breakfast Lar."

"Okay, I'll be down in a minute."

Dean winks at her and rushes down the stairs. He makes a hearty breakfast of croissants, eggs, juice, coffee, berries and yoghurt. A few moments later Lana arrives in the kitchen, her face lights up. "D! You didn't have to do all this!" He hands her a large card, a massive box of assorted Belgian chocolates, a colourful assorted bouquet of exquisite flowers, and a small rectangular gift box. Lana chews on her lip and reaches her arms around his neck. "Thanks D!" she says bashfully and pecks him on his cheek. She sits down and carefully opens the box. Inside sits a stunning 24 carat gold necklace with their initials D and S intertwined. A massive grin appears on her face, she's overjoyed. "Oh, Dean, it's so beautiful! Thank you!" He loves doting on her and is *so* happy when he can see she's happy. He takes it from her, lifts her hair and fastens it gently around her neck.

She walks to the mirror and touches it, gazing at it admiringly. "Wait there!" she points at Dean, instructing him not to move. She runs into the living room to the secret place where she's stashed his gift.

Lana hands him the card and gift. It's quite a small square box roughly the size of his palm. "Is it a basketball?" he jokes.

Lana laughs "Nope!"

"A pair of slippers?" he quips,

"No! Wrong again" giggles Lana,

"I give up! I'm gonna have to open it!" He unwraps the gift paper and opens the box. Sitting inside is a *very* expensive designer watch. "Lar!" he gasps, completely astonished. "I love it!" He takes it out the box and straps it on his wrist. "Thank you, baby," he remarks gratefully, twisting his wrist around to admire it. He pulls her close, grabbing her waist and passionately kissing her lips.

"Let's keep the cards until later when I get back and then we can read them in bed together," she says flirting with him.

Dean raises his eyebrows. "That's a *very* good idea!" He hugs her and kisses her cheek softly. Lana is still only wearing her bathrobe so hurries back upstairs to get dressed as Dean admires his watch.

A few moments later she shouts down to him. "Baby? Have you seen my diary anywhere?"

"Nah, Lar, I haven't, but I'll have a look."

"Alright, thanks!" she replies. A couple of minutes later, she hurries down the stairs. "Did you find it?"

"No, I couldn't see it anywhere, but don't worry, it'll turn up."

"Hmm, I just really needed it for today, I'll have a look in the living room." Lana goes to search as Dean calls the restaurant to book the table for that evening.

Meanwhile, Brad and Jess are just arriving. Brad locks his car as Jess walks up the driveway to the house and knocks on the door. Dean greets her and lets her in. "Hi Jess!" shouts Lana from the other room.

"Hey, Lar!" Jess heads straight to the kitchen, picks up a plate and helps herself to some croissants and berries, then pours herself a large glass of fruit juice.

"Help yourself, Jess!" jokes Dean.

Brad comes in and sits down at the breakfast bar. Jess doesn't stop talking as Lana's rushing around, trying to get ready. She goes into the other room to get her shoes. "Lar you ready yet?" shouts Jess impatiently.

"Yeah, just a second, I can't find my diary." Lana emerges looking flustered, "Maybe I left it in the car," she sighs. "Oh, it doesn't matter, I'll look for it later or we'll be here all day."

She grabs her purse and is just about to leave but Dean stops her. "You need something to eat, honey," he tells her.

Lana picks up a croissant and takes a bite then sips half a cup of juice. "I really want to rush, D, so I can get back. I'll get something at lunchtime." Dean's not impressed but knows the sooner she goes, the quicker she'll be back, so agrees. Lana says bye to Brad and kisses Dean, *intensely*.

"Oh my God, you guys, four years and you still act like newly-weds, it's disgusting!" teases Jess, rolling her eyes. Dean grins and raises an eyebrow to Lana.

She reaches for the handle of the front door but as she's about to open it, The Boss points at Lana through the bubble, Lana suddenly stops in her tracks. She's feeling lightheaded and giddy and nearly faints.

Jess looks on anxiously as Dean rushes to help her. "Lana?" He holds her in his arms then turns to Brad. "Grab that chair!" Brad drags a chair close to her as Dean gently places her in it then kneels down to her level. "Lar, you okay?"

"Yeah, I think I've just been rushing round too much, head rush!"

"Yeah, well everything's going to have to wait, you're not going anywhere until you've had something to eat and I know you're alright," he insists, extremely concerned for her well-being.

The Boss uses his other hand to open another bubble and starts to observe the logging truck moving along the highway. He twists the bubble very slightly and the driver suddenly looks in his rear-view mirror and notices that the logs are becoming unstable in the back. He manages to pull over on to the side of the highway, jumps out and re-attaches all the straps and ropes, then continues safely on his journey.

Dean makes Lana a cup of sweet honey tea and hands her a croissant, she sips it and takes a bite. "You sure you're okay?"

"I'm fine, D," she replies with a sweet smile.

"Alright, well you just drink your tea and sit there for a few minutes, while I go and tidy up."

He kisses her on her forehead and walks into the kitchen. A few moments later he returns. "You'll never guess what I found!" he states proudly.

"My diary!" squeals Lana relived and delighted. "Where was it?" she asks inquisitively.

"It was down the side of the worktop."

"Oh yeah! I remember now, it fell down there the other week when I was making dinner," she realises and tucks it into the inner pocket of her bag.

After about half an hour, Lana is feeling much better and is ready to go to work with Jess. "Now, are you sure you're feeling okay?" Dean asks once more.

"Yes, I'm fine," she confirms, gazing adoringly at him.

"Ring me if you feel ill and I'll come and get you straight away, alright?" He kisses her lovingly and she and Jess go to her workplace.

After a few hours, Lana arrives home, and Dean has made her a special Valentine's meal. "Surprise!" he gleams. "I know we said we'd go out, but I thought as you weren't feeling well earlier, we could watch a movie and have dinner at home instead!" While Lana was at work, Dean went to the Caribbean restaurant, brought it all home and made a candlelit dinner for two. He's bought flowers, wine, candles, chocolate and even sprinkled heart confetti all over the table.

Lana is elated! "It's all *so* lovely, D, and *I've* got a surprise for you too!" she taunts secretively.

He looks confused, "Lar, you already gave me a *really* expensive watch and…"

She cuts him off, "No… D, sit down."

Dean becomes concerned. "You alright?"

Lana shines, "I'm absolutely fine, I just need to tell you something."

"What?"

There's silence for a second, as she hesitates then takes a breath. "I'm pregnant!" she blurts out, not being able to conceal the truth for one moment longer.

Dean's face drops to the floor, his pupils dilating. "What? Are… are you sure?" he stammers. Dean is ecstatic at the thought but can't believe what he's hearing.

"Yep!" Lana grins pulling out the positive pregnancy test from her jacket to show him. "That's why I needed my diary, 'cause I've been tracking my dates and I haven't checked it for days, and it's probably why I was feeling faint earlier."

"Lar!" Dean grabs her and holds her tightly, as she closes her eyes deep in bliss. They are both deliriously overjoyed and completely over the moon.

Although The Boss knows he still has to ensure that the link patterns have aligned themselves correctly, he looks on proudly, gratified and relieved at the current outcome.

Chapter 21

Life!

The next fifteen years pass quickly and although still relatively young, Dean and Lana have four daughters together now and live a beautiful and contented life. Sadly, Amadeus is no longer alive, but since they bought him a mischievous playmate to keep him company, his puppies have brought continuous joy and sustained pleasure into their lives.

Due to The Boss having to deal with very similar, sad circumstances to Lana and Dean, he still holds a very special place in his heart for both of them and has vigilantly kept a close eye on them throughout the years. He also previously briefed Tobias to monitor their movements and keep him updated of any situations or unusual occurrences that may arise.

Tobias goes in to see The Boss. "Sir? Lana is deliberating whether or not to become pregnant again!"

"Again!" grins The Boss, but Tobias isn't smiling. His face is rigid like stone and his demeanour calm and deadly serious.

The Boss squints at him, Tobias continues. "Sir, we've had word that the cells and inauguration link patterns in some of Lana's outer chambers are starting to unbalance and are becoming unstable. If she becomes pregnant again, she's *not* going to make it, Sir."

The Boss appears nervous and distraught, as his facial expression alters and drops. "What do you mean she's not gonna make it? It's already written that she'll have a long, prosperous, healthy life?"

"Sir, she will have complications and they won't be able to save her. I've sent several people to warn her. I've sent direct messages, thought patterns, feelings! I've even channelled into her senses *and* dreams indicating the urgency but it's Lana, she's not listening, Sir!"

The Boss quickly thinks back to when he completed the reversal and the last few link patterns weren't aligning. He recognises that this is the same problem rearing its ugly head again, a situation which he was certain he'd already managed to remedy. He steadily becomes quietly nervous. The Boss outstretches an enormous, major visionary future bubble, the largest of them all, then rapidly commands "Lana Smith 7887, future pregnancy, full term." He and Tobias both watch vigilantly as she is taken through to the operating theatre and medics try desperately to save her life, but she bleeds to death and dies before their very eyes. The Boss abruptly snaps the bubble shut, taking an inward gulp. He holds his hand to his head, feeling dismayed and helpless. Tobias bows his head as they both stand there in silence. The Boss is in total disbelief as to what he's just witnessed. "This *can't* be it, not after everything! She has children now and Dean can't lose her again!" he mumbles dismally.

For a few minutes, The Boss hurriedly paces back and forth, deep in thought, desperately contemplating the seriousness of what's happening and how he can rectify a problem he thought he'd already solved. He stops, places his hands on his desk and thinks for a moment. Suddenly, and determinedly, a thought enters his head, he squints. He sits down and pulls his chair in close. Placing his hands together in the middle of his desk, he carefully slides them outward and his wooden desktop miraculously starts to move apart, revealing huge colourful projections containing the link patterns and cell formations.

He starts nodding to himself, now aware his assumption was correct. Realising what now needs to be done, he springs into action. "Alright, there is *one* thing we could do. We could give the *child* a choice."

Tobias frowns. Seeming baffled, he double checks his clipboard, then stutters, "Erm... but, the child isn't created or even confirmed yet, Sir!"

The Boss lifts his eyebrows. "He's already here!"

Tobias remains confused with the whole situation, so The Boss continues to explain what has happened whilst simultaneously typing and moving the projections at speed.

"When Lana died, the link patterns tried to stabilise but for some reason couldn't, so instead they ended up dividing. Cells clustered and got attached, chambers altered and displaced, everything got confused and they all embedded. Her whole life spiralled and was forced into segment displacement." The Boss sporadically looks up at Tobias as he speaks and continues to figure out the complexity of what's transpiring.

"When the error occurred and her accident happened, it was as though her life had ended, which, in the case of cell augmentation, meant that some life events remained undetermined. While she was in limbo, any remnants or any unresolved future events were bought forward and created *anyway*. The boy is not meant to be here, but due to that, he is! I had to continue with the reversal, it was my only chance to change what happened. At that point, the link patterns didn't try to re-align so Lana was never meant to have that choice."

The Boss types even faster and vigorously moves and slides the images from side to side, in all directions and at speed, he squints, completely focused. "The patterns are trying to re-align themselves as we speak!" he whispers. "They must've been sending Lana messages and thoughts as well, which is probably why yours were being counteracted."

Tobias nods in realisation. "But, Sir, why would the patterns start to re-align now?"

"That's a good question, Tobias! It's *extremely* unusual, but patterns *can* try and configure themselves at *any* stage, usually when a significant event is about to take place, which is obviously what is happening now!" he exclaims.

The Boss swivels his chair around to face Tobias revealing to him the patterns and projections as he continues to explain and reiterate in depth. "If any displacement occurs, no matter how insignificant, it should primarily recalibrate itself instantaneously. If more life events occur and they *still* don't change, then it's correct to assume that they'll *never* align. We've watched both Lana and Dean closely over an extended period of time and the situation has remained stable, so I've had no cause for concern. As it's been fifteen earth years, Tobias, this is not a situation I could ever have foreseen happening, I thought the time had long passed."

"When I started the reversal process, one of the link patterns was *still* misaligned. I couldn't wait around to find out which one because it had to complete at that *exact* point on the timeline, or the soul configuration would not have corrected itself and they wouldn't have crossed. The situation would have become irreparable! I waited until the last quarter segment of completion, and as nothing major occurred I didn't see it as a problem. I concluded it would be something trivial, but obviously that was not the case Tobias."

"The crux of it is that only when full completion has taken place can you fully determine what's been displaced, only then can it make itself clear and it was the boy!"

"I didn't find out how significant this was until after the reversal was complete and I could investigate further. *He* was the missing link. We placed him in limbo and surrounded him with lunar soundwaves to protect him."

"Once he'd been brought through, the patterns still didn't try to re-align, they remained neutral, so I had to assign him. Obviously, I wanted to assign him to Lana, but there were far more intricate cell formations associated with her, as she was the main source of the error. She was only less than a *billionth* of a percent after completion, but again the timeline wouldn't allow it, so because he was also Dean's son, I was able to assign him to Dean instead. I named him Saul."

Tobias stands there stunned as The Boss continues. "So, we have to give *him* the choice now." he declares adamantly. "They are *both* meant to live but now only *one* of them can." he states sadly. "We both know how stubborn Lana is, she's *never* going to change her mind, so now we *have* to ask the boy." The Boss declares concisely but with sadness echoing throughout his voice.

"But what if he doesn't choose Lana?" asks Tobias anxiously.

The Boss gazes at him for a moment then sighs. "Then that is what is written. I will continue to try and change her mind for as long as I can, but it's *his* choice and we must remain unbiased. He has Lana's spirit. In my opinion, there is a very high probability that he will choose her, but ultimately, it's *his* decision, so we must lead by example. No matter what we feel, we must not be swayed in any way, we *must* remain neutral." Tobias nods.

"If he does decide to save her, the patterns will automatically stabilise and if not, well... there's nothing more we can do." he notes gravely, his eyes lowering. "Lana and Dean's fate lies with him now." Tobias bows his head woefully. "Please ask Laurie to bring the boy at the eleventh hour." Tobias nods and leaves the room as The Boss continues to try to work on the patterns and get Lana to change her mind.

As the eleventh hour approaches the child enters the room, The Boss turns and stares directly at him. He stands there for a moment, unwittingly observing and absorbing the child's facial features and mannerisms, realising how uncanny his resemblance is to his mother. He snaps out of it... "Hi!" he says, welcoming the child warmly and beckons him to sit in his chair.

"Hello, Sir!" replies the infant, shuffling backward in the seat to get comfortable. The child continues to inquisitively gaze all around the room.

The Boss smiles momentarily but then focuses as he contemplates the urgency and is fully aware that this decision is now entirely out of his hands, but he must do everything he can to help correct it.

"I need to show you something," says The Boss calmly, as he outstretches a huge visionary bubble. "Do you know who these people are?" he asks in a kind and loving tone.

The boy lifts his head slightly and stares deep into the bubble. He smiles upon realisation and points, "Yeah, that's Dean, I'm assigned to him, he's funny! And that's the pretty lady who lives with him."

The Boss looks on with warmth. "Yes, that's right." The Boss pauses for a second then continues, "but... they are also your parents!"

The boy looks astonished. "Dean's my father? And the lady's my mother?" he questions.

"Yes! Your mother's name is Lana." The child grins from ear to ear as he continues to smile at the images, whilst The Boss deliberates the boy's next reaction and the impact his decision will have.

The Boss sighs, "I need to show you something else now," he tells the child downheartedly as he closes the bubble and out stretches another. "This is your birth!" he sadly informs him in a solemn tone.

Momentarily, the boy looks elated, but gradually his face starts to change as he witnesses the doctor frantically try and save Lana's life. He continues to watch as she dies. "I don't understand!" he whimpers.

"Lana's not going to make it Saul," The Boss whispers sorrowfully.

"But why? Can't you help her? Can't you do something?" he begs with emotion breaking in his voice.

The Boss sighs with a heavy heart. "I can't. I really, *really* wish I could."

The Boss leans on the corner of the desk adjacent to him. "We sent her *many* messages, *endless* thoughts and feelings, but she'd already made her decision to have you. Lana's a *very* strong woman and once she's made up her mind, there's little anyone can do to change that. We gave her the choice, but evidently, she wants *you* to live. Even though she hasn't met you yet, it's notably apparent that she already loves you very much."

There's quiet. Everything is still. The boy is tearful and downhearted. "Can't you do anything?" he asks morose and frustrated.

The Boss looks pensive. "*I* can't, but that's the reason I called *you* here. Do you know what link patterns are?"

The boy shakes his head negatively, so The Boss starts to explain. "Everybody has a timeline and that timeline is like their individual story with a beginning, a middle and an end, broken down into chapters, the chapters of their life. Each chapter is then broken down into what we call *link patterns*. Link patterns are like the story of your life and everything that's connected to you. From the instant your soul is created to the moment you arrive in The Waiting Room, your whole life is already mapped out. This means that if you're trying to go down a route that you shouldn't be on, the link patterns will change accordingly. They'll send you thoughts and feelings to try and push you back on the right route. With your mother, regrettably someone here made a *serious* error. She was mistaken for someone else; it wasn't her time, which resulted in the link patterns becoming distorted. When they tried to align and couldn't, they went into automatic consolidation.

Everything that might have happened in her future got pulled in, which produced you!" The Boss puts his hand reassuringly on top of Saul's. "There's no easy way to say this, Saul, and it's through no fault of your own, but you were *never* meant to be born." The boy looks shocked upon hearing this revelation, his eyes dimming slightly. "Lana and Dean would have decided against another pregnancy and carried on with their lives, but as it stands the link patterns have decided otherwise and are trying to change their minds, so we are now approaching the place in time when they are being persuaded to do so, and you *will* be born. Do you understand?" he asks kindly. The boy nods to confirm that he does.

"The patterns have reactivated and are now trying to re-align to stabilise, but because Lana's alive and now your soul is also active and in existence, it means that if you are born, she *will* die. This whole process hasn't occurred yet but is imminent. The only thing we could do to change this situation would be for you to take her place." The boy looks totally baffled. "That would mean you would *never* get to earth, you'd *never* be born, and you'd have to stay here, *but*... Lana would continue to live."

The boy looks distraught, but thoughtful. He hesitates for a second. "Will I ever meet her?" he asks quietly, yet hopefully.

The Boss smiles warmly and nods. "Yes, one day."

Saul thinks some more. "Can I still be Dean's guardian angel?" he asks optimistically.

"Of course, *and* under these unique, exceptional circumstances we should even be able to assign you to Lana as well now." Saul looks up with hope in his eyes, but The Boss doesn't want to sway him so continues in a more detached fashion. "*But*, you know that this must be *your* decision, and yours alone. If you decide to be born and go to earth, you'll *still* see Lana one day. I want you to know that there's no right or wrong answer, and whatever you decide you will have my full blessing. Neither of you has done anything wrong, and no soul is valued greater than another, no matter what stage the physical or mental form. Everyone's life and worth are measured exactly equal, and Saul remember... Lana *wanted* you to live."

Saul takes a gulp and contemplates the situation as The Boss waits patiently for his answer. A few moments of silence pass and then as though a light has been switched on, and an epiphany has occurred, like a sudden burst of optimism and strength has entered and energised his body, Saul declares confidently. "I choose my mother. I want my mother to live!"

The Boss gazes down at the boy and places his hand gently upon his shoulder. He doesn't want him to make a rash or wrong decision based solely on his emotion or love for Lana. "You have to be *absolutely* certain, without a shadow of a doubt, because once this is done, it *cannot* be reversed."

Saul nods confidently. "Yes. I'm certain and I will *not* change my mind!" he proclaims adamantly.

The Boss has a glint in his eye. He smirks proudly. "Well, I thought you might say that, because you're very much like your mother, not just in resemblance, but in spirit and strength... and stubbornness also it appears!"

Saul smiles back. They lock eyes for a moment. "You're sure?" The Boss asks once more in a soft whisper. Saul nods in clarification.

It's approaching 11.11, and as they shake hands, The Boss confirms to him softly, "It is done! You are now also Lana's guardian angel. I'll get Laurie to sort the paperwork." He winks and smiles kindly.

Although the child is confident that he's made the correct decision, he appears somewhat downhearted. His head bowed slightly, saddened at the realisation that he won't ever be a part of their earth family and wonders how long it will be until they're reunited. The Boss stares at him, feeling his low spirits. "Hey, do you want to go and see her now?"

And with that, the boy's face immediately lights up. "Can I?" he asks excitedly.

"Of course. I think she might need you right now!"

Lana has suffered a sudden medical emergency and has had to have urgent surgery to rectify it, which has unfortunately resulted in the diagnosis that she won't be able to have any more children. As she recovers in hospital, she feels depressed, excessively pensive and reflective about it all.

Curiously, Lana's been placed into a side room, *Room 8*, and Laurie has been assigned as her nurse. As she checks Lana's observations and vital signs, she asks if there's anything she needs. Lana suddenly feels at peace, in fact, she always seems to feel at ease whenever Laurie is around. She smiles gratefully but tells her she's alright, then turns her head to look out towards the vast double glass windows. Before Laurie closes her door, Saul walks passed her. She winks at the little boy reassuringly, and cheekily he winks back. Lana's sad and withdrawn, still lying on her side staring out the window. The boy stands next to her bed and places his hand on top of hers, as Lana watches the sun break through the clouds. Although she can't see him and is still saddened, suddenly she feels hopeful and at peace.

Just then, Dean enters the room, he consoles her, and they start to talk. "Lar, we've already got four beautiful daughters. You being here is all that matters to me!" They count their blessings as he holds her lovingly in his arms. Saul looks on and all three are united in soul once more. Dean stays a while then leaves as Lana has to stay in overnight.

As morning breaks, Lana is just starting to awaken, at that split second in between sleep and consciousness. As she blinks, she notices a little boy standing there in the doorway. The little boy smiles caringly in her direction, she smiles back, still blinking, trying to focus on him. Just then, Dean arrives, completely oblivious to the child.

"Hey, Larnie! I missed you! You feelin' alright?" he asks attentively, kissing her softly on her forehead.

Smiling back, she pushes herself up the bed, lowering the covers down to her waist. She glances back towards the door, but the boy is no longer there. Dean walks around the bed emptying all the magazines, flowers, food and gifts he has brought onto the bedside table, as he continues to talk, but she calmly interrupts. "Who was that little boy?"

"What boy?" he replies, completely mystified.

"The boy you just walked past in the doorway!" she says pointing in the direction he was standing.

He looks over to the door, with a frown. "Huh? I didn't see a boy!"

"You just went past him!" she insists.

"Lar, I dunno!" Dean chuckles. "I didn't see a boy, maybe people are bringing visitors and he wondered in before I got here!"

"No! You literally just walked straight past him!"

Dean shrugs, "I don't know what to tell you!"

"Could you please go and look, D, because he could be lost or something."

He nods then scours the corridors and asks a few people, but no-one has seen, or is missing a child. "I asked around, Lar, but there aren't any children out there!"

Lana blinks a couple of times then shakes her head in confusion and defeat. Dean gently sits on the bed next to her, placing his arm tenderly around her shoulder and pulls her close as they watch television together and plan a vacation for when Lana is well again.

Chapter 22

Over the Rainbow...

Many, many years later...

Lana arrives in The Waiting Room. Immediately upon entering, all of her memories of previously being there instantly come flooding back to her. She recollects *everything* that happened the first time she was there all them years ago. Liliana is there to greet her once more.

"Hello, Lana, it's *so* good to see you again!" she gleams with heartfelt sentiment and joy echoing throughout her voice.

"It's good to see you too!" Lana agrees with an expansive grin, but at the same time feels a little disheartened that Liliana is *still* in The Waiting Room after so many years have passed, and hasn't yet secured her golden wings.

Liliana beckons her to follow, so Lana clasps her ticket and manual securely under her arm and shuffles with the help of her cane to the front row of seats. She slowly lowers herself and Liliana sits down next to her.

"So, *now* you have the manual!" quips Liliana.

"Well that's because Laurie *gave* me one this time!" Lana claps back wittily as they both giggle.

"So... you know why you didn't get on the tram right?" Lana frowns slightly and tilts her head.

"No, not really."

"Well our superior here, *The Boss*, he wanted to give you another chance at life." Lana squints, unsure what she's talking about. "With everything that happened to him, he decided to give you a different avatar, a new entity so that *your* soul would still remain complete and intact."

Still totally confused, Lana queries. "A different what? And *what* happened to him?"

"You're not aware of any of this, are you?" queries Liliana in a surprised tone.

"No!" she confirms, with a negative shake of her head.

"What happened to you, happened to The Boss!" Liliana exclaims. "Someone made a *very* serious error and it wasn't your time, and the same thing happened to his wife. She was taken when it wasn't *her* time either. He tried *everything* to save her, but he couldn't." Lana looks saddened and feels so sorry for him. "I think that's why he tried so hard to help you, because he saw his own situation in yours." Lana gulps as tears gradually form in her eyes. Liliana explains everything in great detail, as Lana realises the lengths The Boss went to, to help save her. He didn't let her die and if it weren't for him, she wouldn't have had the beautiful life she did with Dean, n*or* would she be sitting where she is right now. "You know, I probably shouldn't be telling you this either, but you appear to know everything else now, so..." Liliana expresses humorously.

"There's a limited time on Earth when it's more likely to see angels, the moment upon awakening before realisation of consciousness, it's called *crossover*. Well you probably won't remember, but many, *many* years ago when you were ill in hospital and Dean came to visit you, there was a little boy standing there in the doorway when Dean came through the door?"

Appearing enlightened, Lana gasps. "Yeah, I do remember that! He waved at me, but Dean didn't see him!"

"Yes! Well, not only is he Dean's angel but he's also your angel and... your son!"

Lana's completely stunned. "Wait, what? But I don't have a son!"

Liliana smiles widely. "See, the thing is, occasionally people are sent choices, and the alternatives are laid out to them, sometimes blatantly and sometimes very subtly, but situations are *always* put into place to give options, and no matter what was placed in front of you, you were still willing to go forward for your child, irrelevant of the outcome, so... The Boss decided to ask *him.*"

Looking lost, Lana queries, "ask him what? How could he ask him anything? I don't understand."

"There is no time here, so his soul is projected as a child." Liliana clarifies. "The Boss showed him what would have happened if you'd have given birth to him... *you* wouldn't have made it, Lana!" she whispers. Lana is stunned. "Without a moment's consideration, the child said he wanted *you* to live, so The Boss made it possible. I just thought you would want to know."

The moment is poignant as Lana nods gratefully and becomes emotional. "My son!" she mouths to herself.

"There's something else, something *very* special," Liliana grins. Lana's fascinated and intrigued. Liliana opens her coupled palms as Lana moves a little nearer for closer inspection. Inside her hands sits the *Legerdemain stone*.

Lana's inquisitive and extremely curious, "It's *exquisite*! What is it?"

"It's an elysian vow, embedded inside an enchanted precious gemstone." Lana has absolutely no idea what *any* of that means but is totally mesmerized and overwhelmed by the astounding beauty of it. "Lana, you need to understand the *extreme* importance and *power* of this, it is *beyond* legendary! I really can't even believe I have this is my hands!" Liliana continues to eagerly clarify. "Every nine hundred and ninety-nine chiliad earth years, this stone is extricated from the heavens and bestowed upon *one* exceptional soul, and *you* have been chosen Lana!"

Still perplexed by the whole situation, she continually stares at the gemstone in amazement and awe. "Me! But why me?" Lana questions.

"As you now know, a terrible error was made which affected your life line, but against all odds, you and Dean still managed to find each other, and as love overrules *everything*, the higher forces believe that *you* are deserving of such a precious gift, as they are confident you will choose wisely, and so it is yours!"

"Choose wisely? But wh... what do I do with it?" Lana stammers anxiously.

Liliana simplifies it. "This stone is specifically assigned to *your* life, *your* timeline and all things within it. It has the ability to give you *one* thing and *one* thing only, but the power of it is *beyond* imagination. *Anything* you wish for *will* happen, without fear of consequence. You have the power to go anywhere, do anything or change *anything*. There are no limits to this stones power or reach."

Lana sits up alert. "Anything? So, I could live my life over and give birth to my son, and we could *both* live?"

"Yes!" confirms Liliana confidently. "The power of this enchantment is sent from the heavens, and that power now lies within *your* hands. A*nything* you desire will be yours, so please, think carefully!"

Liliana waits patiently as Lana stares at the stone, considering her options. She deliberates, ponders and contemplates, thinking of all the things she could change. She reminisces about everything she could do *again*, but hasn't she lived such a blessed life *already?* She glances in Liliana's direction and thinks how she could finally make her wings golden. She thinks of all the people she has loved as her thoughts then turn to her son. She smiles proudly to herself as she considers his selflessness and envisages what he might look like. She reflects back over her life and how she could live it with Dean all over again, but this time with their son as well, and how wonderful that would be. She thinks back on everything Liliana told her and the intense admiration and pride she feels for the selfless sacrifice that her son made for her.

She reflects some more, then there's a moment of pure emotion as her eyes start to become misty with tears. Having finally made her decision she lightly nods to herself, "I know what I want to do!" she whispers calmly, beaming with pride. She informs Liliana.

Liliana grins from ear to ear, appearing extremely excited and abundantly overjoyed. "Are you sure, Lana?"

"Yes, I'm sure." she corroborates firmly.

"Well then, all you need to do is take the stone, wrap your hands tightly around it and close your eyes. Think it, and it will happen!"

Liliana places the stone gently into Lana's palms and encases her fingers very carefully around it. As she closes her eyes and conceives her wish, her hands start to glow warmly. As she opens her eyes, instinctively she gradually unwraps her fingers. She is stunned and taken aback as the stone is no longer there but instead a magnificent, breathtaking golden butterfly flutters from her hands and vanishes from sight into the heavens. Liliana grins intently and nods at Lana knowingly, confirming that her wish is now complete.

Meanwhile, Tobias goes to see The Boss. "Sir, I thought you might like to know, Lana Smith... she's in The Waiting Room!"

The Boss glances up, deep in thought. Pausing pensively for a second, he portrays a nostalgic smile. "Thank you, Tobias." Tobias nods back respectfully and leaves.

The Boss takes the misted elevator through to the special passage, leading to the entrance of The Waiting Room. Suddenly, he stops in his tracks as he notices Lana seated there. His mind conjures up a thousand thoughts. Venturing on, he makes his way directly to her. "Hi, Lana!" he says softly as he sits down beside her. Lana stares at him for a second. Although Lana's aged dramatically, she's still *very* beautiful, and her eyes still shine brightly. Her face progressively lights up as memories come flooding back to her when she finally realises who he is. They are both *extremely* glad to see each other again and start conversing like two familiar friends catching up on old times.

"Did you have a good life?" he asks curiously, yet with great affection.

"It was *wonderful!*" she beams. "I did *so* many incredible things. I had a job I loved, which brought me a great deal of joy *and* money," she notes in jest. I travelled the world and visited some unbelievable, extraordinarily beautiful places. I saw some stunning sights, some I never even dreamt possible, but best of all, I was blessed with the most loving husband and beautiful family. I had four daughters you know! Sixteen grandchildren and can you believe *forty-three* great grandchildren and not forgetting my wonderful dogs. I lived to see *all* that! Now isn't that something?"

The Boss grins, his heart warmed. "It truly is!" he replies in agreement, gratified by her beautiful response. He still has a very soft spot for Lana and is feeling highly sentimental.

Smiling back, she caringly places her hand on top of his. "Thank you!"

The Boss seems surprised and taken aback for a moment, but then realises that she must have remembered him from her first time round, and acknowledges that he sent her back. He nods a few times in recognition, kisses her gently on her hand, and graciously beams, "you're welcome, Lana."

"Will I ever see you again?" she asks hopefully, her voice breaking ever so slightly.

He grins and confirms kindly, "you will most *definitely* see me again!" The Boss becomes distracted and side glances as he notices Liliana approaching in the distance. "I think there's someone here to see you!" he says with a wink. The Boss stands and motions his head in her direction, beckoning Lana to look. She turns her head to glance in the direction of his gaze. The Boss carefully and protectively helps her stand but he's not just talking about Liliana, *Dean* is walking towards her too! He's young again and looks just like he did when they first met in the café.

She squints and rubs her eyes; she can't believe what she's seeing. She blinks consecutively a few times trying to heighten her focus, and as he walks nearer to just a few feet in front of her, her heart starts to pound, she can see him perfectly clearly now.

Just before Dean reaches her, he momentarily glances at The Boss, acknowledging him with a meaningful smile and nod, to which The Boss reciprocates. He then turns his attention to Lana. The moment is poignant as he takes her hands in his and their eyes lock. He smiles, his dimples surrounding his huge grin once more. "Hey, Lar! I've been waiting for you!"

"Dean!" she whispers, her voice trembling as she can't contain her excitement a moment longer.

He steadies her as she slowly wraps her arms around his neck; she finally feels like she's arrived home. As they embrace, she progressively starts to turn youthful again. "I've missed you *so* much, Lar!" he declares as he tenderly kisses her.

Lana smiles coyly then bites her lip shyly, as he chuckles then glances down to his side. She follows his gaze. To her amazement and joy, Liliana is happily dancing around, proudly and jubilantly showing off her wings; they're finally golden! "I got my wings Lana, and it's all because of you!" Liliana waves goodbye to them as she flies towards her parents and they all disappear into the heavens together.

As Lana waves back, delighted and proud, she suddenly becomes distracted by a little boy running towards her. It's Saul, he's joyfully playing with a dog, who she gladly recognises to be Amadeus! The dog's mischievously jumping, barking and running all around Saul's feet. Lana stops dead in her tracks and as Saul acknowledges her presence, he instantly stops mid-stride as well, but then gradually continues to walk very slowly towards her. With her heart racing, she bends down to match his height. They stare at each other for a brief moment, then she wraps him in her arms and hugs him tightly. Smiling, he hugs her back; all their hopes and dreams have finally been recognised. She gazes at him fondly and cups his face in her hands, gently stroking his cheek with her thumb. She stares deeply, mesmerized by his features. She recognises both herself and Dean in his facial expressions and he even has Dean's dimples! She is beyond elated and kisses him softly on his cheek as 'Deus jumps onto her knee and barks happily. She picks up the dog and nestles him under her neck, scrunching and stroking his soft fur.

Lana stands to face Dean once more as he devotedly encapsulates her face in both his hands and amorously kisses her lips. He asks attentively, "Lana? Will you dance with me?"

Lana shines, "I'd love to!"

As they start to dance, The Boss twists his fingers in an ascending motion. A wisp of mist carries them upward as they're wondrously transported back to the café. The setting is just as it was all those years ago. The surroundings are exactly the same, as they find themselves dancing to their song *To Be Loved*, playing on the old jukebox. Sam is also there to pour them two cups of cappuccino. The song continues to play as they dance and hold each other's gaze. Everything is complete perfection as Dean twirls Lana around and she giggles. Both of them are finally at peace and exactly where they want to be.

As the song comes to an end, their souls intertwine and become one again as they disappear together into the heavens. Saul and 'Deus run behind them playfully and fade into the distance alongside them, as they are all finally reunited.

The Boss looks on, proudly and lovingly, with eternal love forever in his heart. *"March 15th, 2078, that was a very important day for me... that was The Day I Died!"*

The End.

...or is it?

The Boss touchingly brushes a tear from his eye and returns to his office, where Tobias joins him. As he enters his room, he gets a stark, strange feeling and notices that his chair is spun around in the wrong direction. He frowns at Tobias, then hesitantly walks toward his table and peers guardedly around his chair. There, seated before him is a vision he thought he would never, ever see again.

The Boss opens his eyes *wide*, his pupils dilating, his heart palpitating. He feels as though his legs are about to collapse from under him. He squints intently and swallows hard... "*Draya*?" he gasps. Draya sits before him.

The Boss can't quite believe what he's seeing. Blinking incessantly, he does a double take. She sits with open arms. "Matthew!" she whispers, her eyes glistening.

He breathes hard and stares continuously in her direction. He can't take his eyes off her. "Draya? Is it really you?" he whispers.

She nods. "Yes, my love!"

He reaches out to touch her face, gently prodding her cheek in disbelief that she could actually be real. "How are you here? I don't understand, how can you be here? You were lost! Your soul was gone, dissipated, I saw it with my own eyes! They... They told me it was irreversible!" he stammers.

Draya smiles, a smile he's thought about a million times over. "There was only *one* way I could ever come back and Lana, *she* made it possible."

"Lana?" he queries, frowning and totally baffled. "But how?"

Draya clarifies, "Liliana explained everything. When Lana was in The Waiting Room, because of what had happened to her, the heavens, the angels and the powers that be, decided to give her the Legerdemain stone."

The Boss is totally stunned. He steadies himself on the edge of his desk. "Lana was given the *Legerdemain stone*?" he gasps.

"Yes!" The Boss is completely overcome upon hearing this revelation. He knows how rare it is to have been given such a precious gift and what great importance and influence it holds.

Draya continues. "Lana contemplated changing Liliana's wings, but after speaking to her, she realised that *she* was her link. They were connected by Liliana's mother, but because her mother had already passed, it was obvious to Lana that *she* was the one keeping her here, and as it was imminent that she was going to cross over, she knew Liliana's wings would change anyway. Then she found out that *you* saved her and looked after her son, and although she desperately wanted to go back and relive her life with him on earth, she knew it was only a matter of time until they would be reunited in heaven, whereas *our* situation was eternal, so... she sacrificed that life with him so that *we* could be together."

The Boss is overwhelmed by Lana's selflessness and what she has forgone for them. He shakes his head continuously in disbelief as his eyes well with teardrops. "I can't believe Lana did that for us!" Draya nods compassionately in agreement. He hesitates for a moment, deep in thought. He can't take his eyes off Draya. Tenderly, he takes her hands and wraps them in his. "I just can't get my head around it! I *must* be dreaming!" Reaching out, he touches her face delicately, then strokes her cheek with the back of his hand. "There hasn't been a day that's gone by when I haven't thought about you. I *never* dreamt in my wildest dreams that I'd ever see you again, I'd given up all hope!" he states emotionally, his voice wavering.

"I'm here now!" she whispers, as she also caresses his face lovingly. The Boss pulls her close and they embrace, as he breathes in deeply and catches the scent from her hair. He presses his lips against hers, and as he closes his eyes a tear falls from his face onto hers. Tobias looks on, with tears in *his* eyes, but also accompanied by the *widest* grin.

The Boss gazes at him reminiscently for a second, then strolls over, and much to his surprise, pulls him forward and gives him a lengthy bear hug! Tobias has a startled, shocked expression on his face. The Boss laughs and then begins to remove his bracelet. "Tobias, not only have you been an *amazing* assistant, but you've also been a true friend and loyal confidant." He hands him the bracelet, placing it into his palm and closing his fist securely around it. "And now I'm sure *you'll* make a great leader!" he exclaims with a wink.

The bracelet holds the power to enable him to be *The Boss*, and now that power has been passed on to Tobias. Guardedly, Tobias unfolds his hand and stares at it in astonishment. His eyes ping open, as a rush of adrenalin takes over. "You mean?"

The Boss nods, "*You're* The Boss now! I've got some other place I need to be!" he announces, gazing directly in Draya's direction.

As though a light has just been switched on, Tobias suddenly becomes fearful as the realisation of what's happening starts to sink in. "But I can't do this without you, I... I wouldn't know where to begin!" he stutters anxiously.

The Boss ignores his fears and apprehension and instead directs his hand towards his chair, initiating Tobias to walk over to it. As Tobias moves closer, The Boss removes his elaborate robe and places it delicately around his shoulders. Tobias uneasily lowers himself into the chair, nervously wrapping the robe around himself. The Boss takes the bracelet and fastens it around his wrist and then in an instant, everything suddenly becomes crystal clear. As though he's had amnesia, but now his memory has been restored, Tobias is now completely at ease and fully accepting of his new status. As he basks in awe at the events occurring around him, he scans the table and is undeniably mindful of all the great power that now lies before him. A million and one thoughts whirl around his mind. How he thinks he might give Aaron and Demetrius one more chance or maybe he'll make Laurie his new assistant. He recollects everything The Boss taught him throughout the years, and how blessed he's been to have known this wonderful man.

Draya stands, as The Boss outstretches his hand towards Tobias. "Tobias, it has *truly* been an honour." he declares sentimentally. Firmly shaking hands, they both nod in high regard for one another respectively, then hold each other's gaze for a moment. Tobias breaks into a wide grin then takes a reserved step backward.

The Boss and Draya lovingly wrap themselves in each other's arms as Tobias powerfully enacts an innamorato, eternally binding enchantment, encapsulating them both within the prophetic spell.

He motions his hands animatedly, as it wondrously wraps around them, and steadily lifts them upward.

Tobias looks on with extreme joy, contentment and pride as they're carried up into the heavens, their souls forevermore united.

The End

... and the beginning!

Printed in Great Britain
by Amazon